Miracles
in
Wild Rose
Bay

BOOKS BY SUSANNE O'LEARY

THE SANDY COVE SERIES
Secrets of Willow House
Sisters of Willow House
Dreams of Willow House
Daughters of Wild Rose Bay
Memories of Wild Rose Bay

The Road Trip
A Holiday to Remember

Susanne O'Leary

Miracles
in
Wild Rose
Bay

bookouture

Published by Bookouture in 2020

An imprint of Storyfire Ltd.
Carmelite House
50 Victoria Embankment
London EC4Y 0DZ

www.bookouture.com

ISBN: 978-1-80019-252-2
eBook ISBN: 978-1-80019-251-5

For Agneta

Chapter One

Whenever Tara was hit with a bout of homesickness, she turned to her photo album. Far away from home, in a spacious loft apartment in New York City with the hum of traffic and the occasional whine from a police siren eighteen floors below, she would make herself a mug of Barry's tea. Her twin sister, Kate, would send it to her in her monthly 'Irish Goodies' package, that also contained, among other things, soda bread from the bakery in Sandy Cove and a jar of Old Time Irish marmalade. Curled up on the sofa at the window overlooking the Hudson River, Tara would enjoy her treats and open the album. The traffic noises receded as she flicked through the pages and she was, as always, transported to her childhood and the happy days in the old house in Dublin.

She smiled as she gazed at photos of birthday parties, first communions, confirmations, school concerts and, most importantly, those Irish dancing competitions that she and Kate had won so many times. She still had the medals in a velvet box. She laughed as she came to a big photo of herself and Kate dressed in their dancing costumes. Oh God, they'd been such a hoot. The judges hadn't been able to tell them apart so they had given them the trophy to share. Tara peered at the photo, trying to remember which of the two tall, thin girls with dark hair and huge hazel eyes was her, and which one was Kate. Even she couldn't tell them apart in the grainy images sometimes. They had been nine years old.

It was a whole lifetime ago, it seemed. Her childhood days in Dublin were long gone and she hadn't been there since she'd left over three years ago. And here she was, in New York, pursuing a career in photography, while Kate was on the other side of the Atlantic, a country doctor in a small village in County Kerry. A beautiful place for sure, but so remote. Tara had been there only once last year, when Kate had organised a memorial for their father. Originally from Dublin, his ancestors had come from Sandy Cove and he had always wanted to go back there.

Kate had been so excited about the O'Rourke family history that went back to the eleventh century, but Tara hadn't been able to connect to that at all. Not strange, considering Tara was on a flying visit and hadn't immersed herself in the village and its history like Kate, who had been there for months and had got to know everyone by then. But as Tara gazed out over the heavy grey skies of New York, the image of that beautiful place popped into her mind: the rugged coastline, the shimmering ocean, the bays and inlets, but most of all, the white sands of Wild Rose Bay and the slopes leading down to it covered in a carpet of dark pink flowers. She had promised to go back, but then been so busy in that New York way, with jobs and parties and dating and going to the gym and a million other things big city life entailed.

Tara closed the album and walked to the window, staring out at the river, the skyscrapers and the green square of Washington Market Park below, where she would occasionally play tennis with

Joe. Their relationship was of the kind that could easily be described as 'complicated'. He had once been her boss, but it hadn't taken them long to realise they couldn't work together. Joe had never understood Tara's way of working. Her technique was unusual – based on her feelings rather than what she saw. Instead of clicking away at her target, she would wait a minute or two until she felt emotionally involved with what was in front of her, using all her senses as she waited for the perfect moment to take the shot. It usually resulted in photos that had more depth and feeling than many of Joe's shots, which was why her photos were often chosen over Joe's technically perfect ones.

Once she had left his firm and was working freelance, their liaison had changed to something closer, more intimate. Despite their professional rivalry, they couldn't deny their sexual tension. But even though they had been dating for six months, their relationship never seemed to develop into anything that would last. She never knew what he really thought of her or how much she meant to him. She suspected he liked keeping her guessing so he didn't have to commit.

Tara exhaled and carried her mug to the kitchen part of the loft, where her flatmate, Patty, a stockbroker with a hectic social life, had left the remnants of her lunch in the sink. Tara quickly loaded the dirty plates and her mug into the dishwasher and switched it on, wondering how long she would be able to stand living with this woman. But the loft was spacious and comfortable, with two bedrooms, both en-suite, a large kitchen-diner and living room combined into a bright, airy space with nice views. The location was great, too and well worth the exorbitant rent. The fact that her flatmate was seldom at home made the situation bearable, even if Tara had to tidy up after her.

Tara knew she had fallen on her feet since she arrived in New York three years ago, both with her job and her accommodation. She often had to pinch herself when she thought of her success. It was all about being in the right place at the right time, getting exposure that created that word of mouth that was so important. And it had happened very fast. Despite her occasional homesickness, life in the fast lane suited Tara to a T.

The only problem was her love life, and she was finding it increasingly hard to cope with the on-off relationship she had with Joe. But maybe she was too eager; maybe so far she had been too ready to dance to his tune? It wasn't in her nature to play hard to get, but right now, with Joe, it seemed like a very good option. As she stood there at the window, she suddenly realised: she'd have to be less available. From now on, she'd be more distant and try to be a little mysterious. She nodded as a little smile played on her lips. That was what she would do. Be cool for a while, which meant not answering his texts. Make him guess, wonder and maybe even worry…

But why had she thought so much of Ireland lately? And why was her head full of lilting music, soft air and the smell of flowers? It was probably the time of year, she thought, with the arrival of summer and the heat and humidity that made New Yorkers flee the city at weekends. But Tara had nowhere to flee to, and she was stuck here on a Saturday afternoon waiting for Joe to call, hoping he'd invite her to go to Connecticut where he had a small cottage by the sea. But he hadn't called. Perhaps he had been invited to join someone else's weekend party and had forgotten all about her. Maybe he was miffed that her feature on the old mansions on Fisher's Island had been published in *Harper's Bazaar* last week?

She had gone to this secluded, little-known island north of Long Island, where the old money families had been spending their summers for generations, to photograph the members of one of these families. It had been a surprise assignment commissioned by the magazine and she hadn't even told Joe about it. He found out when the issue was published and demanded to know why she had kept it a secret. Maybe that was why he had disappeared. Tara sighed. She understood his wanting to be the one to shine, but she wished he could be happy for her too.

The call came early on Monday morning. Tara had just left the gym and was on her way to grab a coffee and a bagel at the coffee shop next door. She answered the call at the same time as she stepped inside, nodding to the girl at the counter and whispering, 'The usual, please,' before she sat down at a window seat. 'Hi,' she said. 'Tara O'Rourke here.'

'Hi, Tara,' a woman's voice said. 'I'm Ellie, editor of *The Wild Vagabond*.'

'Hi, Ellie,' Tara said with a dart of excitement, smelling a good project coming her way. *The Wild Vagabond* was a high-profile magazine for the wealthy traveller who wanted to go somewhere different. 'We've worked together before. Remember those photos I did for the feature about hiking in the Canadian Rockies?'

'That's right,' Ellie replied. 'And this time I'm calling you about a feature for our January issue. Something for readers who will be starting to think about their summer vacation trips.'

'Sounds great,' Tara said, trying to appear casual. She loved these kinds of assignments to faraway places. The excursion up the Amazon last year with Joe had been an incredible experience that had given her a taste for more of the same. Tahiti, Australia, she'd go anywhere. 'So where do you want me to go?' she asked.

Ellie said something that was drowned in the noise of a truck outside.

'What?' Tara shouted into the phone, only just hearing what Ellie said. 'Iceland?' she asked, excited at the thought. Wow. How fabulous. She had always wanted to go there. The landscape, the hot springs, the Icelandic ponies… She could imagine the fabulous shots she'd take. 'I'd love to go to Iceland.'

'No,' Ellie shouted back. 'I said Ireland.'

'Oh,' Tara said, her heart sinking. 'Why Ireland?' she asked. 'I mean, hasn't that been done to death already?'

'Not the way we want to do it. We don't want you to go to the well-known tourist spots there but somewhere along that route everyone's talking about. The Wild – something.'

'The Wild Atlantic Way,' Tara said. 'Is that what you meant? The route along the Atlantic coast?'

'Yes, but we don't want you to do the whole thing, just the southern part. Cork and Kerry.'

'I'm not sure that's exactly undiscovered,' Tara remarked.

'I know,' Ellie said with a laugh. 'It's been done before, but we want you to do the hidden parts. Places nobody knows much about.

Not the fancy hotels, but the roads less travelled. You know, the little villages with bed and breakfast places in ruined castles. Trips in horse-drawn caravans and visiting interesting people who live in the old cottages. Places where you can get away from the glam and glitz and discover the real Ireland and the real people. Where you can go and find yourself and walk barefoot on the rocks and be alone. A Lonely Planet kind of thing.' Ellie drew breath. 'We understand from the bio on your website that you're Irish, so we thought you'd know where to go.'

'Hmm,' Tara said while she thought. Okay, so it wasn't a trip up Machu Picchu or a trek through the Mongolian desert, but it could be fun to do something in Ireland. She could combine it with a visit to Sandy Cove and Kate. It would give her the chance to take a break from her problems with Joe. Going to Ireland would give her a chance to look at it all from a distance. She might even forget about him. Never mind the fact that there was someone in Sandy Cove Kate had mentioned that she'd been desperate to meet. Someone she had had a crush on for a long time who just happened to live in that remote little village…

'We think it'd be a huge hit with people who love Ireland already,' Ellie said.

Tara nodded to herself, beginning to warm to the idea. 'I think I know exactly where I'd get some fabulous shots,' she said. 'It's a little place on the west coast that still has that old magic. Not glamorous at all. And the coast is spectacular.'

'Perfect,' Ellie said. 'But we'd like it to be very in-depth and cover a lot of different activities: hiking, horseback riding, surfing, kayaking, even bird watching. Do you think you could do that?'

'No problem at all,' Tara replied.

'Brilliant,' Ellie gushed. 'Of course that'll mean you'll be over there for most of the summer. I hope that won't be a problem?'

'Eh,' Tara mumbled, trying to figure out if it was a good idea to be away so long from Joe. She wanted to be mysterious and play a little hard to get, but being away for so long might be overdoing it. But oh, to spend the summer with Kate, who Tara had missed so desperately! It had felt at times as if half of her was gone. Now they could be together for a whole summer and that suddenly felt wonderful. 'We'll cover your expenses including the flight in business class,' Ellie said, cutting into Tara's musings.

'That's great,' Tara said.

'So you accept this job? We were thinking of asking Joe Mancini, but he's going to Alaska in two weeks. Some kind of assignment for *National Geographic*.'

Tara sat up. 'He is? I mean, yeah, that's right,' she corrected herself, while her spirits sank. Joe hadn't said anything about that to her when they'd had dinner together only three days ago. Why hadn't he told her? And why had he disappeared just like that over the weekend? Was he showing her he wasn't really committed to their potential relationship? Well, two could play at that game. 'I'd be happy to go to Ireland,' she announced. 'Email me all the details and I'll take it from there. I'll book my flight straight away.'

'Fabulous,' Ellie said. 'I know you'll do a fantastic job. We love your work and that slightly different angle you always manage to get. I'll email you the details and the budget for your expenses and your fee. You'll have copyright for all your photos, of course.'

Tara thanked her and hung up with mixed feelings. On the one hand, she was excited and pleased to have been given such a big assignment by this high-profile magazine, but on the other, Joe's obvious indifference to her was hard to take. She knew he had some kind of commitment phobia – he was known as 'no-strings Joe' in the Manhattan dating scene – but she had thought he felt differently about her. Ever since that trip up the Amazon, last year, when they had truly connected, she had felt they had something special. But now they were drifting apart and he was beginning to lose interest. Even though Tara loved New York and her life and work here, she suddenly felt a break away would be the best thing for her, whatever happened with Joe.

She needed to get home for a bit. Home to Kate and that little village in the west of Ireland for some peace and rest and a little Irish craic. She'd come back rested and strong. Maybe it would make Joe commit, but maybe it wouldn't... She was just as unsure about her own feelings as his and the confusion was very stressful. This summer break was just what she needed, and she suddenly felt that the next few months would decide her future. She had to go back to her roots before she could go forward.

Chapter Two

Everything fell into place smoothly; Tara spent the next few days finding a temporary tenant for her room in the loft. The woman was a newly qualified lawyer who would stay until Tara returned to New York and she was relieved to know that she wouldn't lose her room and could move straight back in when she came back at the end of the summer. Tara found a flight with Aer Lingus and she quickly booked it and sent the invoice to the magazine. The only thing taking the gloss off her excitement was her conversation with Joe, who called her two days day before she was due to leave.

'Hi, babes,' he said. She usually found his gravelly voice so attractive, but now it grated slightly on her nerves as she already felt a distance between them. 'How are things with you?'

'Great,' Tara replied, cringing at the word 'babes'. The endearment he used so casually always irritated her. She had tried to tell him it was sexist and patronising and belonged in the last century but it had had no effect on him. She sometimes had a feeling he did it to annoy her. 'How about you? How was last weekend?'

'Pretty good,' he replied with a touch of laughter in his voice. 'I was on this photo shoot in the Hamptons and ended up at a party that went on until early Sunday afternoon. I was still a little hungover on Monday, to tell you the truth.'

'Poor baby,' Tara cooed. 'But I'm sure it was worth it.'

'It was fun, but I missed you.'

'I bet.'

'No, I mean it. But hey, why not do something about it? How about dinner in the Village tomorrow? There's that new place—'

'Sorry, but I can't,' Tara interrupted.

'You can't?' Joe asked, sounding annoyed. 'Why not?'

'I'm going away the day after tomorrow. On a job.'

'Where to?'

'Ireland. I just heard from *The Wild Vagabond*. They want me to do a long feature there, which will take me away from New York for a while.'

'Oh? Well, that's funny, because I'm off on a job too next week. For two weeks. Maybe when I'm back, we can get together and go away somewhere.'

'I'll be gone a lot longer than that,' Tara said.

'Three weeks?'

'Could be more like two months,' Tara said, knowing he wouldn't like it. 'Very nice assignment that I couldn't say no to.'

Joe was silent for a while. 'And you didn't feel like telling me about this?' he finally asked, his voice cold.

'I'm telling you now,' Tara said, trying to stay cool. She knew she was taking a risk going away for so long, but she suddenly didn't care. If he had any feelings for her, he'd accept it and be happy for her. If he didn't, that was his loss. 'You were gone all weekend and I only heard about this on Monday.'

'Today is Friday.'

'I know what day it is,' Tara snapped, tiring of humouring him. 'And how come I had to hear about your Alaska trip from someone else?'

He paused. 'I forgot to tell you, but I was going to, of course.'

'Of course,' Tara said, trying to keep the sarcasm out of her voice.

'What is this?' he asked angrily. 'Have I done something to annoy you?'

'Nothing in particular,' Tara replied with a sad little sigh. 'Just your usual thing of keeping your distance. It's very frustrating.'

'I don't know what you mean, babes. Aren't we good together? It sure works for me.'

'For you, yeah,' Tara said. 'But… Oh, what's the point?' she muttered, exasperated. They had discussed this before, always with the same outcome. Joe would slide away whenever he felt cornered. 'No need to get into this now,' she said. 'We'll talk when I get back.'

'Yes. And we'll keep in touch,' Joe said. 'Or maybe you want to call it a day? Us, I mean.'

Tara's heart sank. He always said things like this to make her feel unsure of their relationship. It was a ploy to get her to stop pushing for a commitment from him. 'Is there really an "us"?' Tara asked, her voice shaking. She thought her leaving would make him fight for their relationship; she didn't think he'd suggest it ended already. 'You don't treat me like I'm important to you. It's not like you've been planning for some kind of future?'

'Maybe it'll be a good thing for us to be apart,' Joe replied. 'Take a break and then see where we stand.'

Tara realised he was sliding away but still wanted to keep his options open. But what did she want? She was wildly attracted to him and they shared a sense of ambition. She had wanted for them to be closer and for him to make some kind of commitment. But she knew he wouldn't stay loyal to her for the whole summer and that he would be flirting with other women whenever he had the chance. Wasn't it better to break it off now and cut her losses? Of course it was. He was wasting her time. She was thirty-six and her biological clock was ticking away. Joe, with his commitment phobia, wasn't the right man for her and she knew it. So why did she still feel she could get him around to her way of thinking? Was she in love with him? Or was it simply a strong physical attraction to a very handsome man? 'I think you're right,' she heard herself say. 'Let's end things now, and see whether we want to get back together at the end of the summer.'

'Oh,' he said, sounding both surprised and disappointed, taken aback that she'd agreed with him. 'Yeah, okay. Let's do that. But we can still keep in touch, can't we? Just to share our experiences job wise?'

'No,' Tara said, steeling herself for the misery she would feel. 'Let's not do that. We should say goodbye now and then meet up in September and see where we stand.'

'September?' he asked, sounding alarmed. 'That's more than two months away.'

'I know,' Tara replied. 'And it'll be a good way to test how we feel.'

'Yeah, but...'

'Goodbye, Joe. Have a nice summer. See you in the fall.'

'What? Wait...'

'Good luck with the job. Ciao,' Tara said and hung up, feeling an odd satisfaction at having shaken Joe even for a few minutes. It would have been a shock for him to have a woman say goodbye to him like this. Tara suddenly laughed out loud as she imagined his sheepish look at the other end. Then she began to panic. Oh God, what had she done? This was probably the end of their relationship... Then she steeled herself, telling herself to keep it together.

A few minutes later, she picked herself up, made herself a cup of Barry's tea and flicked through her photo album, just to remind herself of the good days and that she was going home for a while, home to Kate and to that lovely little village she had only caught glimpses of last year. It would be wonderful to get away and to work in this part of Ireland she hadn't yet discovered. *A new start in an old place*, she thought. *What could be better for me right now? Kate is waiting and we'll have the best summer ever.*

Kate had been over the moon when Tara called to tell her about the summer plans and said she'd be 'on the case' of finding somewhere Tara could stay for the duration of her visit, as their little cottage had no guest room. She decided to give Kate a quick call to find out if she had managed to find a good place to stay for the summer.

'I think I might have found a solution,' Kate said.

'You mean I can stay at the surgery?'

'No. A cottage near mine might be available. The surgery house is a bit upside down at the moment. Dr Pat's wife is moving back in after having lived apart from him most of their married life. So she has the builders in and the house is being restored from top to bottom,' Kate explained.

'Oh?' Tara said, surprised by this news. 'I thought you were planning to buy the surgery and the house when your boss retired. Or did I imagine that?'

'No.' Kate sighed. 'I was hoping to do just that when the time came. I love that house and it would have been so perfect.'

'I know. And if you had been able to buy it, I would have offered you my part of our money that's sitting in the account in the Bank of Ireland after the sale of Dad's house.'

'That's very kind of you,' Kate said, her voice softening. 'But I thought you would use that for a flat in New York?'

Tara snorted. 'That wouldn't buy me a closet here. I'm grand with flat sharing for the moment. Suits me fine with my globe-trotting career. The money will just be sitting in that account. I'm really sorry to hear you couldn't buy the surgery, though. It seemed like it would be possible last time we spoke.' Despite this setback, Tara was struck by how confident and grounded Kate had become since she arrived in Sandy Cove last year. Gone were the insecurity and the hesitancy about her life and her career. It was obvious she had landed in the right spot for her. But not being able to buy the house she had come to love was obviously a bit of a blow all the same.

'I thought so too,' Kate replied. 'But then Helen threw a spanner into my hopes and dreams and announced she was coming back. It's her house after all, so I had no right to complain.'

'I'm sorry to hear that.'

'Yeah, I was disappointed,' Kate said, her voice tinged with sadness. 'But maybe it wasn't meant to be. That's life, isn't it? Helen's planning a lot of renovations so it'll be very comfortable for them when it's ready.'

'What does Mick think about it all?' Tara asked. Mick was Dr Pat's son and a well-known actor at the Abbey Theatre in Dublin.

'Mick? Not really sure what he thinks about anything at the moment.' Kate paused. 'Well, you know what happened, no doubt.'

'No, not really,' Tara replied, wondering what was going on with him. Kate and Tara had seen every single play Mick was in and formed an unofficial fan club when they were younger and when Kate arrived in Sandy Cove and met him, they'd both been so excited. Kate and Mick had made friends and their friendship had spilled over to Tara; they'd connected through Instagram and started to chat, but she hadn't spoken to him recently. 'What's going on with him?' she asked. 'We've been out of touch since last year.' Or since Tara had started dating Joe and Mick had gone to London to work on a play…

'His play bombed,' Kate explained. 'It was slated in the press and the expected audience numbers didn't materialise. And the Abbey haven't cast him in anything new. He's been doing some TV soaps and voice-overs "to keep the wolf from the door", as he says. It's the nature of show business, but he's pretty downhearted about it, I hear.'

'You hear?' Tara asked. 'So he's not in Sandy Cove, then?'

'No, he's in Dublin. He might come down to Sandy Cove during the summer, Pat says.'

'Oh.' Tara paused for a while, thinking about how much fun it would have been to meet Mick in the flesh. But maybe he wouldn't be such great company if he was feeling down about his career. 'Well, never mind him,' she said. 'I'm so excited about my trip. I'll be in Sandy Cove for at least two months.'

'That's wonderful,' Kate said with a happy sigh. 'Can't wait to see you and for you to get to know Cormac. I know the two of you will get on like a house on fire.'

'I'm sure we will,' Tara said, smiling at the memory of Cormac's sweet face and lovely eyes. He was a herbalist and ran an outfit called the Wellness Centre in Sandy Cove, the popular yoga studio, gym and health food store. He and Kate had clashed when they first met, as Kate had been doubtful about the benefits of herbal remedies. But, little by little, she had come around to thinking that the old remedies might have a part to play in the healing process of some illnesses, and then they had fallen in love. It was such a sweet, romantic love story, Tara had thought. When Tara had met Cormac, she'd seen that he and Kate were like chalk and cheese in many ways, but together they formed a unit that seemed unbreakable. How lucky Kate had been to meet him. A case of being in the right place at the right time. Would she ever be as lucky in love as Kate had been?

Chapter Three

Tara's flight landed in Farranfore, the small international airport near Killarney three days later. She was delighted to arrive like this, right into the middle of Kerry instead of having to face a long drive from Dublin or Shannon. Once she had lugged her big suitcase and the smaller one with her cameras and equipment through customs and into the arrivals hall, she spotted Kate, who greeted her with a huge smile. They fell into each other's arms, laughing and crying at the same time.

Kate pulled back and looked at Tara. 'Oh God, look at you! So glamorous!' She touched Tara's hair, cut into a chin-length bob. 'How do you get it to shine like that?'

'Conditioner and a special brush,' Tara said, swishing her hair around. She looked at Kate and laughed. 'But you're positively glowing. I thought you'd be worn out by all that hard work, but here you are, looking as if you've been on holiday.' Tara kept staring at her sister. Kate's slightly tanned face glowed with health and happiness and her short haircut suited her outdoorsy, sporty look. She was dressed in a pair of faded jeans, a white T-shirt and trainers, a great contrast to Tara's Ralph Lauren chinos, black Armani linen shirt and Chanel ballet flats.

'And you look as if you've just been for a weekend at a spa,' Kate shot back.

'I had to dress up for business class,' Tara explained. 'I brought a very simple wardrobe for this trip. Jeans and cargo pants and T-shirts and stuff like that.'

'All designer, I bet,' Kate said with a laugh. 'But hey, we'll soon rough you up a bit. Sandy Cove is not exactly a hotspot of fashion and glamour.'

'That's why I picked it for my base,' Tara said and picked up her bags. 'But where's the pony and cart?'

Kate laughed. 'I've turned all modern and came in my car.'

'Oh, that's a relief,' Tara joked. 'I'm dying to get settled. Did you manage to get me a place to stay? I'm not picky. A B&B will be fine as long as they have Wi-Fi. I don't mind if it's not a five-star hotel.'

'We'll squash you into our spare room for a few days and then we thought you could house sit a little cottage for the summer. It's close to ours and right on the beach, which I'm sure you'll love. It's a great place for swimming.'

'That sounds lovely,' Tara replied. 'Who owns the cottage and why don't they want it for the summer?'

'It's owned by Jasmine and Aiden, Sally O'Rourke's daughter and son-in-law. They're working in Paris until August,' Kate said, trying to grab Tara's smaller case. 'I'll carry this one for you.'

Tara snatched it back. 'No, it's my camera equipment. I never let go of that one. You roll the suitcase instead.'

'Okay,' Kate said and started to pull Tara's big suitcase behind her. 'Let's get going, then.'

They exited the airport terminal and walked to the car park where they loaded Tara's luggage into Kate's little Renault and drove off into the early summer day. A recent shower had washed the dust off the trees and wildflowers along the road and made the air feel fresh and clean. Tara rolled down the window and looked out at cottages and houses, quaint pubs and shops that lined the road. 'How fabulous to be here,' she said with a happy sigh. 'New York is hell in the summer. Hot and humid and dirty. This feels like paradise. The air smells of flowers and grass. So lovely.'

'Well, it can feel like that sometimes,' Kate replied as she stopped at traffic lights. 'But I can assure you that there are as many ups and downs here as anywhere else. Except it's easier to cope with them here, of course.'

'I'm sure it is. But I'm not sure I could do what you did. I love New York, but maybe not in the summer. Any other time it's a fantastic city.'

'It seems to suit you,' Kate said, glancing at Tara. 'But you must be tired and hungry. Do you want to stop on the way for breakfast? We can get something in Killarney.'

'I'd love to, but don't you have to get back to the surgery?' Tara asked.

'Pat took the morning shift,' Kate explained. 'So I don't have to be back until after lunch.'

'Oh, great.' Tara yawned. 'Sorry. The jetlag is kicking in. I managed to sleep for a few hours on the plane but that doesn't seem to have helped. Breakfast sounds great. It'll wake me up so we can talk while we drive.'

'There's a nice little café with a garden just after Killarney.'

'Great,' Tara said and yawned again. 'Oh, God, I can't stop yawning. I think I'll snooze for a bit until we get there.'

'Good idea,' Kate said as she turned into a wider road with dense traffic. 'It'll take about half an hour to get through this. The tourist season has just started and the good weather lured a lot of people away from the bigger towns.'

'Mmm,' Tara said and, unable to keep her eyes open, drifted off.

'Here we are,' Kate said what seemed like only minutes later.

Tara opened her eyes and peered at an enchanting little house with a sign that said 'Leonora's Cottage Café'. The house was surrounded by a garden full of flowers. Small round tables under colourful umbrellas were dotted all over the place and people were carrying trays out of the house to sit down in the warm sunshine. 'Gorgeous,' Tara mumbled and groped for her bag. Not fully awake, she followed Kate down the garden path and sat down at a table under a large oak. 'Could you get me some coffee and… whatever they have that's nice?' she asked. 'I'm too zonked to think.'

'I'll see what they have.' Kate put her bag on a chair. 'Try to wake up while I'm gone.'

'Okay,' Tara said and sat back in the chair, looking around, enjoying the wonderful garden and the air that smelled of flowers and grass, the leafy landscape and the green hills against the powder-blue sky. The light was wonderful here, and she felt a sudden dart of pure joy as she thought of the photos she'd take in this beautiful part of Ireland. She'd find simple little places like this, away from the glitzier restaurants and hotels in Killarney that had been purpose built for rich tourists. The road less travelled was what she wanted to follow and this might be the start.

'Give me a hand,' Kate said, coming towards the table with a loaded tray.

Tara shot up and took the tray and put it on the table. 'Wow,' she said, looking at the two mugs of coffee, soda bread with marmalade, croissants and chocolate muffins. 'You went to town on the goodies.'

'I was hungry,' Kate said and sat down. 'I had to get up at six to go to the airport.'

'I'm sorry,' Tara said. 'And I didn't even say thank you. But I really appreciate you coming to meet me.' Tara felt a tiny bit of awkwardness between them for a moment – it had been such a long time since they'd been together. 'I could have got a taxi or something if it was too much of a hassle to pick me up,' she added, trying to gauge Kate's mood.

'Don't be silly. Of course I'd come and meet you,' Kate said and took her mug and a slice of soda bread from the tray. 'Come on, dig in.'

Tara did as she was told and it didn't take her long to finish the soda bread and start on the croissants. 'Lovely,' she mumbled through her mouthful. 'Aren't we lucky we don't put on weight easily? Remember how we used to stuff ourselves before the Irish dancing classes? But then we burned it all off in the jigs and reels.'

'Fun times,' Kate agreed. She swallowed and looked at Tara. 'Tell me more about your assignment.'

'It's a big one that'll take up most of the summer,' Tara said. 'It's for a series of articles about hidden corners of a country many people already know. The magazine are featuring a lot of different countries around the world and they picked me to cover Ireland. I wanted to go somewhere a bit more exotic, but then I realised I could spend some time here with you, so it seemed perfect.'

'Perfect for me too,' Kate said with a happy smile. 'Hidden corners?' she asked. 'What does that mean?'

'Places that are off the beaten track that aren't the usual tourist spots. So I thought Sandy Cove would be perfect. Quiet little village with stunning countryside to wander through. The mountain tracks, the beaches, Wild Rose Bay with the wild roses…'

Kate stared at Tara. 'That's a well-kept secret, you know.'

'Is it? But that'll be so fabulous for my article. I can imagine the photos I'll be able to take, and—'

'Hold on,' Kate interrupted, looking shocked. 'You're not going to lure hordes of tourists to Sandy Cove, I hope?'

Tara laughed. 'Not hordes, of course, just those who love hiking and roughing it in gorgeous places that are hard to get to.'

'But that could be a lot of people,' Kate argued. 'I've seen your photos, Tara. They are so incredibly enticing. You could make a rock in the middle of nowhere look like paradise.'

'Thank you,' Tara said even though she knew it wasn't meant as a compliment. 'But I don't see why you think my photos in that magazine would damage this area at all.'

'The peace and tranquillity of Sandy Cove would be wrecked,' Kate explained. 'I'm not sure the locals would be that happy to see an influx of tourists. We find it hard to cope with the ones who come there as it is.'

Tara stared at Kate. 'What do you mean? Wouldn't anyone who runs a shop or restaurant there be delighted to make more money?'

'I'm not so sure about that. The village has only two pubs, a restaurant and a café, and a few other shops, plus the Wellness Centre that's pretty basic. The people who run these places are happy with the business they get as it is. But if it becomes some kind of hotspot, it'll wreck the unique atmosphere of the place. And there's nowhere to stay since Willow House was closed for guests. A very nice family lives there now.' Kate drew breath. 'Can't you do some other place in Kerry?'

'What other place?' Tara asked. 'This is the Ring of Kerry. Everything around here has been written about a thousand times already. Your village is the only place that still has that unique, unspoilt Irish charm.'

'Exactly,' Kate said, her mouth pinched. 'And we'd like it to stay that way, thank you very much.'

Tara rolled her eyes and sighed. 'I get your point, but I still don't see—'

'Let's talk about that later,' Kate interrupted with a stern look that said she didn't want to start an argument there and then.

'There's plenty of time. I'll be staying here until the end of August.'

'Wonderful,' Kate said with a smile that made Tara feel better despite Kate's obvious worry about Tara exposing her beloved village to tourism on a large scale.

'You'll be sick of me by then,' Tara joked, trying to lighten the mood.

'Oh yeah, of course. And we'll bicker and fight and it's going to be fabulous.'

Relieved the atmosphere had improved, Tara touched Kate's hand. 'Yes, it will. I've missed you so much.'

'Me too.' Kate leaned over and kissed Tara's cheek. 'You have no idea how much. Especially when I first came here and tried to fit in. I was like the proverbial square peg.'

'Why?' Tara asked, taken aback. 'Was it because you're from Dublin? Or that you can be a bit superior at times?'

Kate bristled. 'What do you mean? Superior?'

'I meant, you know, that you tend to lecture people and that might have got up their noses,' Tara explained, knowing she was stepping on a very sore toe. But it had come out of her mouth without thinking, as Kate's reaction to her assignment and what it might lead to had annoyed her.

'I haven't lectured anyone,' Kate snapped. 'In fact, both Pat and Bridget have said I have excellent people skills.' She glared at Tara for a moment, looking offended.

'Of course you do,' Tara said, backing down immediately. 'I know you're a brilliant doctor and I'm sure all your patients love you. You probably only lecture me a bit because I need it,' she added, eating a large bite of humble pie for good measure. She didn't want their reunion that she had looked forward to with such joy to turn sour the very first day.

'I don't mean to lecture you,' Kate said, sounding mollified. 'But you do need someone to tell you when you take risks that might put you in a lot of trouble.'

'I suppose I do,' Tara replied. 'Though it can be hard to take.'

'I know.' Kate smiled apologetically. 'I might be a little overbearing with you sometimes.'

'Maybe. But I'm sure that wasn't the problem with the people in the village,' Tara continued. 'It was probably more about being a Dubliner.'

Kate sighed. 'That, and being a woman and a lot younger than they expected and not knowing how to handle country people and so on and so on. But now all is well and I seem to be part of the furniture.'

'And you love it,' Tara said, smiling at Kate.

'Oh yes, I do. I feel this is truly my home. There are so many O'Rourkes here and some of them remind me of Dad and his family. The eyes, the black eyebrows, the set of their jaws, their voices.' Kate looked suddenly sad. 'How Dad would have loved to come here and see it all and connect with the people.'

'I know,' Tara agreed, feeling her eyes well up as always when they talked about their father. 'I can see him in the little pub on the main street chatting away to them all and feeling like the Kerryman he always was.'

'That would have been such a joy for him,' Kate said wistfully. 'The village is full of people who look like him. You'll see. With your photographer's eye you'll notice a lot more than me.'

'Can't wait.' Tara looked up at the hills behind them, turning away from her sad thoughts. 'The light here is amazing. I can't wait to start taking some great shots.'

'Just don't go mad around the village,' Kate warned. She picked up her mug. 'You know, when you told me about your assignment for Paddy's Day, it struck me that it might tie in with our own family history. I've always wanted to know why our great-grandfather, Daniel O'Rourke, left Sandy Cove. I've tried to find out, but nobody knows. It was so long ago, they say. But someone hinted at a family feud about a hundred years ago. Wouldn't it be fun to find out what happened?'

'How could we do that? Everyone's dead,' Tara said, her interest waning. She'd never been one for history lessons and had never been interested in what happened in the past. The present was a lot more intriguing to her.

'I found out about the early history of the family,' Kate said. 'And it was fascinating.'

'You told me all about that,' Tara reminded her. 'The healers in the Middle Ages and how they were revered by the chieftains and all that. I know you love folklore and Celtic legends, so that would be right up your street. Interesting, but so far away in time. I found it hard to connect with that, to be honest.'

'I know you did,' Kate replied. 'But this is about what happened only a hundred or so years ago. And I know Dad tried to find out but none of those people were still alive so there was nobody to ask.'

'Oh, yes,' Tara said, trying to remember what their father had talked about through the fog of her jetlag. 'He did say he never knew what happened.'

Kate nodded. 'Exactly. It's the last piece of the jigsaw. I've learned all about the people who lived in the old village that's now in ruins from Sally, who you'll meet soon. That brings us up to the early nineteenth century. So all we have left is our story, the people who left to go to Dublin a little over a hundred years ago. But why did they? That's what I'd love to find out.'

'Well, maybe we can try,' Tara said, trying to sound enthusiastic. 'But let's leave it for now. I'm too tired to think.'

'If you've finished, we can get going.'

'I've eaten every crumb,' Tara said with a laugh. 'And I'm dying to get back on the road.'

'Okay. Come on then.' Kate put everything on the tray and got up.

Tara followed her sister to the cottage café, her camera ready. This place was so enchanting and so very Irish in its simplicity and old-world charm. When they got inside, she went straight to the counter where a rosy-cheeked woman in a frilly white apron was putting a tray of muffins into the chilled cabinet. 'Hi,' she said. 'Are you the owner?'

The woman closed the cabinet and wiped her hands on a towel. 'I am,' she said. 'What can I do for you?'

'Oh, nothing,' Tara replied. 'My sister and I just had the best breakfast ever.' She gestured at Kate, who was putting the tray on the counter. 'That's Kate. My twin sister.'

The woman looked from one to the other and laughed. 'You didn't have to tell me. You look exactly alike, except for the hair.' She held out her hand. 'I'm Leonora.'

Tara shook her hand. 'I'm Tara. Great to meet you.' She held up her camera. 'I'm a photographer and I'm working on a story for a magazine in America. All about Kerry and places a bit unusual and out of the way. I love your café and I thought it would be great to include it in my article. Would you mind if I took a few shots?'

Leonora beamed. 'Not at all.'

'Be careful,' Kate said behind them. 'Say no if you don't want this place invaded by Americans.'

'But that would be grand altogether,' Leonora chuckled. 'I love Americans and I even have family there. In Boston,' she added. 'Wouldn't they be impressed if they saw me in a magazine.'

'Fabulous,' Tara said and got her camera ready. 'Forget about me and just do what you were doing.'

She backed away so she could get the whole café into the shot, the polished wooden floor, the wainscoting painted a light green with a white trim, the old-fashioned counter and the cute little windows adorned with flowers in ceramic pots. Then she stood there for a while, trying to get that feel she needed before she had the perfect angle, the light and the friendly atmosphere the place exuded. Leonora, who had gone back to the counter to serve a customer, glanced up just as the sun came out of the clouds outside, casting golden beams into the little café. The perfect moment, Tara knew and clicked away, catching the soft, slightly dim light that only lasted a second. It gave a timeless feel to the café and Tara knew it would look lovely on the page. The only thing she didn't manage to get into the shot was the heavenly smell of baking. 'Thanks, Leonora,' Tara called when she had taken her photos. 'I'll do a few of the garden too, if that's okay.'

'Great,' Leonora called back and waved. 'Lovely to meet you, Tara. Let me know when the article is published and I'll get all my cousins over in Boston to buy a copy.'

'I will,' Tara promised. 'Thanks a million for being such a great subject.' She followed Kate out the door. 'That was great,' she said. 'I'll just take a few shots of the garden and then I'll be with you.'

'Oh, God,' Kate said with a sigh. 'Now you'll start a stampede to this quiet little café.'

Tara glared at her. 'The owner was happy for me to take photos.'

'She doesn't know your powers.'

Tara stopped taking photos and turned to look at Kate. 'I'll ask permission wherever I can and if anybody protests, then I won't do it. I won't take any photos of you or your house or your boyfriend or even your cat, I swear to God.'

'I don't have a cat,' Kate said glumly.

'That makes it easier,' Tara retorted, taking another shot as a light breeze made the roses sway. 'The light here is so fantastic, you see. Difficult to resist.' She turned to look at Kate again, but she was wandering back to the car.

Tara put the camera back in her bag, feeling disappointed. She had been looking forward to her reunion with Kate and thought it would make them both so happy to spend the summer together. But Kate's reaction to her assignment and her obvious fear of the village being exposed to tourism both dismayed and surprised Tara. It wasn't like Kate to be so worried and tense or so negative towards her twin sister. They had been nearly inseparable as they grew up and been devastated when they had to part and had missed each other so much it hurt. What had changed to make Kate so distant and suspicious? Was it Tara's fault? All these thoughts whirled through Tara's tired brain during the rest of the journey, and even though the conversation was good-humoured again, there was a niggling feeling that the summer would not be the wonderful break she had been looking forward to.

Chapter Four

Tara forgot her worries as they arrived in Sandy Cove. She looked at the hedgerows full of wildflowers and was entranced by the beautiful gardens of the little houses all painted different colours and the quaint shopfronts lining the main street.

'I had forgotten how gorgeous this village is,' she said with a happy sigh.

Kate waved at someone in the street and laughed. 'It's a true little gem.' She pulled up and rolled down the window beside a woman carrying a baby in a baby carrier on her chest. 'Hi, Eileen. How's the baby?'

Eileen bent down carefully, her hand on the baby's head. 'So much better, Dr Kate. It was just an upset tummy as you said.' She glanced at Tara. 'Hi, you must be Dr Kate's sister. Welcome to Sandy Cove.'

'Thank you,' Tara replied, craning her head to see the baby. 'What a lovely little girl you have there.'

'He's a boy,' Eileen corrected.

Tara put her hand to her mouth. 'Oh, sorry. Those long eyelashes made me think he was a she.'

'I know,' Eileen said with a laugh. 'They're amazing. I'm nearly jealous of them myself. But shh,' she said as the baby started to squirm. 'He's waking up. I'd better keep walking to get him to drop off again. He's been awake most of the night. But now he's settled and the tummy ache seems to be gone, all thanks to the doctor here. Don't know what we'd do without her.'

'We'll be off too,' Kate said and waved. 'Glad to see he's better. Give me a call if he gets another attack.'

'Attack of what?' Tara asked as Eileen walked away.

'Colic,' Kate replied as she turned into a narrow lane. 'But I think she started him on solids too soon. Should be fine now that he's gone back to more digestible food.'

'Oh,' Tara said, impressed. Her previous visit had been so short she hadn't had time to notice that Kate was obviously a very competent and much-loved doctor in the village. 'It must be so great to be able to help people like this,' she said as they drove down a narrow lane lined with hedges of fuchsia in full bloom.

'Yes, it's nice to see patients improving.' Kate pulled up outside a whitewashed cottage with a thatched roof and a red door flanked by pots with white and red geraniums. 'Home sweet home,' she said and started to get out of the car.

Tara got out and followed her to the front door, glancing at the view of the ocean and the cliffs. She could see a set of steps leading down to a beach where the blue-green water glinted in the sunlight. 'What a heavenly place,' she said and stopped to look at the view, shielding her eyes with her hand. 'And not a single person on that fabulous beach. I didn't see this part of the beach when I was here last year.'

'It wasn't really beach weather then,' Kate remarked. 'And you only had a few days. This bit of the beach is kind of private because it's hard to get to from the main one,' she explained. 'We share it with Willow House. That's the big pink villa you can see over there above the trees.'

'Oh.' Tara looked over to the right and discovered a large house with a pale pink façade. 'Lovely house. Who lives there?'

'Maeve and Paschal,' Kate said. 'Maeve is a McKenna by birth and married to Paschal O'Sullivan. They have three children. Lovely family. They're away at the moment, visiting her parents who live in Spain, but you'll meet them when they get back.'

'That'll be nice. So that means we'll have this beach to ourselves?'

'Right now, yes.' Kate checked her watch. 'I'll have to get back to the surgery after lunch, so we'd better get you installed and have a bite to eat.'

'Okay,' Tara said and picked up her bag. 'Show me where I'm sleeping and then I'll go and get my suitcase from the car.'

Kate opened the red door. 'Follow me,' she said, walking through a small porch and into a cosy living room where a large red sofa piled with embroidered cushions stood in front of the fireplace. The floor was covered in a multicoloured wool carpet and the pictures on the white walls consisted of various watercolours, a large seascape and various prints. But what attracted Tara's attention immediately was the small antique rolltop writing desk by the far wall.

'Is that the desk from our house in Dublin?' she asked and walked over to inspect it. She ran her hand over the smooth mahogany. 'It's the one from Dad's study that used to belong to our grandad.'

'Yes,' Kate said. 'I thought it would be perfect for this room.'

'It is,' Tara said. 'What else did you take out of storage?'

'Just Mum's old easy chair,' Kate said and pointed at an armchair with green upholstery by the window.

'Oh,' Tara said. 'I didn't know you had taken things from there.' She looked at Kate, a little shocked that she hadn't been consulted.

'I tried to get in touch with you when we moved in here to tell you,' Kate said, looking defensive, noticing Tara's sadness. 'But you didn't reply so I went ahead. I didn't think you'd mind. I'm sorry. I should have made sure you knew and that it was okay.'

Tara shrugged, knowing it was true that she was sometimes too busy in New York to answer her phone. 'It's fine. It just gave me a bit of a start to see it here. No big deal.'

'Great,' Kate said, looking relieved. 'I had it re-covered as it was very worn.'

'It looks lovely,' Tara said, slowly getting over her pang of jealousy. Why shouldn't Kate have a few pieces from their childhood home for her new house? 'Perfect for looking out at the view with a book and a cup of tea.'

'But everything else is still there,' Kate assured her. 'The furniture in Dublin, I mean. So once you have a house of your own, you can pick whatever you want.'

'That'll be a while,' Tara said with a laugh. 'I'm not ready to settle down just yet. But it's nice to know all of Dad's stuff is there waiting, though.'

'Some of it belonged to Mum,' Kate remarked.

'I know. Like the chair. But this desk belonged to our grandad and it was in the study by the window in our house in Dublin. We never got to look inside.' Tara pulled up the rolltop. 'What's in here? In the drawers and slots?' She looked at piles of papers and envelopes. 'Haven't you looked through all this?'

'No, I just got it from Dublin. Haven't had the time yet. But maybe you could sort it all out while you're here?'

'I'd love to go through it,' Tara said as she opened an envelope and discovered some faded black-and-white photos. 'Especially the photographs.'

'You're welcome to get started.' Kate opened a door. 'This is our spare room. You'll be sleeping in here for the next few days. It's a bit cramped. Hope you don't mind.'

Tara joined Kate at the door and peered into a small, sunny room with a single bed, a wardrobe, a bookcase crammed with books and a chest of drawers. The wooden floor was bare and the room smelled of dried flowers and herbs that came from a shelf by the window full of jars with what looked like dried rose petals and all kinds of leaves and roots. 'It's a nice room,' she said and put her case on the bed. 'And it smells great.'

'It's Cormac's room, really,' Kate said and opened the sash window. 'He puts some of the plants here before he makes up his special teas and other remedies. I think he's planning to make up essential oils from some of these.'

Tara took a deep breath. 'Gorgeous. He should make a bath oil. I'd certainly buy it.'

'Why don't you tell him tonight?' Kate suggested. 'He'll be home then and will love to tell you about his work. He's done so much since last year. But he needs guinea pigs to try things out on. Dr Pat's wife, Helen, runs a pharmaceutical company and after a lot of negotiations, they came to an agreement last month. They are now working with Cormac on a line of natural health and beauty products.'

'Really?' Tara said, intrigued. 'That's amazing.'

'Yes, he's very excited about it.' Kate smiled, looking suddenly more relaxed. 'I'm so happy for him. This way he gets to do what he loves at his own pace. He's such a free spirit but he needs focus and this has given him exactly that.' She turned and walked out of the room. 'I'll go and make us some sandwiches for lunch and then we can sit on the bench outside. It's such a heavenly day.'

'Great,' Tara said, happy that the discord about her assignment had been put aside. They'd have to clear that up later. But now all she wanted to do was have lunch and then a nap. After that, she'd go for a walk around the village to familiarise herself with her surroundings, and possibly take some preliminary shots. She'd do what she had come here to do, even if Kate didn't like it. She'd just have to get used to the idea.

Tara walked back to the car to get her suitcase, standing in the front garden for a while, mesmerised by the beauty of the landscape, the golden light and the smell of the soft, clean air. *This place,* she thought. *How heavenly it is. And what wonderful photos I could take. Would it be such a sin to put it on the tourist map?*

Chapter Five

Later that day, when Kate had gone back to work, Tara woke from her nap and walked into the living room to have another look at the desk. It touched her to see it in Kate's living room which made it feel that their father was here in some way. Their mother's chair in the sunny window was another thing that sparked memories of a happy childhood in that old house in Dublin. Their time there may have been shattered by their mother's long illness and subsequent death when Tara and Kate had been fifteen, and their father's more recent death, but it still held happy memories. And she and Kate still had each other.

Tara felt a pang of dread as she thought of Kate's reaction to her assignment. Would she have to choose between her work and her relationship with her sister, the person she loved the most in the whole world? No, of course not. Kate would come around and see how unreasonable she was being and how terrible it would be to try to hide the beauty of Sandy Cove. If Tara didn't spread the word, someone else would. It was only a matter of time.

Tara shook off the worrying thoughts and went to the desk, opened it and started to take out the letters and photos shoved into drawers and compartments. It wasn't the many old letters that had intrigued her, but the envelope full of old photographs. Images of a world gone by, faces of people long dead but so alive then, frozen in that moment when they had been in the middle of life, not knowing what the future held. Old photos had always fascinated Tara and it was often through them she found her inspiration. Now she took out that envelope she had glanced at before and went to sit down in her mother's chair.

The sunlight streaming in was perfect for looking at the images, some of them blurred and yellowed, some surprisingly sharp and detailed. She looked at families dressed up for weddings and christenings, summer parties and Christmas dinners, recognising familiar features in the faces of people she had never known. The O'Rourkes had high cheekbones, thick eyebrows and large, dark eyes and she and Kate had inherited some of those traits. How strange to see those details and recognise some of her own features in faces from so long ago. It was eerie and wonderful at the same time.

Some of the photos were especially intriguing to Tara, as they were taken against the background of a large farmhouse overgrown with ivy. The house had two storeys and quite a lot of land from the look of it, so Tara knew that it belonged to a well-off family. It was unusual for such a place to be built in Ireland in the old days. It must have been an important farm, Tara thought. 'Kerry' was written in captions scribbled on the back of the photos, so she knew it must have been nearby, but where? Around here, in Sandy Cove? Or somewhere else in Kerry?

Tara picked up the last photo in the envelope and stared at a good-looking young man wearing a tweed jacket and a flat cap standing in front of the house which had granite steps leading up to an ornate front door. His hair was dark and curled around his ears and he carried a shotgun. His smile was infectious and she found herself smiling back, thinking of her father, whose smile had been very similar. Who was he? She turned the photo and found something written in pencil at the back. *Daniel at the farm in October 1920,* she read. Was this Daniel O'Rourke, her great-grandfather? The man whose history Kate had wanted to know all about? The man who had left for Dublin and become a policeman? She didn't know, as she had never seen any photos of him. But if he was – and the likeness to her grandfather and her father strongly suggested this was the case – why had he left? And who had written those words?

Tara looked through the photos again but this young man wasn't in any of them, except if he was one of the children, which was hard to make out. There was only that one photo of the young man and she picked it up again, marvelling at the quality and sharpness of the picture. But it was not only that she found so intriguing; it was the look in his eyes and the startling likeness to her father in photos she had seen of him when he was young. She couldn't take her eyes off his face and suddenly had that feeling deep inside she got sometimes when a photograph pulled at her emotions. It was suddenly as if this young man with the expressive eyes was looking straight at her across the many years that separated them. Despite her lack of interest in history, she suddenly knew she simply had to find out who he was and what had happened to him. Not only for her late father, who she missed so much, but also for herself and Kate. This young man's destiny was their family history and would provide that missing piece of the jigsaw they had always wanted to find.

Tara put all the photos except the one of the young man back in the envelope. Then she put it where she had found it and propped the one of Daniel against a candlestick on top of the desk. She walked back and looked at it from a distance.

The young man looked eerily familiar but seemed at the same time like a stranger. But he had to be who she thought – her great-grandfather. 'Did you do something to break up your whole family?' she asked, her voice echoing in the stillness as she remembered what Kate had said. If he had caused some kind of scandal, she continued her reasoning, it would have impacted not only on his own life but on the lives and futures of his children, their children and – her and Kate's lives, too. These thoughts made her nearly dizzy as she imagined what life would have been like had she grown up on a farm in Kerry, rather than in an old house in Dublin. If this was indeed her great-grandfather, what had he done to change all of their lives so drastically?

Cormac arrived home late in the afternoon bringing fresh fish wrapped in newspaper and a bag of new potatoes. He smiled broadly as he discovered Tara sitting in a deck chair on the back lawn reading *The Irish Times* that she'd found on the kitchen table. She shot out of her chair as she spotted him. 'Hi, Cormac,' she exclaimed and threw her arms around him.

'Hi, Tara,' he said and kissed her cheek. 'It's so lovely to have you here again. Welcome to Sandy Cove.'

'Thank you. Lovely to be here at last. And I adore this little cottage you're renting.' She looked at him, amazed by his handsome face, the sweet expression in his beautiful green eyes and how unaware he was of his looks. He was dressed in a faded green linen shirt, baggy shorts and sandals that would look nerdy on anyone else but which he carried off with effortless elegance. 'You look well,' she added.

Cormac laughed and dropped his burden on the grass. 'It's all thanks to this fantastic weather. I'm so glad you came. Kate has been longing for you to come and stay.'

'Me too. I won't be staying long here though,' Tara continued, 'but in some little cottage that needs minding, Kate told me. Belongs to a couple called Jasmine and Aiden, she said. They can't come over from their jobs in Paris until August, I believe.'

'That's right,' Cormac replied. 'The cottage is nearby, so we'll be neighbours. Hope you don't mind, but I think that spare room is a little cramped for a longer stay.'

'God, yes, it's tiny,' Tara agreed. 'And I need space to work and spread out a bit. It'll be perfect and I won't be in your hair. But near enough if I get lonely. Hey, sit down and we'll have a chat.'

'Okay.' Cormac pulled another deckchair over to where Tara had been sitting. 'I have to cook that fish for dinner, but I have time to sit down for a bit until Kate comes home.'

'You do the cooking?' Tara asked, sitting down again. 'Thank the Lord for that. Kate can't even boil water.'

'I know,' Cormac said. 'But that's not a problem. I love cooking and she loves my food, so that works for us. Bridget used to cook for her when she lived at the surgery, but now we're together, I'm in charge of the food.'

'She's a lucky woman,' Tara remarked and lay back in her chair, closing her eyes. 'What a lovely day. I'm just lazing around, recovering from jetlag. I might even go for a swim.'

'You should,' Cormac said. 'But wait for Kate, she'll come with you. She loves her swim before dinner.'

'I bet she does. We both love swimming and always have, ever since we were kids. Couldn't get us out of the water, even if it was freezing.'

'The water is warmer here than on the east coast,' Cormac said. 'And I just heard on the radio that the postman in Donegal has predicted a hot summer this year.'

Tara laughed as she remembered this man and his yearly predictions which were usually a little hit and miss. He was a well-known character in Ireland and people often joked about his predictions. 'The postman in Donegal? Is he still around?'

'Oh yes, and he's been pretty accurate with his predictions lately as well.'

Tara looked out over the shimmering water. 'I hope he's right. This place is lovely, and with this good weather it's as close to paradise as you can get.'

Cormac smiled. 'Better than New York?'

'In the summer, yes,' Tara replied with feeling. 'New York is pure hell when both the temperature and the humidity soar. But in the fall, it's wonderful, of course.'

Cormac laughed. 'The fall? You sounded very American there.'

Tara smiled. 'Yeah, I know. It kind of rubs off on you very quickly. The lifestyle, the accent, the whole way of living. I love it. But I'm glad to be here for the summer all the same. Glad to be in Ireland generally. Roots are hard to pull up, you know.'

'I can imagine.' Cormac lay back in the deckchair, studying Tara for a while. 'You and Kate are so alike in one way, but so different in another. Fascinating that. Twins, I mean.'

'I know. It's strange sometimes how we think alike but then have such different reactions to a lot of things. Kate has always been the big sister, even though she's only two minutes older than me. I'm the wild, bold girl who never thinks before I leap. Kate has always had to pull me out of scrapes. Yeah, we look identical but that's an illusion. When we've been apart for a long time, like now, it gives me a bit of a start to look at Kate again. Like looking into a mirror. But now our hair is different, of course.'

'Are you going to cut yours short like Kate's?' Cormac asked.

Tara touched her smooth bob. 'No. I don't think so. I like it on her, but it's not really my style. In any case, that would make us look too identical and then people might ask me to examine their tonsils or something.'

Cormac laughed. 'That might cause a few problems all right.' He paused, watching her for a second. 'Did you never want to study medicine with Kate?'

Tara laughed and shuddered. 'Ugh, no. I'm not good around sick people. And I nearly faint at the sight of blood.'

'Hmm, interesting,' Cormac said, looking intrigued.

'And I love cooking,' Tara continued, changing the subject to take the spotlight off her relationship with Kate. 'Do you need a hand with that fish?'

'No, but you could make the salad. Just lettuce, tomatoes and a simple vinaigrette. I grow everything myself,' he said proudly.

'How amazing,' Tara said, beaming at him. She sat up as she heard a car pull up at the front of the house. 'I think Kate's back.'

Cormac got up. 'Great. Go for that swim with her and I'll put on the spuds and then start grilling the mackerel when you come back.

We can eat outside.' He pointed at a table and chairs by the stone wall that separated the back garden from the cliffs and the path to the beach.

'How lovely.'

'You want wine?' Cormac asked as he walked to the back door. 'I think Kate put a bottle of white in the fridge this morning.'

'Perfect.' Tara followed him inside, and continued to the living room, where Kate was putting her bag on the sofa. 'Hi,' she said. 'We're rustling up some dinner. Fish and potatoes and salad. But we have time for a swim first, Cormac said.'

'Fabulous,' Kate said and smiled at her sister. 'You and Cormac had a chat?'

'Yes, we're getting to know each other. Much better than FaceTiming.'

'That's for sure.' Kate ran her fingers through her hair and took a deep breath. 'Hectic afternoon. It was the mother and baby clinic today. Lots of crying and squirming babies and frantic mothers. But they were all happy in the end.'

'Must be tiring,' Tara said sympathetically.

'A bit, but very nice, too.' Kate smiled. 'So what have you been up to?'

Tara shrugged. 'Not much. I took a nap after lunch and then I looked at some of the photos in the old desk. Amazing, but a bit sad not to know who these people were. I'm pretty sure that one of them is Daniel, though.' Tara pointed at the photo she had put up on the desk. 'You didn't see that one, did you?'

'No.' Kate walked to the desk and picked up the photo. 'Oh my gosh, it's an incredibly sharp picture. Just look at him. A true O'Rourke. He had the same eyes as Dad. And the thick eyebrows.'

'Like ours. And we're forever plucking them,' Tara said.

'That's for sure.' Kate studied the photo. 'But where is he standing? This house… I've never seen it before. She looked at the photo and read the text aloud. '*At the farm?*' she said, looking confused. 'What farm?'

'The family farm, here in Kerry. Perhaps in Sandy Cove?' Tara suggested. 'The farm he left to go to Dublin.'

'*Daniel at the farm in October 1920,*' Kate quoted. 'What does that mean? And who wrote it?'

'That's what I asked myself, too,' Tara replied. 'I was wondering about the family feud you mentioned.'

'I don't know that much about it. Just that something happened to make Daniel leave to go to Dublin.' Kate gave Tara a surprised glance. 'What's this all of a sudden? I thought you weren't a bit interested in history, even if it's about family.'

'I know,' Tara said with a laugh. 'History always made me yawn. But the strangest thing happened when I looked at this photo. The expression in his eyes, that little smile… It was as if he was looking at me, sending me some kind of message. Silly, I know, but I suddenly felt I just had to find out who he is and what happened to him. And I realised that you were right. It's not just boring old history, it's about us.' Tara tapped the photo. 'What happened to him made us who we are. That's what I felt anyway.' She drew breath. 'If we could find that house, we might get some clues.'

'It looks quite big for a farmhouse around here. I doubt it's in Sandy Cove,' Kate said, looking at the photo again. 'Do you remember Granny? She was a real Dubliner, but perhaps there was a reason she wasn't really interested in her husband's family back in Kerry? Do you remember what she said when Dad asked?'

'"Let the dead rest in peace",' Tara said darkly. 'That's all she ever said. And then nobody dared ask after that, not even Dad.'

'And both she and Grandad died when we were small, so we never really knew them,' Kate remarked. 'I always felt sorry for Dad. He had no family of his own, really, except for his brothers, but they weren't close.' She looked at the photo again. 'Daniel O'Rourke was a handsome lad, don't you think?'

'Really good-looking,' Tara agreed. 'But there's something wild about him, a bit of a devil-may-care look in his eyes.'

Kate peered at the photo. 'Yes, maybe. But you have a better eye for those things than me.'

'I do love looking at portraits,' Tara said. 'And I love photographing people's faces.'

'You're so good at that.' Kate sighed and shook her head. 'You're good at all types of photography, really.' Kate paused thoughtfully, looking at Tara. 'I still don't want you…' She stopped. 'No need to go into that tonight.'

'Or ever,' Tara said hotly, knowing what Kate was about to say. 'I heard what you said about protecting the village and I know how you feel. Point taken.'

'But not accepted,' Kate filled in. 'I see that stubborn look in your eyes. But I don't want to argue with you.' She put the photo back on top of the desk. 'We should celebrate our reunion and go for that swim before dinner. It'll be a gorgeous evening. Wait till you see the sunset. Spectacular. And then, when it gets really dark and we can see the stars, you'll be gobsmacked.'

'I'll get my gobsmacker camera ready,' Tara said, relieved that the argument wasn't going to be picked up again. But the feeling that it was going to be an ongoing disagreement between them stayed with her like a niggling worry. Kate wouldn't be placated until Tara changed her mind and focused on another part of Kerry altogether. But how could she, when the beauty of Sandy Cove constantly amazed and delighted her, even after a few short hours? And if the Donegal postman was right, this would be a summer like no other with endless possibilities for spectacular photos. She only hoped it wouldn't end in tears.

The tension eased while they got ready to go down to the beach for a swim, both wearing navy swimsuits crossed over at the back. 'Identical,' Cormac said, laughing, as they prepared to leave, both with a white towel across the shoulders.

'Not quite,' Kate said. 'My togs are from Marks and Spencer. Tara's have to be from some fancy designer beachwear collection.'

'Nope,' Tara countered. 'It's an old pair I bought in Macy's last year.'

'Ah well, on you it looks so fab you'd swear it was something glamorous,' Kate replied.

'Thank you, my lady,' Tara said and curtsied, which earned her a shove from Kate's elbow.

'Funny how you picked the same style though,' Cormac remarked. 'But I suppose that's what twins do.'

'It is,' Kate agreed. 'Come on, then, sis. Last one in is a rotten egg.' She started a half-run down the path to the beach, with Tara following behind trying to keep up. Once they jumped onto the sand, they raced to the water's edge and ran, side by side, into the waves, laughing and splashing each other, screaming as they threw themselves into the water.

Tara slowly got used to the cold and felt a surge of pleasure as she continued to swim behind Kate in the crystal-clear water. She could see fish swimming below her and gave a start as she spotted the outline of a stingray against the sand below. But then she realised it was the harmless box stingray, common in these waters. She watched as the ray slowly glided away under her and then resumed swimming, her strokes stronger as she tried to catch up with Kate, who was racing ahead. But it was no use. Kate had always been the stronger swimmer and Tara slowed down, watching Kate's steady progress out towards a rock sticking out of the water. She arrived at the rock as Kate was already sitting there, her face turned to the sun.

'Oh, God,' Tara said, panting as she hauled herself up onto the smooth rock. 'I'm a bit out of shape.'

'Ah well, it has to be the jetlag,' Kate said sympathetically, helping Tara get up to sit beside her. 'That's bound to knock a bit off your form.'

'I never managed to beat you,' Tara said. 'Even when I wasn't tired. But that's okay. It has to be some kind of talent you were born with that I didn't get.'

'You've got a lot of talents that I don't have,' Kate said. 'But I think we complement each other.'

'We do,' Tara agreed. She lay back on the hot rock and enjoyed the warmth of the sun on her skin after the cold water. 'This is heaven,' she mumbled, closing her eyes.

'It's my favourite spot,' Kate said, leaning back. 'I love swimming here and then lying on the rock to feel the heat of the sun. And then, when I'm too hot, I get into the water again and swim back. After that, I have Cormac's dinner to look forward to. I feel so blessed.'

Tara turned her head to look at Kate. 'I'm so pleased for you,' she said, meaning every word. It was wonderful to see Kate so happy with a man like Cormac. *True love*, she thought. *Will I ever find that, too?*

'What about you?' Kate asked as if reading Tara's thoughts. 'You and Joe, I mean. Last time we talked you seemed very happy, too, even if a little uncertain.'

Tara sat up. 'I'm even more uncertain,' she said, staring out at the horizon. 'I don't know how he feels about me, really. Or me about him. He never seems to want to move on with our relationship. So I thought I'd test him and told him I wanted to take a break for the summer. From us, I mean.'

'Oh.' Kate sat up and put her hand on Tara's shoulder. 'I'm sorry. That must be hard. How did he take it?'

'On the chin. Well, kind of. He pretended to be cool but I could tell he was annoyed. It's not that he's committed to whatever it is we have, it's more that he can't stand being rejected. Bad for his self-esteem, I think. The thing is, we're dating but there's no real mutual understanding, if you see what I mean. So it's good to be away for a bit and then see how we feel when we meet again. Better than being in some kind of limbo.' Tara looked at Kate over her shoulder. 'I know what you're going to say, so don't. I'd prefer if we didn't talk about him, if you don't mind. For now, I mean. I just want to settle into this gorgeous place and then do my job. I can't wait to get started. And I'm so happy to be here with you and to get to know this village. I'm really looking forward to the next few weeks.'

'Me too,' Kate said. 'I think it'll be great to have you practically next door. I would have loved to have you stay with us, but there simply isn't room.'

Tara smiled. 'Oh, that doesn't matter at all. I think it's the best solution. We can see each other all the time anyway and not get in each other's way. You know what I'm like when I'm working, up all night sometimes and then sleeping late or vice versa. And anyway, you and Cormac need a little space. You only just moved in together, didn't you?'

'We did,' Kate said with a dreamy smile. 'And we're only just getting used to each other. But so far it's working beautifully.'

'I can see that. So you don't want me to be there all the time, do you?'

'Well, no,' Kate confessed. 'That'd cramp our style a little, I think.'

'Of course it would.' Tara dipped her toes in the water. 'But now I think we should get back, or Cormac will start sending smoke signals.' She slid down the rock into the water. 'Oh, this feels nice. Let's not race this time.'

'Okay,' Kate laughed and pushed herself down into the water beside Tara. 'We'll swim back slowly.'

Tara floated on her back, enjoying the cool water on her scalp. She looked up at the sky before kicking off beside Kate, looking at the fluffy white clouds drifting across the blue sky. How heavenly this was. She felt she would always remember this first day in Sandy Cove and the promise of a wonderful summer stretching ahead.

Chapter Six

Tara moved into the cottage three days later. It was a cute little house along the same cliff path as Kate and Cormac's home, with a white stucco façade, square windows with trims painted blue which matched the front door that was the original half-door where you could keep the top open while the bottom part was closed.

'It used to be to keep animals out,' Kate explained. 'I think this little house had hens running around in the garden so the half-door would have been handy.' She ducked her head as she went in carrying Tara's suitcase, with Tara in her wake with her camera bag, plus her laptop. She had left the other case with bits and pieces like make-up and accessories behind in Kate's house. They had seemed essential when she left New York, but it had only taken her a few days in Sandy Cove to realise that life here was simple and such things were completely unnecessary. She had also slimmed down her wardrobe even more, to two pairs of jeans, a pair of khaki shorts, a few linen shirts, an assortment of T-shirts and two swimsuits. She had left the rest in Kate's wardrobe, feeling oddly liberated to have such a minimalist collection of clothes. There was no need to dress to impress, even if her jeans were from Armani and the deceptively simple linen shirts from the latest Ralph Lauren summer collection. But nobody around here would know that.

'Here we are,' Kate said as she stood in living room, putting the suitcase on the floor. 'What do you think?'

Tara looked around the room with its wooden floorboards that had been painted white, the blue rug on which stood a cream sofa, two small easy chairs and the simple fireplace with a mantelpiece made of a thick piece of driftwood on which were assembled a collection of seashells and two glass jars with candles stuck into sand. The curtainless windows let in the dappled sunlight from the garden and there were small lamps with linen shades on little tables dotted around the room.

'Oh my God, it's gorgeous,' Tara said with a happy sigh. 'I love it. And the light is wonderful.' She went to one of the windows and peered out at the view of the bay and the islands. 'I can see the beach and the top of Willow House. And the headland behind it and...' She turned and smiled at Kate. 'What a great little place. Jasmine and Aiden did a wonderful job. I must give them a call and thank them.'

'They're happy you're here to house sit for them,' Kate said. 'They would normally be here now, but Aiden is running this big restaurant in Paris and Jasmine had a lot of new clients at her financial consultancy, so they couldn't spend the summer here as usual.'

'Couldn't they let it?' Tara asked.

'They don't want to do that. When Jasmine's mother Sally heard you were coming, she suggested you stay here. She and her husband will be back from visiting Jasmine in Paris in a few weeks. She's another O'Rourke, actually.'

'Really? Are we related?'

'Not as far as we know, but I'm sure the families were one and the same around two hundred years ago. Another branch, I'd say. This area is full of O'Rourkes.'

'Maybe she can help us find that farm,' Tara suggested. 'The one Daniel O'Rourke stood beside when that photo was taken. I'm still wondering where it is. Has to be somewhere nearby, don't you think?'

'No idea,' Kate replied. 'But I'll ask John, Bridget's husband. He knows all about the history around here. We can talk to him tonight when we go over there for dinner.'

'Great,' Tara agreed. 'Nice of them to ask us to come for a meal.'

'They're a lovely couple. Bridget is the surgery nurse. She was living in Pat's house when I came here, but now they live in their own house nearby. Pat has his dinner there every evening, so you'll meet him, too.'

'I can't wait,' Tara said. 'Let's see the rest of the house,' she suggested and opened a door which she thought might lead to the kitchen. But it was the door to the bedroom, where a large double bed and a small wardrobe took up most of the space. The bed had a headboard that was made of pieces of driftwood and it was covered in a white crocheted bedspread with a pile of lacy pillows.

'Oooh, how cute,' Tara exclaimed and threw herself on the bed. 'I'll be having very sweet dreams here, I'm sure.'

'Of course you will,' Kate said, laughing. 'But not yet. Let's see the kitchen and the bathroom and then I think we'll have seen the whole house.'

Tara got up and followed Kate around the rest of the dwelling. The kitchen was tiny but had everything one would need to cook a meal. There was even a little table for two beside the window that overlooked the back garden with its small lawn and a flowerbed with roses and peonies just beginning to bloom. 'This will be where you earn the rent,' Kate said. 'The flowerbed will need weeding and the lawn mowed.'

'No problem,' Tara said, looking forward to having her breakfast out there when the weather was warm. 'Bathroom?' she asked.

'Here,' Kate said and opened a door beside the bedroom. 'It's gorgeous,' she reported after having stuck her head in. She moved aside to let Tara pass. 'Take a look. You'd think you were in France.'

Tara ducked her head under the low lintel and went into the enchanting bathroom with a roll-top bath, a vintage wash basin shaped like a shell with old-fashioned taps and a tiled floor that looked like a mosaic with the motif of a dolphin. Seashells and tiny pieces of driftwood adorned a shelf over the bath, along with a glass jar full of turquoise bath salts and a little bowl with a heart-shaped soap. 'This is incredible,' Tara said with a happy sigh. 'I'll be here every night in that bath. And look,' she said, pointing at the window, 'it has a sea view.'

'Fabulous,' Kate said. 'Jasmine and Aiden worked so hard to do up this cottage. It took them over a year before it was finished.'

'And now they can't enjoy it because of work,' Tara remarked, turning to look at Kate.

'That's only this year. They're going to try to organise their work so they can spend more time here in the future,' Kate explained.

'But what if they have a family?'

'They have applied for planning permission to extend,' Kate replied. 'And there is plenty of space at the side to add at least two more rooms. Sally showed me the plans. I think they might even get started at the end of the summer.'

'I'm sure they'll do a lovely job to make the bigger cottage just as nice as this one,' Tara said as she stepped out of the bathroom. 'Right now it's a beautiful little love nest.'

'Oh, yes, it is. And they're such a romantic couple,' Kate said, giving a start as her phone rang. 'Oh, that must be Pat. He said he'd call if he needed me.' She answered the call, and after a short conversation hung up and put her phone back in her pocket. 'I have to go to a house call. Old man up the road feeling unwell. Can you manage now?'

'Of course,' Tara said, delighted at the prospect of settling into this wonderful little place. 'Go on. I'll see you tonight.'

'Great.' Kate moved to the door. 'Seven o'clock. No need to dress up. We can walk to Bridget's house together.'

'Great.' Tara waved at Kate. 'Go on. I'll be fine.'

Kate laughed and waved back. 'Okay, sis. See you later, so.'

Tara watched Kate walk off down the path, disappearing as she rounded the corner of her own house. Then she laughed and did a little dance around the pretty living room, enjoying the freedom of being in her own space, on her own terms. She had never lived truly on her own before and had always longed to. And here she was, all alone but not in the slightest bit lonely. And why would she be, with Kate only a stone's throw away? This way she could find her feet and get a feel for being independent in the best circumstances.

Tara stopped dancing and went to unpack her suitcase and settle into her new home. But before she did anything else, she took the photo of Daniel O'Rourke and put it on the mantelpiece among the seashells and beachcomber collection. 'There,' she said as she looked at his handsome face. 'I hope we'll get to know each other in some way or other.'

She studied the photo again, especially the backdrop of the ivy-covered farmhouse with the ornate front door and noticed something above it she hadn't paid attention to before. A small plaque with the year 1860 written in faded letters. So this was quite an old house, then. It had to be somewhere in the neighbourhood. But where was it? And who lived there now? She was suddenly very excited at the prospect of finding out more. And maybe she could even combine her search with her assignment in some way. Perhaps there was a trail by Wild Rose Bay to this mysterious house that would suit the adventurous hillwalker who wanted something different. Or maybe it could lead to a historic tour of the area? That would introduce a new attraction for people who loved to discover a path to the past. It was a great idea, whatever Kate might think. But first she had to find it.

Dinner at Bridget's house turned out to be most enjoyable. Bridget, a large woman in her late fifties with curly red-blonde hair and rosy cheeks, greeted Tara with a warm hug. 'I feel I know you already,' she chortled as she released Tara and looked her up and down. 'So like Kate, but with a different twist. But if you cut your hair, I'm not sure I'd be able to tell you apart.'

'I won't,' Tara promised. 'I like my hair the way it is.'

'It's lovely. But come in,' Bridget urged and pulled Tara into the hall. 'And then out again,' she added, laughing. 'We're eating on the patio out the back as it's such a warm evening. John is doing the drinks and Pat's already out there. I just have to go and check on the lamb and then I'll be with you. Right through the living room over there and out through the patio door. You can't miss it. Kate, will you show the way?'

'Of course,' Kate said and walked ahead, Tara and Cormac behind her, into a bright living room and then through a set of French doors onto a patio with a round table. Bridget's husband, John, a softly spoken man with kind eyes, was mixing drinks while he talked to an older man with grey hair and glasses who sat at the table sipping what looked like a gin and tonic. They both looked up as Tara, Kate and Cormac arrived.

The man at the table got up and kissed Kate on the cheek. 'Hello, Kate,' he said and pushed his glasses up his nose. Then he held out his hand to Tara. 'And this is Tara. We meet at last. I'm Pat. Welcome to Sandy Cove.'

'Thank you, Pat,' Tara said, smiling at the man. 'I've heard so much about you.'

'Me too,' Pat said. 'About you, I mean. And now you're here. Kate must be so happy.'

'We both are,' Kate said, putting her arm around Tara. 'It's good to be together again.'

'And you're here to work, I hear,' Pat continued. 'Taking pho-tographs for an article, is that right?'

Tara glanced at Kate. 'Yes. All over this area,' she said to relax the tension she felt was beginning to mount with Kate every time her assignment was mentioned. 'I'll be travelling up and down the coast.'

'Will you rent a car?' John asked as he handed her a glass of white wine. 'Is this okay? Kate likes a glass of white, so I thought…'

Tara laughed and took the glass. 'You thought right. I love a glass of white before dinner. And to answer your first question, no. I thought I'd see if I could hire a bike. I love cycling. Or even buy one if I can. Is there a bike shop in the village?'

'Why didn't you tell me?' Kate chided. 'You can have mine. I don't have much time to use it. And it's nearly brand new.'

'Oh great,' Tara said. 'Perfect. Thanks, Kate.'

'It's in the little shed out the back,' Kate said. 'I'm glad it'll be used. I thought I'd go with Cormac when he cycles to Dingle to see his family, but I have only been able to go twice.'

'I'll give it back to you when you need it,' Tara promised. 'I'm looking forward to cycling on the country roads around here. Much better way to see the countryside than from a car.'

'Maybe you'll find that old farmhouse,' Cormac suggested as he poured himself a glass of lemonade from a jug. 'The one in that old photo, I mean.'

'What old farmhouse?' Bridget asked as she arrived on the patio carrying a platter of sliced lamb and new potatoes. 'Go get the gravy in the kitchen for me, please, Cormac.'

'We found an old photo in our dad's desk,' Kate said to Bridget. 'We think it's our great-grandfather, Daniel O'Rourke. And he's standing in front of a farmhouse that seems to be the family farm in Kerry, according to what's written on the back. But I don't recognise the house and can't figure out where it is. It has to be somewhere nearby, though. Dad always said the family originally came from Sandy Cove.'

'Did you bring the photo?' John asked.

'No, but I took a shot of it with my phone,' Tara said and pulled her phone out of her pocket. She quickly located the picture and held it out for John to see. 'There it is.'

'May I have a look?' John asked.

'Of course.' Tara handed him the phone. 'You can enlarge it a bit but it makes the image a little blurry.'

'Hmm,' John said as he peered at the screen. 'It looks familiar, but I can't quite place it.' He enlarged it slightly with his fingers. 'That front door... Could it be...? Take a look, Bridget,' he said and gave the phone to Bridget. 'Could it be Cois Abhainn Farm?'

'Quiche – what?' Tara asked.

'Cois Abhainn. It means riverside,' Cormac said as he brought the gravy boat to the table. 'Riverside Farm, eh? That kind of rings a bell, but a very faint one. I'm not from around here, so I don't know every single house.'

'It's an old farmhouse,' Bridget said. 'Down a back road off the Ballinskelligs road. Isn't that right, John?'

John nodded, still studying the picture on Tara's phone. 'It is. And it did belong to an O'Rourke family as far as I know. But I think the last owner was a bit of a hermit and didn't come into the village much. In fact *those* O'Rourkes were always a bit strange.' He handed the phone back to Tara. 'This farm had a lot of land, nearly a hundred acres of good grazing land. It's been let to farmers around here for years. I think they also own the land around O'Rourke's tower above Wild Rose Bay. The land around the house is very close to those fields.'

'Oh yes,' Kate exclaimed. 'I remember now. You told me about that when I'd just got here and we were trying to figure out who had permission to forage for plants there, remember, Cormac? It was owned by someone called Liam O'Rourke.'

'Yes, that's right. But we decided to leave it alone and not ask questions,' Cormac remarked and pulled out a chair. 'Bridget, please sit down. You've made us such a delicious meal and I think we should dig in before it goes cold.'

Bridget laughed and sat down. 'You're right, Cormac. And I have to confess I'm starving.'

Everyone pulled out chairs and sat down, passing around the platter and the gravy boat while John poured wine for them all except Cormac, who stuck to the lemonade, explaining to Tara that he didn't drink anything alcoholic, simply because he had been 'too fond of it' in his wild youth. 'Not quite an alcoholic but I was afraid I was heading that way,' he explained.

'He keeps an eye on me, too,' Kate joked as she took a sip of wine. 'But I have no head for too much of it, so I'm careful.'

The conversation turned to the weather and how the postman in Donegal had been right yet again, even though his forecast for last winter had been wide of the mark. 'He said we'd have a dry, cold winter,' Pat remarked. 'Then we had nothing but rain for two months. But he's redeeming himself this summer.'

'Long may it last,' Bridget said with a wistful sigh. 'I like a bit of warmth on my old bones.'

'Old?' Pat snorted. 'You're just a spring chicken compared to me.' He pointed at Cormac, Kate and Tara. 'And these are children compared to the rest of us.'

Tara laughed. 'That's lovely to hear. Made me feel young instead of middle-aged.'

'Middle-aged?' Kate said, giving Tara a little shove. 'I'm not there yet, thank you very much. Nor Cormac, but he's a little younger than us. He's only thirty-three. Nearly a teenager.'

'I'm her toy boy,' Cormac joked.

Tara laughed and concentrated on the food on her plate. The lamb was perfectly cooked with just a hint of pink, the new potatoes with butter and chives the most delicious she had tasted for a long time. She dug in with gusto, feeling a surge of pure joy sitting there with such nice people who had welcomed her so warmly and made her feel instantly at home. She could understand why Kate was so happy here and never wanted to leave. Even though village life would never be one she would choose herself, she knew it was perfect for her sister.

Tara had a different agenda, however and didn't see herself settling down for quite some time. But she didn't want to stay single forever, and she hoped that Joe would miss her so much he would want to commit to something more permanent once she came back to New York. He was the type of man she always thought would be perfect for her – a free spirit. She sighed and put another sliver of tender lamb into her mouth, feeling both happy and sad as she wondered if it would be possible for her to ever find what she was looking for.

Chapter Seven

A week later, Tara was cycling along the road that led to Ballinskelligs, a village about twenty kilometres from Sandy Cove which was famous for its wonderful views of the legendary Skellig Islands. These islands, the largest of which was Skellig Michael, could be seen in the distance, looking like little mountains rising out of the ocean, surrounded by flocks of seabirds hovering around the cliffs where they were nesting. Tara had to stop several times to take photos, the light and the views constantly changing as the clouds drifted across the sun. She had been happy to find Kate's bike in the shed and discovered it was brand new with many gears to cope with the steep roads going up the hills. She felt cycling would keep her fit and give her a better feel for the landscape than driving, giving her the experience of this mode of travel for the more adventurous tourist. She was, after all, on a quest for a different holiday, something a little more challenging than touring by car or bus.

She had taken a quiet road known as the Skellig Ring, away from the more travelled Ring of Kerry and a lot less busy. There was no traffic at all today, Tara discovered to her delight and cycled on slowly, enchanted by the landscape of cliffs and inlets and the view across the intensely blue ocean. Her rucksack held her camera equipment, sandwiches, a thermos of tea and a large slice of carrot cake from a café in Sandy Cove called The Two Marys', run by two women who were cousins with the same name. Tara had already met them when she went around the village the day after her arrival and been highly amused by their repartee with each other. Their cakes were famous and rightly so, Tara thought, as she tasted some of them when she went in for her eleven o'clock cup of coffee.

She had got her bearings in the village very quickly and been greeted warmly by the locals, who were intrigued to meet Kate's twin sister and absolutely amazed by their likeness to each other. 'If it wasn't for the hair, I'd think I was talking to Dr Kate,' a woman had declared, adding that she hoped Tara wouldn't get the same haircut and cause people to think they were seeing double. 'Then we'll be rushing to the eye doctor to make sure there is nothing wrong,' she added with a laugh.

Tara stopped and got off her bike for a moment, as steep slopes covered in wild roses in full bloom could be seen in the distance. Above it rose a headland with a ruined tower. *Wild Rose Bay,* Tara thought. *How beautiful it looks. And that must be O'Rourke's castle that Kate told me about.* Promising herself to go there the following day for a closer look, Tara cycled on thinking about her other quest: of finding that old farmhouse. John had told her how to find the 'boreen' that led to it, using the old Irish word for back road. 'There is a large boulder just before, and there used to be an old signpost but I think it's fallen down,' he had explained. 'It used to say *Cois Abhainn Farm.* I haven't been up that way for years, so I can't guarantee the road is still even walkable. It's probably just a track. You could leave the bike there and walk the rest of the way. It's about a kilometre and a half or so.'

Now Tara kept her eyes on the edge of the road to see if she could find that large boulder. It was supposed to be about halfway to Ballinskelligs and she started to wonder if she had come too far and missed it. But then, when she rounded a bend, she saw it, standing about two metres high at the side of the road with a pole beside it that could have held a sign. She got off her bike and set it down behind the boulder, making sure her rucksack was secure on her back. Then she took a quick swig from her bottle of water and started down the lane that was now just a track. As she walked on, she saw that some kind of vehicle had recently driven down the lane, judging by the tyre marks in the mud. Someone who'd got lost, or had come up here to walk further up the mountainside, she assumed. Or perhaps a farmer come to check on his sheep that she could see dotted all over the steep green slopes above her.

As Tara walked on, she slowed her pace to look at the trees, their foliage forming a green canopy above her head, the dappled sunlight illuminating the path lined with wildflowers. She breathed in their sweet scent, feeling she was in an enchanted place where only birdsong and the soft whisper of the breeze broke the silence. She stopped and found one of her cameras in her rucksack and took a shot of the path ahead, feeling she wanted to capture this moment. The stillness, the scents and the sound of birds were impossible to record, but she knew the photo would hint at the atmosphere if she succeeded in taking the perfect shot. She waited a moment, and, when the light changed as a cloud drifted across the sun, shot a series of photos she knew would be slightly different from the first ones – slightly misty, giving a faint paranormal feel. Satisfied, she put away the camera and walked on, wondering where the house was. Then she came to an old cast-iron gate hanging off its hinges and knew this had to be the entrance to the front garden of the old farmhouse.

Walking through the gate, Tara came to a drive that had once been covered in gravel but now consisted of mainly weeds and clumps of grass. This would once have been neatly raked, the lawn on either side mowed. A well-tended entrance to a large farmhouse where people had lived and worked so many years ago. Intrigued, she walked faster around a bend and stopped suddenly as a house came into view. In a flash of recognition, she knew this was it. The house in the photo. Cois Abhainn Farm, the house her great-grandfather had left when he was young after some kind of family feud.

Tara stood there for a moment, looking at the house covered in ivy, worn and withered by age and neglect. But it was still beautiful, with the graceful proportions of Victorian architecture. How strange that it stood here, in the wilds of Kerry, where farms were usually small and the houses much more modest. She took out her camera and lingered for a while, waiting for the perfect light to settle to take a shot that suited her. She closed her eyes to get into her feelings, to tap into what it was deep inside that had made her want to come here and see the house. Then she looked up and walked to the side, to get the exact angle of that old photo. Daniel would have stood here, slightly to the side of the front door… She pretended he was there, standing in front of her, looking at her with that slightly quizzical air she had noticed. Then, suddenly she got that feeling she was after, which was nothing more than a slight draught across the back of her neck that made her shiver. Without hesitating she took a series of shots, the clicking of the camera echoing in the stillness of the warm summer day. There. Done. Those shots would be amazing, but she decided not to look at them until she could see them with Kate. The unravelling of the family history was a journey they would take together.

Tara put away her camera and walked closer, her feet crunching on the bit of gravel that remained. The ornate front door, its green paint flaking off, was half-open. She glanced at the little plaque above it that said *1860*, just like in the photo, and suddenly felt an urge to go inside. It was nearly as if the house was beckoning her to come in. She took a tentative step across the threshold and peered into a dark hall with wide floorboards that still looked solid enough to walk on. There was a musty smell of damp plaster and a whiff of smoke from the fireplace but there was still a feeling of freshness from the air blowing through the broken panes of the sash windows. A half-moon table stood at the far wall and a dusty mirror hung above it, reflecting Tara's pale face and eyes wide with excitement.

She walked further inside, through the hall and into a corridor that had an open door on either side, one that led into a room that must have once been a living room with a pretty period fireplace, a sagging sofa and two easy chairs that stood on a dusty carpet, the colour of which was barely discernible. The other door led into what must have been a dining room, judging by the large oval table. Tara walked further down the corridor, towards an open door that led to a kitchen with a solid fuel stove and a pine table with matching chairs. She noticed a collection of crockery through a half-open cupboard door. The back door was one of those old-fashioned half-doors, the top hanging open, letting in a ray of sunshine.

Tara went to the door and peered outside, discovering a back garden that despite its neglect was a pure delight with roses rambling all over the walls and clematis in a riot of pale pink across the roof of an old farm building. A jasmine bush had gone wild all over the rest of the garden. The scent of flowers was nearly overpowering and the sound of birdsong and humming of bees added to the peaceful atmosphere. Tara stepped out into the sunshine and, suddenly remembering the sandwiches and thermos of tea in her rucksack, decided to have her lunch right here, in this enchanted, forgotten garden. She sat down on the back step and slowly ate her delicious chicken sandwiches while she looked at the flowers gone wild, and planned the photos she would take. It would illustrate the lushness of Irish gardens and how flowers thrived in the rich soil and the mild climate. The photos she had taken of the overgrown path she had walked on would also be included, making it a great feature in her article about hidden places to walk.

Tara had finished her lunch and was taking close-ups of the roses when she heard a noise. She stiffened and listened to some kind of vehicle slowly lumbering up the rough path. She quickly repacked her rucksack, slung it on her back, and made her way to the rear of the old shed, her camera still in her hand. She might get away by a different path than the one she had used before and not be discovered by whoever had just arrived. Aware of the fact that she was perhaps trespassing, she felt it would be better not to be seen rather than be confronted by some angry sheep farmer. But she gave a start as a car door slamming shut broke the silence and before she had a chance to find an escape route, a man was coming around the corner of the house, stopping dead as he spotted Tara.

'What the…' he said, looking both startled and annoyed. 'Who are you and what are you doing here? This is private property, you know.'

Momentarily speechless, Tara stared at the tall man with black curly hair and blazing blue eyes. He was dressed in jeans and a crumpled checked shirt and carried a shotgun broken over his arm. He looked to be about her age, maybe a little older and she couldn't help noticing that he wasn't bad-looking at all. Or that standing there against the backdrop of the old house with the shotgun, he looked so wild and handsome, and wouldn't have been out of place in a movie. Without thinking, she took a picture of him and then lowered the camera and smiled. 'Sorry. I was taking some shots and—'

'Shots of what?' he asked, looking puzzled.

'The landscape and the roses, and… well, I was out walking and then I saw the house and wanted to take a look at it and saw the amazing little garden with all the flowers, so I thought I'd sit here for a while and have my lunch,' she babbled on. 'I thought it was abandoned, so I figured it would be okay.' She drew breath and looked at him to see if he believed her story. 'Don't shoot me,' she added with a nervous laugh.

'Shoot you?' He looked at the shotgun. 'With this? It's a rusty old thing I found in the hall. Must have been my old uncle's. He lived here until he died five years ago. In fact, this old wreck is for sale.' He leaned casually against the wall of the house, an amused look in his eyes. 'You want to buy it?'

'No,' Tara said and took a step back. 'I don't like guns.'

'I meant the house,' the man said and smiled suddenly, showing even white teeth against his tanned face. 'I think I scared you. I'm sorry, didn't mean to at all, but I got a bit of a fright myself when I saw you.'

'Oh,' Tara said. 'Of course. I'm sure you didn't expect to see anyone here.' She paused. 'So you're the owner of this house?'

'That's right.' He held out his hand. 'I'm Liam O'Rourke. Owner of this wreck.'

After a brief hesitation, Tara shook his hand. 'Tara,' she said. 'Uh, um, Tara O'Rourke, actually.'

He stared at her, still holding her hand. 'O'Rourke? How strange. Are you from around here?'

'Not really, but my father's family is originally from Sandy Cove,' Tara replied, the heat of the sun on her back making her perspire. She pulled her hand out of his grip, took off her rucksack and put it on the ground.

'From Sandy Cove?' Liam said, looking surprised. 'Really? Maybe we're related,' he suggested, leaning the old shotgun against the wall. 'So you're from Kerry, then?'

'No, I'm from Dublin,' Tara said. 'Originally, I mean. I live in New York now.'

'Dublin, eh? I see.' He folded his arms and stared at her. 'So what are you doing in these parts? Come to check up on your ancestors?'

'I'm here to take photos for an article about the west coast for an American travel magazine,' Tara explained. 'But I'm also interested in finding out about my ancestors. They left for Dublin about a hundred years ago.'

'Like a lot of people,' Liam said. 'This area was crawling with O'Rourkes in the old days. We must all have been one happy family hundreds of years ago. But then we kind of split up into different branches.'

'Right,' Tara said. 'And your family? Who were they? This farm must have been quite important in the old days,' she continued, wanting to test him before she revealed her connection with the farm through her great-grandfather.

'It was. Once.' Liam looked at her, his eyes narrowing as if he had just realised something. 'Dublin,' he said slowly. 'There was some old story I heard about this family and how there was a huge row just after the Rising…' He stopped. 'But let's not go into that.'

Tara was dying to know more but Liam seemed reluctant to go on. 'But you grew up here?' she asked.

'No, I didn't,' Liam replied. 'I'm from Limerick. This farm belonged to my grand-uncle and he left it to me in his will, for some reason. Quite a surprise at the time, I have to tell you. I was called after him, so maybe that was why.'

'And now you're selling up?' Tara asked.

'Yes. The land is let, but the house was too rundown to do anything with, so I'm putting it up for sale to see if anyone would like to take it on and do it up.'

'Oh,' Tara said. 'I see. I heard someone called Liam O'Rourke owned this place. So that would be you, of course.'

'Or my great-uncle. Though I'm not sure anyone in town knows much about him. He didn't go into Sandy Cove much. Didn't like it, he said.'

'Why not?' Tara asked.

'Some old row, I expect. Drunken brawl, stolen donkey, that kind of thing that people got excited about in the old days,' Liam said as if he was trying to close the subject.

'Maybe,' Tara said with a feeling he knew more than he let on. 'But this *is* Riverside Farm?' she asked, just to make sure she was in the right place. 'Or Cois Abhainn Farm?'

'It is,' Liam said. 'There was a sign at the crossroads years ago but it seems to have disappeared. But yeah, this is the O'Rourke family farm – or what's left of it.'

Tara looked up at the house. 'It could be a lovely place for someone who'd have the means to do it up,' she remarked.

'And the courage,' Liam said with a laugh. 'It'd be a huge undertaking.'

'The roof looks solid enough, though,' Tara remarked.

'It's okay, I suppose. But there are so many other things that need doing. But yeah, it's a blessed place, I have to admit.' His eyes suddenly brightened. 'Did you say you were doing a piece for an American magazine?'

Tara nodded. 'Yes, I am.'

'Maybe you could feature this house in the article and slip in that it's for sale? Could attract the attention of some rich Yank who'd love to own something like this.'

'Well, this is not going to be an article for rich people. It's meant to describe hidden corners and undiscovered trails for hiking and maybe even camping.'

'Or glamping?' he asked with a grin. 'I could put up those yurt things on that field by the river and they'd have running water right there beside them.'

'The river?' Tara asked, looking around. 'Where is it? It's called Riverside Farm, after all.'

'If you walk behind the shed over there, you'll see it,' Liam explained, pointing at the back of the little garden. 'Be careful of the nettles, though.'

'Okay,' Tara said and hitched her rucksack higher on her back. 'I'll go and take a look. And then I think I'll be going. I have to get to Ballinskelligs and do the whole round trip and maybe walk a bit up the hills behind that village to take some more shots.'

'I suppose you've already taken a lot of photos around Sandy Cove,' Liam suggested. 'Very beautiful places around there.'

'Well, yes, I've done a few. But I'm not going to feature the village in my article particularly. It appears it wouldn't be popular with the locals.'

Liam shrugged. 'Yeah, that doesn't surprise me. They like to keep themselves to themselves. A stuck-up lot, my great-uncle used to say. Didn't go there much and neither have I.'

'Is that so?' Tara said, studying him.

'Yeah, well, not my turf. No need to go raking up old stuff.' He looked at her blandly. 'Not that I know much about it, of course.'

'Of course,' Tara said even though she had a feeling they both knew there was more to it than he let on. She had a feeling that if she mentioned her connection to the farm, he'd shut down the conversation altogether. 'Well,' she said and started to walk away. 'I'll be off then, when I've had a look at the river. Nice to meet you, Liam. Sorry about trespassing on your property.'

'No problem,' he said and shot her a lopsided smile. 'It was great to meet you.' He groped in his shirt pocket and produced a dog-eared card. 'My contact details. You might send me that photo you took of me.'

'Sure. No problem.' Tara took the card and stuffed it into her back pocket, happy he hadn't been annoyed that she had taken his photo. 'Bye, then,' she said and walked to the shed behind the roses. 'Would you mind if I took a few shots from the river?' she asked.

'Not at all. Go ahead,' Liam said. 'It's a nice spot. There's three acres of scrubland down there. And you'll love the wildflowers that are in bloom at this time of year.'

'Oh, great.' Tara waved and walked off around the shed and down a small incline to a clump of trees from where she could hear the noise of water. She glanced up at the side of the mountain that rose above the trees and gasped at the sight. The whole slope was covered in heather in full bloom, all the way to the top. The mass of purple flowers looked stunning against the blue sky. Oblivious of the nettles that stung her ankles, Tara hauled her camera out of her rucksack and took shot after shot until she was satisfied she had covered every angle and used every single shift of the light.

Tara put away her camera and made her way down to the trees where she found another delightful vista. Behind the trees she discovered the river that gave the farm its name. Not much more than a stream in the summer, it meandered its way through the valley and this little glen where orange and red montbretia flowers grew in profusion on the banks. The water gurgled and gushed over the rocks, and a weeping willow dipped its branches into the river. Tara sat down on the bank, took off her shoes and slipped her feet into the cool, soft water, closing her eyes, listening to the birdsong and the sound of the water washing over the rocks and boulders. She suddenly felt a whisper of wings and opened her eyes to discover a heron that had just landed on the opposite bank. Knowing she wouldn't get her camera out in time, she slipped her phone out of her pocket and, moving as slowly as she could, managed to take a shot of the bird before it turned its head and gave her a haughty stare, flapped its wings and gracefully flew away, following the line of the river until it disappeared.

'Magic,' Tara muttered to herself, 'pure magic.'

When she put her phone back in her pocket, she found the crumpled card Liam O'Rourke had given her. She looked at it and discovered the Aer Lingus logo along with his name, phone number and email address. So he worked for Aer Lingus and lived in Limerick. He was probably based at Shannon airport, she assumed and put the card back in her pocket. She didn't quite know what she felt about him; their encounter had been too brief for her to form an opinion. Nice enough, she supposed, but there was something about him that had raised a few questions in her mind. He hadn't seemed to want to talk about the history of his family but what he said did suggest that his grand-uncle was involved in a scandal. Was he the reason why her great-grandfather had left the farm and Sandy Cove forever? She had an odd feeling that Liam knew more than he let on. Tara suddenly felt that she simply had to find out what had happened all those years ago. She had always loved a mystery. She stood up and looked back at the house, the roof of which was sticking up above the sheds. *Riverside Farm*, she thought, *what secrets are hiding inside?*

Chapter Eight

Dark clouds gathered over Sandy Cove the following day and more than a rumble of thunder could be heard in the distance. Not a day for cycling, Tara decided and stayed at home to go through the photos she had taken and get started on the first draft of the article. She found that the words didn't come as easily to her as creating images did, and knew she'd be struggling to paint a picture of the beautiful landscapes and wonderful walkways. She wished she hadn't suggested she'd do the writing as well, but she had wanted the practice so she could develop her skills. She had signed the agreement and there was no going back. In any case she didn't think the magazine would want the extra expense of hiring a writer on top of the fee they were paying her, so she had to do her very best. The editor would probably be able to improve her efforts and make it into something more readable in any case.

She hadn't been able to talk to Kate last night or shown her the photos of the old house, but they were meeting for dinner at Kate's house this evening, which Tara was looking forward to. She was dying to tell Kate about Liam O'Rourke. She was sure Cormac would be interested in what he'd said too. Cormac had told Tara he would try to find out something by talking to people who came into the

Wellness Centre and perhaps see if the library had anything on the local history around the time just after the Civil War.

The thunderstorm moved closer and a sudden crash and violent lightning made Tara jump up and close the living-room window that she had left open. As the forked lightning illuminated the bay, she grabbed her camera and waited for the next one, which came right on cue. She managed to catch the next flash of lightning before the thunder rolled away leaving torrential downpour in its wake. The rain smattered on the roof and splashed on the terrace for around five minutes and then stopped as suddenly as it had started, leaving a newly washed garden with the leaves dripping and glistening when the sun came out of the clouds.

Tara laughed and opened the window, breathing in the sweet scent of grass and flowers, enjoying the freshness of the air after the rain. The clouds at the horizon were nearly black and the contrast with the now-sunlit beach was beautiful. Tara grabbed her camera and ran down to the beach to take some shots of the headland and the waves that crashed onto the rocks, sending white foam into the air. Seagulls and gannets glided above, screeching at each other. Tara stood there and looked at the scene, taking shot after shot, not waiting for the perfect moment as she knew she wouldn't have much time before the light changed.

And then she noticed footprints in the wet sand and realised someone had just walked across to the rocks. She peered ahead and saw the figure of a tall man walking barefoot, slightly bent over, hands in the pockets of his shorts, a white shirt billowing around him and fair hair blowing around his head. She took a shot of the footprints just as the waves washed over them and knew she'd get a kind of Robinson Crusoe effect which might look good on the page of the magazine. Maybe an introductory shot, just above the headline? She pointed her camera at the figure ahead and clicked a few times, hoping the lonely feeling would come across. She wanted to give the impression of a deserted beach for those seeking solitude and peace on this beautiful coast. She lowered the camera and looked at the man, who was now standing at the water's edge, staring out to sea. As she walked closer, she saw there was something familiar about that head of shaggy fair hair and the line of the jaw. Then it dawned on her who he was and she ran towards him despite his stance that said he wanted to be alone.

'Mick!' she shouted. 'Hi!'

He turned and looked at her as she approached, his eyes wary and a little confused. Then he smiled. 'Hi, Kate,' he said. 'Long time no see. You've let your hair grow. Looks nice.'

Tara touched her hair. 'Thanks, but I'm not Kate. I'm Tara.'

He looked taken aback and stared at her for a moment. 'Tara? Kate's evil twin?'

Tara laughed, remembering how she had joked about being the evil twin when they had talked on the phone a few times over a year ago. 'That's right.'

'What on earth are you doing here?'

'If you had bothered to keep in touch, you'd know that.'

He shot her a contrite look. 'I suppose I would. Sorry about that. I've been away a long time and not been in touch with anyone. Things have been a bit difficult lately.'

'Oh, that's too bad,' Tara said, remembering what Kate had said – just how much had his acting career suffered? She kept looking at him, amazed to see him in the flesh, when she had dreamed about meeting him ever since she had been one of his fans. She kept staring at him, noting both that he was even better looking in the flesh, but also that he looked oddly sad and dejected. What had happened to give him that bitter twist to his mouth and the forlorn look in his gorgeous brown eyes? 'Welcome home,' she said, feeling awkward.

'Thanks,' he said. Then he looked out across the sea again. 'I'm not great company right now, I'm afraid. I just arrived from Dublin and then decided to go for a walk when the rain stopped. Didn't expect to meet anyone here. Are you staying with Kate?'

'No,' Tara replied. 'I'm house sitting for a girl called Jasmine, who I haven't met yet. But she won't be here until August.'

He turned to look at her, a glint of interest in his eyes. 'So you're on holiday here?'

'No, I'm here for work. I'm taking photographs for an article about the west coast. It's for *The Wild Vagabond* magazine. Hidden spots, unknown trails, secret hideaways, that sort of thing.'

'Oh, great. That's a very well-known magazine. You must have been happy to get that job.'

'Oh yes, I was,' Tara replied, relieved that her chatting seemed to cheer him up a little. 'This way I get to spend time with Kate and I'll have a chance to explore this area. There are so many undiscovered paths and trails here. And the light and the landscape and the fabulous flora and fauna are all so incredible for a photographer. I only just arrived but I've already got a lot of material.'

Mick nodded. 'Sounds great. I'm sure it'll be great for tourism in Kerry. As long as you don't draw too much attention to this place.'

Tara looked at him. 'Why do you say that?'

He shrugged. 'No reason, other than that this is my home and I wouldn't want to see it turned into Blackpool.'

'What?' Tara bristled. 'Blackpool? Isn't that going a bit far? I'm just going to do an article about the beauty of the west coast and feature some of the hidden parts that haven't been explored before. It's aimed at the backpackers and hikers and people who want to experience something wild and beautiful. What's wrong with that?'

Mick laughed ironically. 'Yeah, right. Your amazing photos will be in one of the most popular travel and lifestyle magazines in America. It must have a circulation of several million.' He went on, barely drawing breath. 'And you're standing here pretending it won't have any effect at all and that only a handful of hikers and walkers will turn up here to experience the paradise you will have dangled in front of them.' He turned to face her. 'Just stop to think for a moment, okay? Think of something other than your career and consider the people in this village and how what you do today will affect them tomorrow. It could all go viral and cause a minor tsunami of visitors to here.' He made a wide sweep with his arm to encompass the coastline and the mountains. 'This place has a unique beauty, but it's fragile.' He stopped, looking sad.

Tara stared at him as what he said began to sink in.

Mick sighed. 'Oh God…' He paused. 'I'm sorry. That was a terrible thing to say… I'm not in the mood to be optimistic. About anything,' he finished.

'I can see that,' Tara said, taken aback. Kate had said he was feeling dejected, but she hadn't thought it would be this bad. His words stung her, but she could see it was more about him…

'I didn't mean to upset you.' Mick touched her shoulder. 'I'm afraid you've caught me on a bad day. Not that I've had any good ones lately. Anyway, it was nice to meet you in person finally. But now I'm going to walk back home. Maybe we could meet up sometime for a drink or something?' he added, his voice softer. 'Just for a friendly chat and to make up for me barking at you just now.'

'That would be nice,' Tara replied, touched by the contrite look in his eyes. 'You have my number.'

'I certainly do,' he said with the flicker of a smile. 'Bye for now, Tara.'

'Bye, Mick,' she replied. 'Take care.'

'Thanks.' He waved and walked off, his back straighter and his steps lighter than earlier, which cheered Tara up a little. Maybe giving out to her had given him some kind of boost, even if it had annoyed her. But this was not how she had imagined their first encounter. She had been sure they'd meet some day but she hadn't expected it to be when he had lost his confidence and belief in himself. Tara suddenly felt an urge to help him, or at least let him know she would be willing to listen should he need someone to talk to. She looked at his retreating figure and sighed, disappointed that her first meeting with Mick O'Dwyer had been so full of conflict and arguments. She hoped they'd be on friendlier terms the next time they met.

Chapter Nine

Later that night, over dinner on Kate's terrace, Tara told Kate about her visit to Riverside Farm the day before, and her meeting with Liam.

'Amazing,' Kate said when Tara had finished her tale and shown her the photos she had taken that she had downloaded to her laptop. 'Look,' she said and passed the laptop to Cormac. 'Have you ever been to that little valley?'

Cormac looked at the screen and went through the photos one by one. 'No, I haven't. Funny how it's hidden from the land around the tower, but I suppose the headland is in the way.'

Tara nodded. 'That's right. You can only see towards Ballinskelligs from there.'

Kate pulled the laptop back across the table. 'That man in the photo, is that him? Liam O'Rourke?'

'Yes,' Tara replied.

'Good-looking,' Kate remarked. 'So he inherited the farm from his grand-uncle?'

Tara nodded. 'Yes, so he said. He seemed to think it was a bit of a burden and not a gift at all. He's putting the house on the market. He doesn't want to live there. He works for Aer Lingus and is based in Limerick. I'm guessing he's at Shannon airport or something.'

Kate nodded. 'Could be. Sad to think the house won't be in the O'Rourke family any more.'

Tara shrugged and started to collect the plates. 'I don't feel sad about that. They're such distant relations and we don't know that family. I have a rough idea about the times and dates and I think Liam's great-uncle would have been the same generation as our grandfather. So… if that's true, then his great-grandfather must have been roughly the same age as Daniel. But why did he inherit and not Daniel? That must mean that somehow, our great-grandfather was rejected by his family. Now I'm dying to find out more. And I'd also love to go back there and examine the house in more detail. I just walked through it yesterday and then Liam appeared and didn't seem to want me to go back inside.'

'Yes, but you can't barge in there again without permission,' Kate argued.

'Hmm,' Tara said and looked at Kate with a mischievous little smile. 'I might be able to sneak back when he isn't there. He must be at work most days. Yesterday was Sunday, so…'

'So tomorrow he'll be at work and the coast will be clear?' Cormac asked, looking as if he didn't quite approve.

'That's what I was thinking, yes,' Tara said.

'You'd be trespassing,' Cormac warned. 'I mean now that you know who owns the place and that he has it up for sale and so on…'

'No, on the contrary, that's a very good idea,' Kate cut in, looking excited.

'But that's not quite legal,' Cormac argued.

Kate snorted. 'Who cares if it's legal or not?' She looked at Tara, her eyes sparkling. 'I'd love to come with you.'

'That would be great. Can you take the day off?' Tara asked, excited at the thought of them exploring the house together.

'Not tomorrow, but the day after I could take the morning shift and then we could go together and bring lunch. I'll take Cormac's bike. That'll be okay, won't it, sweetheart?'

'Sure, but I hope to God nobody sees you,' Cormac said.

'Why would that be so bad?' Kate said innocently. 'I'll just be out cycling with my sister.'

'And then the two of you will be breaking into that old farmhouse,' Cormac said darkly. 'Nice behaviour for the GP of Sandy Cove, I have to say.'

'They'll just think I'm on a house call,' Kate said, waving away Cormac's concerns. 'Please don't be such a stick in the mud, Cormac.'

'You get your herbs and stuff from that guy's land,' Tara reminded Cormac.

'Yes, but that's different,' Cormac argued. 'The path to it is a right of way, which means anyone can use it. The land isn't used for anything either.'

'We're just going to have a little look,' Kate cut in.

'Not quite correct,' Cormac muttered. 'But I can see there's no stopping you.'

'Yeah, but remember we're O'Rourkes,' Tara added with a cheeky grin. 'The rebel streak in us is coming out.'

'How could I forget,' Cormac said, as if to himself.

Tara beamed at her sister, ignoring Cormac's frown. 'Brilliant. And *he* won't be there as it's the middle of the week. He'll be busy at the Aer Lingus office in Shannon. I'm sure that's where he works.'

'But maybe we should check just to make sure?' Kate said. 'Google him or something to find out if that's what he does?'

'Or we could see if we can find him on Facebook?' Tara suggested, logging in to her profile on the laptop.

'Great idea,' Kate said and moved her chair closer to Tara. 'Type in his name.'

Cormac laughed and picked up the plates Tara had stacked. 'I'll just tidy up here,' he said. 'Who wants some tea?'

'Both of us,' Kate said, her eyes on the screen. 'Make us that special herbal one you just put together, please.'

Cormac stood there with the plates, looking at Kate and Tara sitting close together watching the screen, and smiled. 'You two,' he said. 'What a combination. I never realised how twins are always half of each other when they're apart and then such a unit when you're together.'

Tara returned his smile and winked. 'On our own we're amazing, but together we're *dangerous*.'

'Don't try to frighten me,' Cormac said and went inside.

Tara turned to the laptop where Kate had just typed Liam's name on Facebook. Several links came up, but the second one seemed to fit.

'It says Limerick,' Kate said and clicked on the name. They both stared at the profile that came up with a man in uniform in the photo.

'That's him!' Tara squealed.

'Is he a pilot?' Kate asked.

'Must be.' Tara stared at the image. It was the man she had met, even though he looked a lot more polished in the photo. 'His hair is shorter and he's shaved his beard,' she said. 'It's him, though.'

'He's really good-looking,' Kate remarked.

'I preferred him a bit messy like he was when we met,' Tara said, staring at the face.

'If he's a pilot, we can't be sure he'll be working normal hours,' Kate muttered, scrolling down the page. 'But it looks like he's not very private with his posts…' Her voice trailed away as she looked, Tara leaning over to see.

'Look,' Tara exclaimed, pointing at the top post. '*Off to Greece tomorrow for work. Hoping to do a little island hopping while over there,*' she quoted. 'So he's on a flight to Greece and will probably be away a few days. Could be gone until after the weekend. What do you think?'

Kate nodded. 'Yes. That post is from today. I'd say we'll be safe.'

'Safe from what?' Cormac said as he carried a tray with cups and a teapot to the table.

'From being discovered as we snoop around on O'Rourke property,' Kate said, her look daring Cormac to argue.

Cormac put the tea tray on the table with a clatter. 'I hope you're right. But don't look at me like that, Kate. I won't try to stop you. I wash my hands of the whole affair. You two go and play the Famous Five, and I'll be at the Wellness Centre minding my own business.'

'Thank you, sweetie,' Kate said and rose to give him a kiss. 'I knew you'd understand.'

'I understand that you want to go and see that place,' Cormac replied. 'Why not just ask this O'Rourke guy if you can look around the house? I'm sure he wouldn't mind.'

'Yes, but he seemed to know something he didn't want me to find out,' Tara said. 'So we'll need to go there without him looking over our shoulders.'

'And it'll be an adventure,' Kate filled in. 'I know this is a bit juvenile, but it'll be fun.'

'Great fun,' Tara agreed, happy that they were so in tune. The arguments and bad feelings about Tara's article seemed forgotten and now they were looking forward to finding out more about Daniel and what had happened to him all those years ago. The story they'd discover might be tragic but they would at last know the reason for his flight to Dublin.

Tara smiled at Kate with a surge of hope. They were united again, doing something together, just like in the old days. They had once been so close, nearly inseparable but the bond between them wasn't as strong as before. Kate's disapproval of Tara's assignment had driven a wedge between them, which had both surprised and saddened her. It had seemed unbelievable that Kate was not on the same wavelength about this and that she didn't trust Tara to have the right motives. Could they patch things up while researching the story of their great-grandfather?

But there was something she hadn't shared with Kate. Her meeting with Mick and that strange jolt she had felt when she had looked into his troubled eyes. She knew Kate would ask questions. But she wasn't ready to answer them. It had been so brief but so strangely emotional, his sadness so enormous. She didn't know what was troubling him and had made this fun, gregarious, charming man so morose. Depression? Mid-life crisis? Or was it simply the failure of the play that had upset him, as Kate had said? Whatever it was she felt he wanted it to remain private. She had accidentally bumped into him when he had needed solitude. It would be better not to talk about him until he was ready to come out of his shell.

Tara glanced at Kate and wondered if she knew Mick was back home. Tara opened her mouth to ask, but changed her mind. She felt she needed to keep it secret.

Kate looked back at Tara. 'What?' she asked.

'Nothing important,' Tara said. 'It can wait.'

Kate nodded. 'We'll leave it alone for now, I think.'

'Good idea.'

They exchanged a look with that old feeling that they were reading each other's thoughts. It used to be a comforting thing in the past, but now Tara wasn't so sure.

The next morning the dazzling sunshine and warm breeze lured Tara onto the beach in her swimsuit at seven o'clock. Kate was working all day today to make up for the free afternoon tomorrow, when they'd go back to the old farmhouse to see if they could find anything that would throw a light on that old family feud that had torn the family apart.

Tara dropped her towel on the sand and without hesitating ran into the waves and threw herself into the cool, clear water, swimming fast at first, then slowing down and switching to breaststroke while she looked down at the fish a few feet below her. A ray undulated gracefully away as she swam and a shoal of tiny fish darted this way and that in a kind of underwater ballet. Delighted by the sights below her, Tara swam on then turned on her back and floated, looking up at the sky, letting her thoughts drift to Riverside Farm.

Just being there had been amazing to Tara, in a way she hadn't expected it would be. As she walked across the creaking floors, knowing she was walking in her great-grandfather's footsteps, she'd tried to imagine what life had been like for that family in those turbulent days in the early nineteen hundreds, just after the Irish War of Independence and the bloody Civil War that followed. Family against family, brother against brother – was that what it had been about? The story they might unravel could be tragic but she felt strongly that they had to know. It had been swept under the carpet and kept there all this time. Even her own father hadn't known what had happened and he had often said he wanted to find out but there was nobody left to ask. His mother, Tara's grandmother, had apparently said, 'Let the dead rest in peace' and then changed the subject which must have been like coming up against a brick wall. But now both Tara and Kate felt enough time had passed and the truth just had to come out. That old house held the key to the mystery, all they had to do was to find it.

When Tara had reached the middle of the bay, she turned and swam back with steady strokes, reaching the shore and wading out of the waves breathless but happy. She was wringing out her hair when she felt a tap on her shoulder. She twirled around and discovered Mick in a pair of swimming shorts, his hair dripping too.

'You're hard to keep up with,' he said, panting. 'Are you training for the Olympics?'

She shook her hair and laughed. 'No, I don't think I'd qualify. I love swimming though.'

'I can see that. Me too. Hang on, I'll get my towel.' Mick walked away and then quickly returned with a big towel that he spread on the sand beside the one Tara had dropped earlier. 'I take it this one is yours?'

'Yes.' Tara arranged her towel and sat down, looking up at him as he smoothed back his wet hair. 'You get up early.'

'Not normally, but the seagulls woke me up. Noisy bastards.' He sat down on his towel and leaned back on his elbows, studying her. 'Did you tell Kate I'm here?'

Tara frowned. 'No, but I thought I wouldn't have to. You must have bumped into her at the house as soon as you arrived.'

'I've been keeping away from the surgery. I haven't seen her since I arrived. That's why I thought you were her yesterday.'

'Oh. Okay.' Tara looked at him, squinting against the sunlight. 'Do you want me to tell her? Or not?'

'I'll look into the surgery later today and say hello. Thanks for not… you know.'

'I wasn't sure if you wanted her to know you were here, so I said nothing.' Tara lay down and closed her eyes. 'But I think she knows anyway.'

'How?'

Tara didn't open her eyes. 'Telepathy.'

'Oh yeah,' he said incredulously.

'Twin telepathy is real, you know. We do seem to read each other's minds sometimes,' Tara said, turning her head to look at him.

'How strange.' Mick eased himself onto his back, lying so close their noses nearly touched. 'Your eyes are slightly different to Kate's. Darker and a little rounder. And that little dimple beside your mouth is all yours. Apart from that, you're incredibly alike. Even your voices are identical.'

Tara moved away. 'Stop looking at me as if I'm rabbit in a laboratory. Have you never seen twins before?'

'Not this close,' Mick said, not taking his eyes off her face. Then he blinked and sat up. 'I'm sorry. I'm acting really strange.' He ran his hand over his eyes. 'I didn't sleep very well.'

Tara put her hands under her head. 'You're having problems?'

'Yes. And no. I mean I did, but I'm better now. I came here to rest for a bit after a long and dark spring. Things happened to me, one after the other and it seemed as if there was some kind of curse on me.' He laughed and shook his head. 'That sounds mad, but it's how I felt. Jobwise and love-wise everything came crashing down all at once. I couldn't cope with it all, so I ended up having therapy.'

'Did that help?'

'Sort of. Lying on a couch talking about me and having someone listen to my woes was a great comfort. But it was expensive. I realised living in denial is cheaper in the long run, so that's what I'm trying now.'

'And that's working for you?' Tara smiled.

Mick shrugged. 'I'm not sure. Self-pity is very rewarding. Wallowing in it can be so therapeutic.'

Tara had to laugh. 'I like your black humour. That sounds like you're getting better. If you were in real trouble you wouldn't be able to joke about it.'

'Maybe I'm just looking for sympathy?'

Tara shook her head. 'That's not your style. But I might be wrong. I hardly know you. And you don't know me.'

'I know Kate.'

'I'm not her.' Tara sat up. 'We look identical but what's in our heads and our hearts is not.'

'Oh yes, I forgot. You're the evil twin,' he said with a laugh.

Tara looked back at him. 'I'm the wild one, in any case. Kate is older than me by two minutes. Sounds weird, but she was always like a slightly older sister. More grounded and less impulsive than me. I got into trouble and then she had to get me out of it.'

'Interesting,' Mick said as his brown eyes studied her. 'So twins aren't really carbon copies of each other?'

'No, not at all. I think we complement each other rather than being exact doubles.'

'Like bookends?'

Tara laughed. 'More like ice cream in various flavours. Vanilla and chocolate. Different and a great combination.'

'Which one are you?'

'You'll find out when we know each other better.' Tara got to her feet and picked up her towel. 'I have to go. Breakfast, and then I have to do some work. I have to write this article and that's a real headache. I take great photographs but writing is not my strongest point.'

'I might be able to give you a hand with that,' Mick offered, still sitting on the sand. 'I enjoy writing, so give me a shout if you get stuck.'

'I will. Thanks.' Tara stood there looking at him, feeling confused. Their conversation had been flirty and fun, but then she felt it was getting too close for comfort. Mick had figured in her fantasies when she was younger. But the real Mick was different to the glossy image he presented. He was still as good-looking with that deep actor's voice, but with a sad, disillusioned look in his eyes and lines and shadows in his face that told of sleepless nights full of dark thoughts.

And the real Tara? She was also a little worn and battered by life's twists and turns. She was unsure of herself and what she was doing – her emotions just as wobbly as his, she suspected, even if she hadn't put herself on a therapist's couch.

'Take care,' she said as she walked away.

'You too, Tara. I'll be in touch about that drink.'

'Great.' She waved and walked slowly back to the house, feeling his eyes on her. The subject of her highlighting Sandy Cove in her coming article hadn't come up and he had been very friendly, so maybe that outburst the day before had just been because of his bad mood? It was difficult to figure out, but she would know more once they had spent some time together, which seemed very likely.

He had said he'd ask her out for a drink and she was sure he would. He and Kate had become close friends during Kate's first year in Sandy Cove and Tara was sure they still were. But she didn't want him to think she was Kate's copy – a problem that often cropped up when they were friends with the same person. It had been the reason they had asked to be in different classes at school and had had different circles of friends. The relationship they had with each other was something so personal it could never be shared with anyone else. And they hadn't had the same taste in men, which could have caused problems.

Tara smiled as she thought of Kate's boyfriends. They had often been slightly nerdy types who shared Kate's interest in science and medicine. But in contrast to them, Cormac was no nerd. His amazing good looks combined with being self-contained and in tune with other people made him uniquely attractive and perfect for Kate. Tara was sure they were meant to be together for life. And what about Joe? Was he the perfect man for her? Tara wondered. Would absence make his heart grow fonder? And would it do the same for her?

Tara shrugged off those thoughts and turned her mind to tomorrow and that house she and Kate were going to explore. Solving the mystery of what had happened to their great-grandfather was the perfect antidote for her feelings about Mick and her complicated love life.

She walked up the path in the sunshine and arrived back at the little cottage, her mind on only one man – Daniel O'Rourke. She saw him in that photo, standing in front of the farm that should have been his home. What had he done to lose it?

Chapter Ten

Tara and Kate set off on their bikes at eleven o'clock the next morning under cloudy skies, ignoring the promise of rain. Kate had managed to leave the surgery early as Pat had wanted to take over and also expressed a wish to do the house calls later that afternoon.

'He loves the house calls,' Kate said to Tara as they pedalled off down the main street. 'And he's much better than me at doing them. I don't have the patience for the endless cups of tea and the long chats about the weather and "Auntie Maura's cat that lived to be a hundred and one and my cousin up the road with the gammy leg that you might want to go and take a look at". But Pat revels in them. It's the cream on the cake for him.'

Tara laughed. 'I can't see you doing all that. But if Pat loves it, why not? I'd say that sort of thing is what keeps him happy and youthful.'

'Oh yes, it is,' Kate agreed. 'But I love the surgery and trying to find out what's wrong with people. And the contact with the specialists and the hospitals is really my strong point. We're a great team.'

'It's good to see you so happy,' Tara said. 'Even if you look tired sometimes.'

'Being a country doctor can be very challenging. I always feel I'm on duty even when I'm not.' Kate smiled. 'But oh, God, I can't think of any other job that would suit me so perfectly. Or any other place I'd like to live. I have really landed, you know?'

'I can see that. And Cormac is dreamy,' Tara added.

'He is,' Kate said as they reached the open road. 'He loves me and I love him.'

'He loves you?' Tara said laughing. 'Are you kidding? He worships the ground you walk on.'

Kate glanced at Tara and pushed playfully at her. 'You're getting far too romantic. Must be those soaps you keep watching.'

'I'm not into those any more,' Tara argued. 'Except the Irish ones. But I only watch those because I'm homesick.'

'I bet.' Kate slowed down as the road narrowed. 'Get behind me so we won't be knocked over if there's a car.'

'Okay.' Tara stopped for a moment to let Kate pass and then cycled behind her.

'Do you watch *Dubliners in Love*?' Kate asked over her shoulder.

'Yes, I can get it on RTÉ Player when I'm in New York. Very good show for a soap opera. And I love seeing the bits filmed in the streets of Dublin.'

'Have you seen the episodes Mick was in?'

'No, not yet. Why?'

'You should. He's very good.' Kate stopped suddenly, making Tara swerve.

'Yikes! I nearly fell off.' Tara got off her bike and stood beside Kate. 'Why did you stop like that?'

'Because of that. Look!' Kate exclaimed and pointed down the slope.

Tara followed her gaze and gasped as she saw a huge bird with an enormous wingspan gliding over the bay. 'An eagle,' she whispered in awe and fumbled in her pocket for the small camera she had taken with her at the last moment before they left.

'An osprey,' Kate corrected, her eyes on the bird.

'Beautiful,' Tara mumbled, trying to focus on it as it slowly flew across the bay below. She managed to adjust her camera and took a few shots in quick succession and then switched to video to capture the graceful flight of the osprey as it glided on the wind, turning its head, staring down into the still blue water. Then it turned and soared higher, so high it was only a speck against the sky before it disappeared.

'So fantastic to see it,' Kate said as she straightened her bike. 'They're very rare but it's nice to see they're coming back to Kerry.'

'Such a beautiful creature. And the light was perfect.' Tara put her camera away. 'Thanks for pointing it out to me. I wasn't paying attention.'

'Too busy thinking about Mick?' Kate asked with a suggestive little smile. 'He told me you've met.'

'Yes, we have. Twice,' Tara confessed. 'I didn't tell you because I thought—'

'I know. He's very down at the moment. Never seen him so bad. He's usually so positive and I know he'd be embarrassed if everyone knew. I think it's all the work stuff he's been through lately and then, of course, turning forty soon.'

'Mid-life crisis?' Tara suggested, happy that Kate understood why she had kept quiet about meeting Mick.

'Yes, something like that, I suspect.'

'What happened to him?'

Kate shrugged. 'Lots of things. I told you about the play. It was so important to him and it was a huge blow when it failed. Also Pat told me he was dating someone, but that ended around the same time. Then he came back to Dublin and took that part in the TV soap that he hates doing. He's come here to rest and regroup, he says.' Kate looked at Tara. 'I think you'd be good for him. And he for you. You'll cheer each other up.'

'I don't need cheering up,' Tara said stiffly. 'I'm here to do a job and spend time with you.'

'And to try to find out about that family mystery,' Kate filled in. 'Let's go, then. We have no time to lose.' She got back on her bike and pedalled quickly up the road.

'Hang on, I'm coming,' Tara shouted, following Kate as fast as she could, her legs aching as she tried to keep up.

As she cycled on, her thoughts drifted to what Kate had said about Mick. Failed relationship, career going downhill, mid-life crisis. That must have dented his confidence a lot and made him feel like a failure. What a come-down for the once-bright shining star of the theatre. But how could she help him? Cracking a few jokes and giggling wasn't enough. She would have to tread softly and give him time, try to listen and provide some kind of comfort without judging him. Not easy for someone as impulsive and impatient as her.

She looked at Kate cycling ahead and tried to forget about Mick and his problems. They were on an adventure, a quest to solve a mystery. The thought made Tara increase her speed and when they reached the crest of the hill, they freewheeled down it, squealing in unison, ending up at the crossroads breathless and laughing, ready to tackle what lay ahead.

When they had hidden their bikes behind the big boulder, Kate and Tara walked swiftly down the lane that led to the farm, both deep in thought, wondering what they'd find at the old house. Tara had just seen part of the ground floor the other day, and she was dying to explore further. It had looked as if the old man had slept downstairs and only used the kitchen towards the end of his life. She assumed that Liam hadn't done anything to it in the years he'd owned it. He didn't seem that attached to the place as he hadn't spent much time there as a child, according to the little he had said to her. Odd, Tara thought, as she had felt a real emotional pull herself when she walked through the house and sat in that beautiful little rose garden, as if the memories of her ancestors were in her genes.

As they walked on, Kate looked up in awe at the fuchsia hedges and elderberry bushes full of white flowers that lined the trail. 'The elderberry flowers are so abundant here,' she said. 'I must pick some for Cormac on the way back. He'll make some of his cordial with it.'

'Wait till you see the little rose garden behind the house,' Tara said. 'Those roses must have been planted early last century.'

'Maybe by Daniel's mother?' Kate suggested.

'That's a lovely thought,' Tara said as they arrived at the old gate. 'Here we are. The grand entrance.'

Kate touched the gate. 'It would have been quite grand once, I think.'

'Very,' Tara agreed as they walked across the overgrown front garden. 'But look, here we are,' she said as the house came into view. 'At Riverside Farm. The old homestead.'

Kate stopped dead and stared at the old house. 'It's changed since that photo was taken,' she said. 'It looks so sad and abandoned.'

'I know. I feel sorry for it,' Tara said as she studied the ivy-covered façade, the broken windows and the crumbling bricks of the porch.

'The door is open,' Kate said.

'That's because it's impossible to close it. The timber has warped.' Tara walked up the front steps and peered in. 'Anyone home?' she called.

'Stop it,' Kate said with a shiver. 'You're scaring me.'

Tara laughed. 'Sorry. Just messing. There's nobody here. Let's go inside. I want to go upstairs.'

'Are you sure we should?' Kate asked, her voice uncertain.

'Of course. How else are we going to find anything?'

'I don't think we will.'

'Come on,' Tara urged and stepped inside, Kate following close behind.

They walked together across the hall, Kate peering into the rooms on either side of the corridor. 'That must have been the living room,' she said as they passed the open door.

'There's a sofa bed, so I think the old uncle must have slept there,' Tara said. 'Probably couldn't make it up the stairs if he was very old and ill. And then there's a dining room across the corridor, but there's nothing much there.'

Kate looked around. 'It must have been a lovely house once. Just look at those floorboards and the cornices. And the fireplaces are beautiful.'

'Oh yes, I'm sure it was a gorgeous house,' Tara agreed. She stopped for a moment, taking in the feeling of calm. 'And there's a nice sort of atmosphere here. You know, like good vibes. Do you feel it?'

Kate closed her eyes for a moment. 'Yes,' she whispered. 'And weirdly, there is no smell of mould. Just a little dampness. It smells of the dried rose petals you get in a potpourri.'

'That's from the little garden behind the kitchen,' Tara explained. She looked up the staircase that curved gracefully to the top floor. 'Let's go upstairs.'

'Is it safe?' Kate asked.

'I'm sure it is,' Tara replied, already halfway up the stairs. 'The floorboards feel steady enough.'

'Yeah, but I meant…' Kate said, her voice hesitant.

'You mean are there ghosts up there?' Tara laughed but stopped as there was a loud creak.

'What was that?' Kate asked, her face pale.

Tara listened for a moment. 'Just one of the steps creaking. Come on,' she said, continuing up. 'It's okay. It's very bright up here. There are two windows on the landing and all the doors to the bedrooms are open. Quite draughty, though.'

'That's because most of the windows are broken,' Kate said as she joined Tara on the landing.

'I know.' Tara peered into one of the bedrooms. 'This must have been the master. It's big and has a large window.' She walked carefully inside with Kate close behind. 'Look, it still has a big bed. No mattress.'

'Thank God for that,' Kate said. She touched the mahogany frame of the fourposter and looked at the ornate headboard. 'Quite a magnificent piece, don't you think?'

'Yes,' Tara agreed. She looked around the large airy room with its sloping ceiling and sash window overlooking the garden below. The sun came out of the clouds and cast a warm light on the old floorboards, the torn wallpaper with tiny blue flowers and the panelled doors. Tara spotted a small chest of drawers with a mirror attached near the window. 'This is lovely,' she said and ran her finger over the dusty surface. 'Victorian, I think.'

'I wonder why it's still here,' Kate said. 'I mean, it could fetch a good price in an antique shop.'

'Not that much,' Tara argued. 'This kind of stuff isn't popular any more.' She tugged at one of the drawers but it wouldn't budge. 'Can't open the drawer. It must have warped.' She pulled at another one. 'This one is better.' The drawer slowly slid open revealing something inside. Tara looked at it. 'It's a book. No—' she said as she pulled it out. 'It's a photo in a leather folder.' She blew the dust off it and sneezed several times, handing it to Kate. 'Here, take a look while I blow my nose.'

Kate took the folder, not looking very happy. 'Not sure we should do this. It's not our property.'

Tara wiped her nose with a tissue. 'I know, but we'll just take a look and put it back. It could give us a clue.'

Kate handed the album back. 'You open it.'

'I will.' Tara looked at the worn green leather of the folder and slowly opened it. 'Look,' she said to Kate. 'A wedding photo. Must be from the turn of the last century. Or earlier perhaps. The couple look older than the usual bride and groom.' She looked at the faces of the couple gazing into the camera. 'Funny how they had to sit like that for ages without moving or they'd blur the shot.'

Kate leaned closer to look. 'The groom is very handsome. Looks a little like our great-grandfather in that photo we found.' Kate studied the writing underneath the photo. '*Mary and John's wedding in 1904.* Who are they? Can't be Daniel's parents. He'd have been four years old then.'

Tara looked at the people in the photo: the bride and groom sitting stiffly on a sofa flanked by two young boys in dark suits and a little boy cross-legged at their feet. 'Who are those two lads? And the little boy?'

'Maybe the little boy is Daniel?' Kate suggested. 'He has those big eyes and the dark hair…'

'I know.' Tara looked at Kate. 'It has to be him. Maybe he was some kind of ring bearer at the wedding? I mean those people might have been an aunt and uncle or something. And the two lads… But why are there no bridesmaids or flower girls or something?'

'We could try to find out,' Kate said. 'Look at church registers in the area. They might have been in a different parish, Ballinskelligs or Cahersiveen. The marriage has to be recorded somewhere.'

'That's a brilliant idea,' Tara said. 'Why didn't I think of that?'

'Because I'm cleverer than you, of course,' Kate teased.

'Of course you are. Let's see if there's anything else here.' Tara pulled out another drawer, but found it empty as were all the others. 'Nothing. Let's see the other bedrooms.'

'And then we'll go outside,' Kate said with a little shiver. 'It's a little creepy up here. So quiet, as if the house is holding its breath.'

'Don't be silly,' Tara said as she pulled her phone from the pocket of her jeans and quickly took a shot of the photo before she put it back in the drawer. 'I want to see the rest of the rooms up here.'

She walked out through the door, down the corridor, opening doors to three further rooms that were empty. 'Nothing,' she said, feeling disappointed.

'Nice rooms though,' Kate said. 'Lovely fireplaces in each room and the cornices and original shutters are still intact.'

'You could make it into a gorgeous house with a bit of work,' Tara said.

'And a truckload of money,' Kate remarked.

Tara looked out the window at the view over the river and the mountains rising up behind it. 'Fabulous view.'

'I feel at home here,' Kate said as she joined Tara at the window. 'Even though it's a bit eerie. Isn't that strange?'

Tara turned to look at Kate. 'I do too.'

'Can we take a look at the rooms downstairs?'

'Yes. Good idea. And then we can go and have our sandwiches by the river.'

They ran down the stairs and walked through the rooms on the ground floor, admiring the wide oak planks on the floors, the period fireplaces and the heavy shutters beside each of the tall windows.

'There is no bathroom or loo in the house,' Kate remarked as she looked around the old-fashioned kitchen.

'No, but there's an outside toilet in one of the sheds,' Tara said as she walked to the sink and turned the tap, jumping away as the water gushed out over her. 'Yikes!' She turned off the water and looked down at her wet clothes and trainers. 'I'm soaked through.'

'That'll teach you to turn on a tap in a strange house,' Kate said, laughing.

'Ha ha.' Tara walked to the half-door. 'Come on, let's go outside and let the sun warm us. It's a little chilly here.'

'Especially if you're wet,' Kate remarked. 'But yeah, let's go outside. I want to see the rose garden and the river.'

They walked through the half-door and stood in the garden for a while, admiring the roses, breathing in their scent.

'Gorgeous,' Kate said. 'Even if it's overgrown.' She walked over to the shed, a long, low building opposite the house, opened the door at the far end and peeked in. 'You were right. There's a loo here. Incredible to think that nobody bothered to put a bathroom into the house.'

'The old man mightn't have had the money. He was a bit of a hermit, Liam said. Maybe the new owner will do it up.' Tara glanced up at the roof. 'The structure seems to be in good nick.'

Kate followed her gaze. 'It looks fine. No missing slates on the roof. And most of the window frames look okay.'

'I suppose,' Tara said, losing interest in the state of the house as her stomach started to rumble. 'It's past lunchtime,' she said, taking off her rucksack. 'And I'm dying to eat the sandwiches I made for us this morning. How about you?'

Kate nodded. 'Yes, I'm suddenly starving.'

'And I want to sit in some sunny spot and get my clothes to dry.'

Kate looked around and then sat on the step outside the kitchen door. 'Right here would be fine. It's sheltered and the stones are hot.'

'Great.' Tara sat down beside her, took the sandwiches out of her backpack and handed one to Kate. 'Chicken with a lovely onion chutney I found in that little shop in the village. Hope you like it.'

'Thanks,' Kate said and bit into the sandwich. 'Gorgeous,' she mumbled through her mouthful. 'You make lovely food.'

Tara took a big bite, enjoying the flavours. 'I love cooking. Funny that you don't.'

'Never had the time to learn. Besides, why bother when you were so good at it? And now I have Cormac, who's a real gourmet chef.'

'You're so lucky.'

'Does Joe cook?' Kate asked.

'Yes, he does,' Tara replied, reluctantly turning her mind to the problems she had left behind. 'His family is Italian, so...'

'You never told me much about him.'

Tara finished her sandwich and wiped her mouth. 'I know, but...' She paused. 'Things weren't so great between us and that's part of the reason I'm here doing this job and being with you.'

'I see.' Kate put her hand on Tara's shoulder. 'I'm sorry. I won't mention him again. We can talk about it when you're ready.'

Tara patted Kate's hand. 'Thanks, sis. I thought I'd go away for a bit and see if...'

'If he'd come to his senses and realise how much you mean to him?' Kate filled in.

Tara looked down at her feet, trying to sort out her feelings. 'Yes, that's it. But I might be wrong and he'll find someone else while I'm gone.'

'Then he doesn't deserve you.' Kate took a sip from her water bottle. 'Maybe it's good for you to have some time on your own to find out what you want?'

Tara blinked away the tears that suddenly welled up.

Kate looked at her with eyes full of empathy. 'Tara, if it doesn't work out, there's nothing you can do.'

'I know.' Tara wiped her eyes with the back of her hand. 'Never mind. Let's not sit here and feel sad.'

'No.' Kate drained her bottle of water and got up. 'Let's go and look at the river.'

'Good idea.' Tara put the wrappings and the bottles into her rucksack. 'Did you bring coffee?'

'Yes.' Kate put her rucksack on her back. 'I have a thermos and mugs and some chocolate cupcakes from The Two Marys'.'

'With icing?'

'Yes, of—' Kate froze as there was a sound from inside the house. She blinked and looked at Tara with alarm. 'There's someone in the house,' she whispered.

Tara stood stock-still and listened as the sound of footsteps on the creaking floorboards came closer. 'Come on,' she hissed at Kate. 'Let's get out of here.'

But it was too late. Before they had a chance to get out of the little garden, the half-door opened, nearly knocking Kate over, and two men stood there staring at them. One of them was Liam O'Rourke. 'What…' he started, looking at Tara. 'You're here again?' He turned to Kate. 'And you…' He turned back to Tara. 'There's two of you.'

'Eh, yes,' Tara said. 'This is my sister Kate.'

'Hi,' Kate said, trying a winning smile.

'Hello,' Liam said brusquely.

'Nice to meet you,' Kate said.

'Eh, yeah. Very nice,' Liam replied. 'But what are you doing here?'

'I wanted to show Kate the house,' Tara said.

'And we thought…' Kate started.

'That you'd be in Greece,' Tara filled in.

Liam looked confused. 'Greece? What do you know about…?'

'I saw you on Facebook,' Tara explained. 'I discovered you're a pilot with Aer Lingus and I thought I'd take a peek at what you were up to.'

Liam looked suddenly highly amused. 'You stalked me on the Internet?'

'Not stalked you exactly,' Tara protested, smiling at him. 'Just checking up on you a little bit. And then we saw that post about going to Greece. Why didn't you?'

'The roster was changed.' Liam's mouth twitched. 'You wanted to see where I'd be today so you could come here and snoop around? But why?'

'Because…' Tara started, trying to come up with a plausible explanation. She glanced at Kate for help.

'Because we're thinking of buying this house,' Kate said very quickly.

Tara blinked and stared at Kate. 'What? I mean, yeah,' she said, realising this was the best excuse. 'You said it was on the market, didn't you?'

'I did,' Liam replied. He gestured at the man standing beside him. 'This is Andy Molloy of Molloy and Sons estate agency. They'll be handling the sale of this property. So maybe you'd like to make him an offer?'

'Uh, eh, not right now,' Tara said. 'We've just had a look around and we need to talk about what we've seen first.'

The estate agent dug in the pocket of his blazer and produced a card that he handed to Kate. 'Give me a call when you've decided and we'll discuss the price.'

Kate took the card. 'I will. Thank you.'

'But now you'll have to excuse us,' Liam said. 'We're going to go through the house to give Andy an idea of how to present it and so on. I expect we'll hear from you soon.'

Tara nodded. 'Of course. We'll get in touch as soon as the house is out there on the market. We need to... discuss a few things between us.'

'Feel free to wander around,' Liam offered. 'And I have no objections to you coming back to take another look.' He checked his watch. 'But now we'd better get a move on, Andy. I have a flight to London at six this evening.' He smiled at Tara. 'Not as nice as Greece, but I'll be back there next week.'

When the two men had gone back into the house, Tara looked at Kate and laughed. 'So now we're buying a house? Are you mad?'

'No, but it was the only thing I could think of,' Kate said. 'We haven't bought anything yet. You can easily pull out and say we've changed our minds.' She pulled at Tara. 'Come on. Let's go and have that coffee by the river. I need it after all that.'

'Me too,' Tara said as the started to walk down the slope towards the copse of trees from where they could hear the sound of water washing over rocks. Halfway there, she stopped and turned to look at the house. The sunlight glinted in all the windows and a dove landed on the roof, cooing. As she stood there, she suddenly felt like she knew what she was going to do. Everything that had happened recently had steered her in this direction she hadn't planned but been guided to by some strange force – or fate. It had been waiting for her all this time, this house, with all its secrets.

Chapter Eleven

Tara spent the following week cycling around the Ring of Kerry, finding hidden spots down back roads and tiny country lanes. She was amazed at how the back country of the Iveragh Peninsula was so deserted, but she assumed it was because everyone wanted to be by the sea and take the most popular routes. Here, further inland, there were mountains and valleys and streams and old humpback bridges with lovely views and an incredible array of wildflowers and birds. She was delighted to find this haven away from the tourist spots and came back every evening with photos she uploaded on her laptop that were exactly what she had wanted.

As there were so many possibilities for a trip to this part of Ireland, she decided to float the idea of a series of articles with the magazine, covering an alternative activity in each one, which they took on board straight away, saying she could go ahead and split her piece into sections – a different area in each, the first being hiking, and then going on to pony trekking, surfing, walking, camping, bird watching and so on. It would be called the 'Irish Wild Vagabond' series and be featured once a month from January onwards. As she never revealed the details of an ongoing project to anyone, she hadn't shared any of this with Kate. In any case, the subject of her assignment was something they avoided, neither of them wanting to rock the boat as they were trying to stay friends and not start arguing about anything.

Despite being busy with her work, she found time to swim every morning at the little beach below the cottage, sometimes meeting Mick, who seemed happy to see her but didn't say much apart from 'good morning', and 'nice day', which it was as the hot weather continued to everyone's amazement. But she left him alone as this seemed to be what he wanted, and in any case, she had other things on her mind, namely the house beside the river.

It had become something of an obsession with her as she went through the rooms, walked through the little rose garden and down the slope to the river in her imagination every night before she went to sleep. It was like a prayer that made her feel happy, as if she had a secret she didn't share with anyone, not even Kate. The idea of buying the house became a wish she hoped would come true, even though it would probably be unwise. The money from the sale of her father's house still sat in their shared account in the Bank of Ireland, but was it wise to blow her part on a wreck of a house in a remote area of Kerry? Probably not, but then the price of that house might not be very high…

Liam had sent her a message through Facebook asking if she wanted to go back to the house for a further look, and she had said she would, thinking she might ask him what he knew about the family history and the people in the wedding photo. Being there might jog his memory. He said he'd take a look at his shifts and get in touch, but in the meantime the house was going up on the property websites so she could see the price and maybe do her sums.

He had sounded as if he didn't quite believe that she would buy it, and Tara suspected he knew it had been a fib. And that's what it had been then, but now it was real possibility.

For some reason she wanted to own Riverside Farm. She knew that she would probably never live there; her life and her career were in New York and she hadn't ever thought she'd want to live anywhere else. So why did she have this idea in her head? Why was part of her so hooked on the house and the idea of it belonging to her? And why hadn't she discussed all of this with Kate? The answers to all these questions kept whirling around in her head while she worked, trying not to think too much but at the same time feeling irresistibly drawn to the house. The only thing to do was to go back there and take a good look at it and all its problems so that she would get it out of her mind once and for all.

A few days later, Mick called Tara out of the blue and suggested they meet up at the Harbour pub, sounding a lot more cheerful than he had before, which surprised her. 'I promise not to be gloomy,' he said as she hesitated. 'We'll have a jar and chat and look at the boats coming into harbour. Then, if we feel we have more to say to each other, we'll ask Sean Óg to cook us a steak. He's the owner of the pub and a great cook.'

'I'd love to,' Tara said, his happy voice making her smile. 'I've been cycling up and down the back roads for days taking photographs, meeting people and trying to write. So yes, a break would be good.'

And that's exactly how she felt after a long week of hard work and wrestling with the mystery of Riverside Farm. So she put on a turquoise silk shirt, white jeans and a pair of strappy sandals, applied a little mascara and blusher, noticing that the sun had given her skin a golden glow and her eyes a sparkle. She was astonished that she could look so good without spending the usual amount of time applying make-up and blow drying her hair. She had relaxed her skincare routine and stopped worrying about her hair while she cycled around the area, thinking she would go to a spa before she went back. But now she realised that it wouldn't be necessary. The sunshine, wind and soft Kerry air were the best beauty treatments, combined with sleeping soundly all night and her early morning swims. Happy with how she looked, she walked over to the little pub in the harbour where Mick waited for her at one of the tables on the terrace overlooking the pier where the boats were slowly arriving in the late-evening sunshine.

He looked up as she approached the table and beamed her an appreciative smile. 'Hello,' he said and got up to pull out a chair. 'Thank you for coming and for looking so good.'

Tara smiled. 'Hello, there,' she said, responding to his cheerful tone. 'You don't look too bad yourself.'

He bowed. 'Thank you. That's very kind.'

Her smile widened as she sat down. 'Kindness has nothing to do with it.'

'Thank goodness for that,' he retorted. 'I'm glad you're finding me acceptable.'

'But of course I do.' She met his gaze and felt a sudden flutter somewhere inside as she looked into his brown eyes. Not that she was interested in flirting with him – was she? – but it gave her confidence a lift to see the attraction in his eyes, to see him happy.

As if by mutual understanding, they smiled at each other, and when he put his hand on hers, Tara didn't pull it away, but leaned closer, so close she could smell his aftershave with a hint of citrus. 'And you smell nice,' she added.

'It's not me, it's the seaweed,' he joked, moving away from her as a waiter appeared asking what they wanted.

'Champagne,' Mick said.

'Uh, we don't really do that here,' the waiter said. 'But I think we have a bottle of that Cava stuff. Would that do?'

Mick sighed theatrically. 'I suppose it'll have to. Something bubbly to celebrate with, in any case. Two glasses of that, then, please.'

'What are we celebrating?' Tara asked when the waiter had left.

'My death,' Mick said.

'What?' Tara asked, startled. She stared at him, wondering what he meant. 'Your death?' she asked just to make sure she had heard correctly.

'Not *my* death, of course,' Mick replied with a laugh. 'Don't look so shocked. My character's death. In that God-awful soap I've been in.'

'Oh. You mean *Dubliners in Love*? I haven't seen the episodes you're in yet.'

'Please don't bother. It's all awful.'

'I'm sure it isn't,' Tara argued. 'I've seen some of the episodes and I really enjoyed them. And I've heard it's very popular. Hasn't the series been sold to quite a lot of countries, too?'

'Yes, but that's not a big deal. Irish series are popular these days, including this one. I was beginning to get bored with the plot and the trite dialogue. But now I've been killed off, so I don't have to do it any more.'

'Oh. How come they killed you – I mean, him?'

'I signed up knowing I could renegotiate my contract after six months. So I did and as I had the option to leave I decided that was the best thing to do, and the studio have decided to kill me off dramatically. It's a huge relief, I have to say.'

The waiter arrived at the table with two glasses of chilled Cava and a bowl of nuts. 'Anything else?' he asked as he placed the glasses in front of them.

'Not for the moment,' Mick replied and lifted his glass, smiling. 'So here's to a new beginning.' He clinked his glass against Tara's. 'Cheers!'

'To your death,' she said.

'To my death.' Mick laughed and downed most of the drink in one go.

'So what are you going to do now?' Tara asked when she had finished her own glass.

Mick suddenly looked less cheerful. 'I don't really know. I'm at some kind of crossroads in my life. I'm about to turn forty and here I am still living with my father. And my mother is moving back in and is redoing the house, so it feels even worse now. I have to move out and move on in some way. I can make a living narrating audio books and doing voiceovers, but that isn't really what I want to do for the rest of my life.'

'But you're a great actor,' Tara said, confused. 'I mean, you have a huge talent, you're very good-looking and your voice…' She stopped, not knowing how to go on. She couldn't believe that the great Mick O'Dwyer was sitting here telling her he was finished as an actor and didn't know what to do with his life.

'I might have been good once,' he said with a hint of despair. 'But it's not working any more.'

'Do you feel this way because of what happened with your play?' Tara couldn't help asking.

'So you heard about that? Bad news travels fast,' he said with a hint of bitterness. 'Yes, partly that. But there was something else, too. Someone else, I mean. Someone I thought I could love for the rest of my life dumped me in a very nasty way.'

'That's terrible,' Tara said, wondering how any woman could be so stupid. 'I'm so sorry, Mick.'

He nodded. 'Thank you.'

She could tell that he didn't want to talk about it at length, much like she didn't like talking about Joe. 'But the acting...' she said, changing the subject. 'I mean, you were such a big star. Don't you think you might get back to that in a little while?'

'No,' Mick said glumly. 'It doesn't work for me like it used to, so it's better to quit.'

'You might get back to it when you've had a little time to think and rest,' Tara suggested.

He shrugged. 'Maybe. In the meantime, I'll just keep going like this.' He drained his glass and looked at Tara. 'But enough about me and my miseries. What about you? Anything exciting happening in your life?'

Tara hesitated. She knew he needed something to help him turn his mind away from his problems and his broken heart. 'I'm going to buy a house,' she said, surprising herself. She hadn't even talked to Kate about it, or even looked up the property sites on the Internet to see if the house was on the market yet, but right now, looking at Mick and having heard him pour out his heart to her, she felt a sudden affinity with him.

'What?' he said, the light coming back into his eyes. 'You're buying a house? Here? In Sandy Cove?'

'Not quite. Nearer to Ballinskelligs. It's an old wreck of a farmhouse that is owned by a distant relation. He must be my fifth cousin or something. I've only been there twice but, oh Mick, it's the most enchanting house I have ever seen. And now it's going to be sold and if I don't buy it…'

'You'll die of a broken heart?' he asked in a jovial tone.

'It'll be lost,' she said, a feeling of immense sadness welling up inside. 'To the family, I mean,' she explained. 'It's been in the O'Rourke family since it was built in 1860. But it's not really that, it's the feeling I get when I'm there.' She shook her head. 'I can't really explain it.'

'What does Kate think about this?'

'I haven't told her. It's funny, but she was the one who said we should buy it, but she didn't mean it. And I think she's forgotten about it, actually. But if I told her I do want to buy it…'

'She'll say it's totally mad. Which it is.'

'I know.'

'Tell me more. Did you take photos?'

'Not that many of the house,' Tara said. 'But he – the owner, I mean – said it was going on the market this week.'

Mick picked up his phone. 'Which agency is he using?'

'O'Mahony and Sons.'

'Okay.' Mick turned on his phone and typed something in. 'O'Mahony and Sons...' he muttered. 'Houses for sale, County Kerry...' Then he sat up. 'Here it is. Riverside Farm. Is that the name?'

'Yes,' Tara said, her heart racing. She leaned over the table. 'Is it there?'

'I think so.' Mick showed her a picture on his phone. 'Is this it?'

'Let me see.' She grabbed the phone and looked at the image on the screen. 'Yes,' she said. 'That's it.' She scrolled through the pictures and read the text. '*In need of restoration... Victorian farmhouse with gardens and twenty acres adjoining, beautiful views of the surrounding countryside, ruined tower and access to small bay with private beach.*' Tara looked up. 'Private beach? Where could that be?'

'Must be a part of Wild Rose Bay,' Mick said. 'Have you been there? It's gorgeous.'

'I've seen it from a distance but never been there. Kate said it was impossible to get down there.'

'That's because she didn't want you to make it the tourist spot of the year,' Mick said. 'It's a bit of a scramble but it's not impossible.'

'Oh,' Tara said, still looking at the ad on the phone.

'What's the price?' Mick asked.

'Ninety-five thousand.'

'Well, it says it comes with some land, alongside the beach and the house. It's a pretty cheap price if you get all that.'

'Land?' Tara said, looking at the ad again. 'Must be the slopes down to Wild Rose Bay. That's an added bonus, isn't it?'

'Of course,' Mick agreed. 'Except that bit of land isn't that useful apart from being pretty.'

'I suppose,' Tara said. 'The house is a wreck with no bathroom or indoor toilet, and I suspect, as you said, the land is just scrubland. He's hanging on to most of the fields – they're leased, to a sheep farmer, I expect.' Tara handed back the phone, remembering the animals she had seen while cycling around the area.

Mick looked at the photo of the house again. 'So this is the thing that has stolen your heart? This ruin of a place?'

'Yes,' Tara whispered.

He shook his head with a pitying look. 'You're crazy.'

'I know.'

'Do you even have the money to buy this pile of rubbish?'

'Yes. Kate and I shared the proceeds of the sale of my father's house in Dublin. So it's all sitting there in an account in the Bank of Ireland doing nothing. It's supposed to be our nest egg, our security.'

He looked at her for a moment with a strange expression she couldn't quite decipher. Then he beamed her a huge smile and leaned close. 'Do it,' he said.

Tara blinked. She had expected him to say it was a crazy thing to do and to forget about it. 'What? You think I should?'

'Yes!' he exclaimed with a sudden gleam in his eyes. 'Follow your dream. Buy that place and do it up. Life is so short and you should live it, not sit there and consider the risks and the options. I can tell that this house has grabbed you in an odd way. I can see it in your eyes when you talk about it. So you live in New York, but wouldn't it be nice to have a place to go to in Ireland? Somewhere you can think about when you're homesick. A beautiful, impossibly impractical place you can call your own, where your ancestors have lived for hundreds of years. And you can spend your summers here, bring your family here when you have one, come back when you're old and need the comfort of home and your sister and all the people you will know once this summer's over.'

Tara felt a surge of joy as she listened to his deep voice telling her she should do what her heart desired and forget about being sensible. 'Holy God,' she said with a laugh. 'You're very persuasive. You could sell sand in Sahara if you tried hard enough.'

He winked. 'Oh yes, I'm sure I could. That's why my voiceovers in those ads on TV and radio are so popular. You should hear me when I do the ad for the latest Toyota model. Or the ones for that ice cream brand. Positively orgasmic, I've heard.' He turned to wave at the waiter. 'More Cava and keep it coming,' he shouted. 'Bring us the whole bottle, willya, Conor?'

Tara giggled. 'Stop, I'm feeling a little tipsy already. It's the bubbles.'

'No, it's that house. Now you've been pushed in the right direction, you're drunk with excitement.'

'And when it all turns into that movie *The Money Pit*, it'll be all your fault.'

'Of course it will,' he said cheerfully. 'But hey, won't it be fun?'

Tara looked into his eyes and somehow knew she was going to do it. Not only for herself, but for him and for Kate and for Liam, too. They were all connected in one way or the other. Crazy as it seemed, she felt with all her heart that she simply *had* to buy that house.

Chapter Twelve

The weather had turned to dark clouds and a steady drizzle when Tara made her way to the house the following day. Liam had called and said it was the only time he was free as he was working every day for the next ten days at least. 'London, Rome, Milan, Nice and then Greece twice, followed by several trips to Spain,' he said. 'So if you want to look around the house, it'll have to be tomorrow. It's the holiday season, so we have double the amount of flights until September.'

Tara had agreed and set off on the bike, dressed in waterproofs, feeling it would be good to see the house in bad weather. Maybe it would seem a lot less desirable in the rain. She still hadn't told Kate about her dream to own it, worried that it would be met with a stone wall of disapproval. Kate wanted to find out about their great-grandfather and that was the only reason she was interested in the farm. Once she knew the story, she probably wouldn't feel she wanted to have much to do with the house. Kate had been amazed to find this house, but, being practical, she would be against spending money buying a place that needed so much work. She would never see the romantic side or be so bowled over by the beauty that she'd risk everything she had to own it. Unlike Tara, who had felt a strange pull on her emotions as she walked through the empty rooms where the echoes of the past seemed to whisper in her ears. It wasn't frightening to her in the slightest; it was as if the memories of her ancestors were in her DNA somehow. She had read an article once about how the memories of parents could be passed on to their children, and this now seemed very real to her. That house had a fascinating story to tell and she desperately wanted to hear it.

Not only that, she was also beginning to think that she could do a magazine feature about the house with beautiful photographs that could be published in *Harper's Bazaar* or *Vanity Fair*. *A hidden treasure with a long-forgotten history*, Tara thought, imagining how it would all look in one of those magazines. With Mick's words ringing in her ears, she cycled on through the steady drizzle, breathing in the scent of grass and wildflowers that always seemed more powerful when it rained.

Tara smiled when she thought of her evening with Mick. They had ended up finishing the bottle of Cava and ordered steaks and chips and stayed at the pub until closing time, talking, joking and cheering each other up. Mick walked Tara home to the cottage, refusing to come in as it would ruin her reputation, he said, which made her laugh. But she was happy to say good night at the door as they were both still a little tipsy. Mick had slipped his arm around her shoulders as they walked which she found comforting and sweet. A friendly gesture, she thought, as was the light kiss on her cheek as he said good night and strolled away in the darkness whistling a happy tune. She stood in the little front garden for a while, looking at the stars in the black velvet sky, the soft summer breeze like silk on her skin. She felt that Kate had been right when she said she and Mick would be good for each other. They seemed so in tune, falling into the same jokes and banter as when they had spoken online, only now they could look at each other, breathe the same air and perhaps even feel the same emotions. It was lovely to have a friend like Mick with whom she could be herself without having to impress or pretend to be perfect. The fact that he was wildly attractive was an added bonus, she told herself.

Tara decided not to leave her bike at the crossroads and cycled on down the lane, dodging the dripping branches of the trees, apprehensive about what the farm would look like in this dreary weather. Probably awful, she assumed. She'd forget all about spending her savings on a wreck of a house that would cost even more to do up. But she would at least get some more clues to the family feud that had chased her great-grandfather away for good.

Daniel's face had haunted her ever since she'd found his photo. He was so like her father, the way she remembered him when she and Kate were little girls and they had been such a happy family. Had Daniel been through loss like she had? She had looked at that wedding photo on her phone again, showing it to Mick last night. They both tried to piece the story together. Was that little boy Daniel? And in that case, was the bride his mother? Not really possible, as then she would have had Daniel out of wedlock, which was considered scandalous in those days. So who was she? And the groom? Those questions needed an answer before she could delve deeper into what had happened a hundred or so years ago.

Tara arrived at the farm dripping, hoping Liam would be able to show her around the house, but also give her a bit more information about her family. It was, after all, his family history, too. She got off her bike and stood at the old gate, looking at the house in the gloomy light. It felt so peaceful here, the rain dripping from the trees and the cooing of a dove the only sound. The soft, damp air smelled of wet vegetation and pine trees.

Tara eased off her jacket as the rain stopped, leaning her bike against the ivy-covered wall of the house. She hung the jacket and her bicycle helmet on the handlebars and looked around for Liam's car, but he hadn't arrived yet. Going up the steps and in through the half-open door, she was a lot less nervous than before. The house was still and silent, as if waiting for something – or someone. Tara laughed at herself and pushed those thoughts away as she walked into the living room, where the sofa bed stood all alone, but the floorboards bore marks of other, grander pieces of furniture long before it had been used as the bedroom of an old man. She looked at the wallpaper hanging in strips and the faded velvet curtains and tried to imagine what it would have been like in older, better days. A beautiful room, she deduced as she walked to the window and discovered the lovely view of the little valley and the river. She wondered how they had spent their evenings here, in front of the fire, reading, the women sewing, chatting softly to each other. Or perhaps this room had only been used on special occasions and the families had sat around the old range in the large kitchen where it would have been warmer.

Tara was startled out of her daydream as a car door slammed outside. Liam had arrived. She went out into the hall to meet him, feeling suddenly a little apprehensive. He was, after all, a total stranger, even if they might be distantly related. But her nervousness disappeared as he walked in and beamed her a friendly smile.

'Hi, Tara,' he said. 'Sorry I'm late. There was a lot of traffic on the way here.' He was dressed in a navy rainproof jacket and jeans and his hair was damp and shorter than the last time.

'That's because of the tourist season,' she replied.

'That's right. The planes are packed these days. The Irish craving sunshine and everyone in the rest of the world wants to come to the ol' Emerald Isle.'

Tara laughed. 'Yeah, I know what you mean. I met a lot of that kind of tourist on the way here from New York.'

'I'm sure you did.' He looked awkwardly at her for a moment. 'So, let's go through the house, then, shall we? Anything in particular you want to see?'

'Not really. We could start down here and go through the rooms and you could fill me in on the history, maybe,' Tara suggested.

'Not much to tell you, to be honest. I don't know a lot about it.' Liam walked ahead, crossing the corridor to the room opposite. 'This was the dining room, I suppose.'

'Yes. The table is still here,' Tara said, again running her hand over the dusty mahogany. 'Early Victorian, I think.'

Liam shrugged. 'No idea. Could be. The house was like this when I inherited it. I didn't really know my great-uncle. He was my grandfather's eldest brother and they weren't close, as far as I know. I only met him once when I was a little boy and my dad brought me here to see the house. I can't really remember what it was like. I only remember that I thought the old man was a bit scary. Scruffy and grumpy. There was more furniture though and the garden out the back was in better nick. He gave me a bag of jelly beans and three pounds. That was before the euro,' Liam added.

'Oh.' Tara glanced at her reflection in the antique mirror over the fireplace, noticing her pale face and messy hair, frizzy from the rain. 'So you don't know anything about this house at all?'

'Not much. Except that it was built after one of our ancestors had married the daughter of a rich farmer from Tipperary.' Liam pointed out the window. 'See the shed thing out the back behind the rose garden?'

'Yes?' Tara followed his gaze and looked at the low building with a corrugated roof.

'That was the original farmhouse. Then, when the new, rich bride arrived, she wanted something grander, so they built this house and used the old one as a shed.'

'Really?' Tara peered through the window at the building, and saw that it would have been like the traditional farm cottages that dotted the landscape all over Kerry. Back then it would have had a thatched roof instead of the corrugated one. 'So that was the house that was here before this one was built in 1860?'

'So the story goes. That's all the family history I know,' Liam said.

Tara turned to look at him. 'But what about more recent times? Like the years after the War of Independence and the Civil War? I'm sure there was a lot of conflict then. Fianna Fáil and Fine Gael and all that fighting about the northern counties. Families were split apart by all that and some of them never made their peace with each other.'

Liam looked blankly at Tara. 'No idea about that. I don't think they were feuding much about that in the O'Rourke family. There was some kind of tiff about land and so on, I heard, but nothing serious.'

'Are you sure?' Tara asked. 'My great-grandfather left Kerry and never came back. We never knew why. We didn't even know he came from this farm until we found the photograph of him standing outside this very house. And then last time I was here, I found another photo upstairs of a wedding, taken years earlier, which I think he was in.'

'You found a photograph? Upstairs?' Liam asked, looking alarmed. 'Where?'

Tara felt her face flush. 'In a drawer in the master bedroom. I know I shouldn't have opened it,' she added, 'or even been up there without permission, but I was so curious to find out more about my great-grandfather.'

Liam smiled. 'Breaking and entering, eh? Tut, tut. Maybe I should call the Guards?'

'Yes, maybe you should,' Tara joked, putting up her hands. 'I'll confess straight away. Will you come and visit me in prison?'

'Of course I will.' Liam grinned. 'But let's go and look at that photo and see if I'll recognise anyone.' He started to walk swiftly out of the room and down the corridor.

Tara followed and walked up the stairs behind him, wondering if he would be able to tell her about the people in that photo. He didn't seem that interested but it was probably because he wasn't that connected to this house or this part of his family. He had dodged the subject of a family feud and glossed over any rows or fights that might have happened – she secretly wondered if he knew more that he let on. But why would he hide anything from her? He didn't look like the devious type at all, with that friendly smile and twinkle in his blue eyes. She had instantly liked him when they'd first met, as he hadn't been angry about her barging into his house, nor had he shown any annoyance this second time. Was it because he was eager to sell?

They arrived in the master bedroom after a sprint up the stairs that left Tara breathless. She pointed at the chest of drawers. 'That's where I found it. In the top left-hand drawer.'

'Okay.' Liam walked across the room and pulled out the drawer. He looked inside for a moment and pulled it out further. 'It's empty.'

'What?' Tara joined him and peered into the drawer. 'But it was right here. A photograph in a green leather folder. It said, *Mary and John's wedding in 1904* underneath.'

'You didn't take it, did you?' Liam asked, looking at her suspiciously.

'No, of course not. But...' Tara pulled her phone out of her pocket and looked up her photo app. 'I took a shot of it.' She held up the phone for Liam to see.

He studied the screen for a moment. 'I've never seen it. Don't know who those people are at all.'

'Are you sure?'

He laughed. 'I know I might look a little worse for wear today, but I don't think I've aged that much.'

Tara giggled. 'No, you haven't. You don't look a day over ninety-five. I didn't actually mean that you knew these people personally, just that you might have seen them in photos in some album or other, or heard their names or something.'

He shook his head. 'No, I haven't.'

'Okay.' She looked at the photo on her phone again. 'But seriously... These people must have something to do with this place. Why was it here in this drawer?'

'Are you sure it was? I mean,' Liam explained, 'you might have seen it somewhere else, maybe in with those photos of that young man you said was your great-grandfather.'

'No. It was here,' Tara insisted. 'Kate was with me and she saw it too. Told me I had to put it back, which I did.'

He lifted an eyebrow. 'Really? Are you sure you didn't slip it into your bag by mistake?'

'Absolutely sure. My sister is a stickler for the rules, and I always do what she tells me.'

He leaned against the chest of drawers, his arms folded, looking quizzically at her. 'She's strict? But you're twins, aren't you?'

'That doesn't mean we share the same brain,' Tara retorted. 'We're identical physically, but not mentally. In any case I would have put it back even if she hadn't told me.'

'I'm sure you would,' Liam assured her. He looked around the room. 'Anything else you want to see? The other rooms are empty, so not much to find out there.'

'No, I think I've seen most of the house by now,' she replied, deciding to leave her questions for another time. She suspected he had removed the photo on purpose. 'But I'd love to take a look at the floorplan if you have it, and also the land that comes with the purchase of the house.'

'I have those in the car. But...' He hesitated. 'Maybe we could go and get a coffee and look at the plans somewhere more comfortable?

There's a pub in Ballinskelligs that's quite nice. I could put your bike in the back of my car and drive us there.'

Tara looked out the window and saw that it had started to rain again. 'Okay. And if it stops raining I'll cycle back to Sandy Cove from there.'

'Sounds like a good plan.' Liam held out his hand. 'After you.'

Tara smiled and walked ahead, meeting his gaze as she walked past him. She did feel pleased that she was going to spend more time with him and perhaps get to know more about him. There was something about him that intrigued her. Was it his connection to her family history? To the house? He may not want to tell her about his family, but she decided there must be a good reason. She decided to do her best to find out everything he knew – and make him trust her enough to reveal things he might be hiding.

Chapter Thirteen

The pub in Ballinskelligs had a glassed-in veranda with views of the ocean and the Skellig Islands. The skies had brightened and the rain eased to a light drizzle as Tara and Liam sat down at a table after having ordered coffee and a slice of lemon sponge cake. Liam took the plans he had mentioned out of a big folder he had brought with him from the car.

'This should, strictly speaking, be done by the estate agent, but I thought it would be okay for me to show them to you.' He glanced at Tara. 'Unless you prefer to deal with the agent on your own?'

'No, that's fine,' Tara said. 'I just want to know what comes with the house. Then, if and when I decide to buy, I'll contact the agent and we'll negotiate.' She tried her best to sound as if she was in charge but she knew that it would involve some persuading to get Kate to agree to transfer Tara's part of the money in their shared account. She didn't exactly need permission, but she knew she would have to explain what she wanted the money for. And Kate might try to talk her out of it, as it wasn't exactly a very sensible plan. Not an easy task, but she'd cross that bridge later.

Liam nodded and unfolded one of the plans. 'Here's the floorplan of the house.'

Tara studied it for a moment, familiarising herself with the layout even though she had a very good idea of it already. 'So there's definitely no bathroom, or even a toilet indoors?'

Liam smiled apologetically. 'No. I know this seems very primitive to us, but my old great-uncle managed fine with just that outside toilet and washing himself at the kitchen sink. I think he also washed in the river in the summertime. But he was old and had never had the mod cons we take for granted now.'

Tara shivered. 'Ugh, I can't imagine what that must have been like. Is there even electricity?'

'Yes. As you might have noticed by the electricity poles along the lane. And the lamps in the ceilings and so on.'

'I didn't notice. I just assumed it was there. But I suppose it will have to be rewired all the same.'

Liam nodded at the waitress who brought their order. 'Thanks,' he said and turned back to Tara. 'Yes, I think rewiring would be essential. You'll have to contact the ESB to get connected again, should you want to buy the house.'

'I see. I'm glad I wouldn't have to start from scratch. You never know with these old houses.'

'That's true. Especially as this part of the west of Ireland didn't actually get electricity until the nineteen seventies.'

'Amazing,' Tara said, trying to imagine what it would have been like before that time. 'But it's not just the rewiring that needs to be done to make the house liveable in.'

'Absolutely,' Liam agreed. 'The house needs serious restoring, but at least the roof is quite new.'

Tara sipped her coffee. 'How new? Like from the nineteen thirties?'

Liam laughed. 'No, apparently my great-uncle had the roof redone about ten years ago. I think he was thinking of selling up, but then he got sick and didn't have the energy to organise it. It's sad to think he lived there all alone the past few years. My parents had no idea. They had lost touch with him a long time ago.'

'That's sad,' Tara remarked.

'Very.' Liam unfolded a map from his documents. 'Here is the land around the house and the few acres that will be included in the sale.' He pointed to the middle of the map. 'Here's the house and the slope down to the river, but as you can see, on the other side, the land goes all the way to this rocky area where there is an old tower.'

'O'Rourke's castle,' Tara exclaimed. 'I've seen it from afar.'

Liam smiled and nodded. 'That's right. Not a real castle, but the remains of some kind of tower, and then there's this bit that goes down to this little bay here.' He stabbed his finger at a curve on the map.

'I know,' Tara said, her heart beating faster. 'It's Wild Rose Bay.'

'I think that's what it's called, yes,' Liam replied, not appearing the slightest bit interested. 'Not a lot of land and not much use, but that's all that's left after I sell the rest to the farmer who's been leasing it for years.' He looked at Tara with a quizzical smile. 'I don't think you'll be planning to become a sheep farmer.'

Tara laughed. 'No, that's not one of my ambitions in life.'

'But why do you even want to buy the house?' Liam asked, looking suddenly puzzled. 'Didn't you say you live in New York? And you're quite a successful photographer, I believe.'

Tara stared at him. 'How did you know that?'

'You make no secret of it on Facebook,' he remarked. 'And your Instagram photos are great.'

'Thank you.' She leaned forward, forgetting the maps and the plans. 'Your Facebook page is quite interesting, too. All those trips to fabulous places. Do you ever get bored with flying around the world?'

Liam pondered the question for a while. 'Not bored, exactly. But it can get tiring and a little too hectic at times. Especially in high season. But I'm due two weeks' holidays soon. I'm looking forward to slowing down for a while. I'm planning to go up to Donegal for a bit.'

'With your girlfriend?' Tara asked, suddenly dying to know if he had one.

Liam laughed. 'No. I'm not in a relationship, as they say on Facebook. Not at the moment. How about you?'

Tara hesitated. 'Well... No,' she said, oddly pleased that he wasn't attached to anyone. Not that she was interested in him in that way, it was just that... *What?* she asked herself, meeting his eyes. *I'm trying to sort out my feelings for Joe, so why am I so happy that Liam is single?* She told the little voice inside to be quiet and returned her attention to their conversation. 'I was dating someone,' she tried to explain. 'But we're on a break.'

'Interesting,' he said, looking at her intently.

'Not really,' Tara said with a non-committal shrug. 'But – back to the house,' she continued. 'I have to think about it.'

'Of course. It's a big decision. Lots of money at stake. And then all the work that has to be done.'

'I know.' Tara's gaze drifted to the plans on the table and saw the house again in her mind's eye. Cois Abhainn Farm was so beautiful, even in its dilapidated state. Seeing it in the rain hadn't put her off, quite the opposite. The grey light, the raindrops against the roof, the little rose garden where the colours of the roses had been even more vivid in the rain, the kitchen with its old range and the old floor tiles… Tara imagined the walls painted white, with Shaker style cupboards, the range polished and a large black dog snoozing in front of it. The living room with a big rug on the polished floorboards, a blazing fire and a big sofa in front of it, piled with cushions. And the dining room with friends sitting around that big table, and… *Stop it*, she told herself, trying to rein in her imagination. But oh, what a cosy holiday home it could all be…

It wasn't only the house that excited her, it was the little bit of land attached to it. The tower, the slope covered in wild roses all the way to that little beach… It would once again belong to her family – if she took the plunge and spent all her money buying it. And what a feature she could write about all this, once she found out more about the history of the farm.

But what about Kate? She couldn't exclude her sister from this venture, even if buying it and featuring the farm in a magazine would be met with a lot of resistance from her. She looked up from the plans and noticed Liam's eyes on her.

'You're miles away,' he remarked with a smile. 'I think you need a little time to digest all of this.'

'Yes, and I need to talk to my sister. This should be a family decision. Something we'll do together.'

'Of course,' Liam agreed and gathered up the plans. 'I could make scans of these and email them to you if you want. Or, better still, why don't you just use your camera right now?' He put the plans back on the table, pushing the cups and plates aside. 'There. I think the light's good here, so you'll get all the details in.'

'Thanks.' Tara got her phone out and took shots of the plans. Then she pointed the camera at Liam. 'Smile,' she said.

He shot her a lopsided smile, looking amused. 'I'm not part of the property.'

'No, but you looked so good there, against the views of the ocean. Your eyes are so blue. And you have a very interesting face.'

'Thank you.' He reached out and grabbed her phone, pointing it at her. 'Now you smile.'

Tara laughed as he clicked. Then she took the phone back and moved around the table to sit beside him, holding it aloft. He put his arm around her and with their heads together, they looked at the screen while Tara took the photo. She showed him the shot. 'We have such different colouring. You with your curly black hair and blue eyes, and me with lighter brown hair and hazel eyes. And…' She stopped and stared at him. 'You don't have the O'Rourke freckles. Or the straight hair, or…'

'I think I look more like my mother's family,' Liam said. 'The O'Rourke genes must have been diluted through the years. It's just the name we share, after all.'

'I suppose,' Tara said, wondering why he had, for a moment, looked oddly uncomfortable. It might just have been that he felt awkward about her commenting on his looks. But he didn't seem like the shy type. Quite the opposite. At first glance she had thought he oozed confidence with that cheeky smile and the twinkle in his eyes. And the way he had put his arm around her for the selfie had seemed quite practised, as if he had a habit of flirting with any attractive woman who happened to cross his path.

'Send me that shot,' Liam said. 'I'd love to have it as a memento.'

'Of course,' Tara said. 'I'll just edit it and adjust the light and contrast when I get back home.' She looked out the window and noticed the weather had improved. 'I think I'll head back now,' she said. 'It has stopped raining so the cycle ride should be lovely.'

'Pity,' he said, looking disappointed. 'I'd have enjoyed driving you back. I've never been to Sandy Cove.'

'Why don't you come some other day? I'll show you around,' Tara suggested. 'It's a gorgeous little village.'

His eyes brightened. 'I'd love to. But I have to get going too. I have to get to Farranfore for the flight to London later today.'

Tara gathered her things and got up. 'Okay. Let's just get my bike and rain gear out of your car and then we'll say goodbye.'

'For today,' he filled in, also getting to his feet. 'I'll be in touch when I'm on leave and you can give me the grand tour of Sandy Cove.'

'Great,' Tara said. 'Thanks for coming today and showing me those plans.'

'It was a true pleasure. I really enjoyed the day.'

'Me too.' She hesitated for a moment. 'I should tell you, though, that it'll be a while before I can decide about the house. So if someone else is interested, you should go ahead and sell. I couldn't expect you to hang around and wait for me to make up my mind.'

He stood for a moment, looking at her. 'That's very kind of you. But I think the house is special to you for some reason. When you were there today, there was a look in your eyes…' He stopped and smiled apologetically. 'Maybe it was just my imagination.'

'Yes,' Tara said. 'Maybe it was.' She suddenly felt uncomfortable under his probing gaze and worried irrationally that he might be able to read her thoughts. 'But we have to get going,' she breezed on. 'Let's go and get my bike and stuff.'

She started to walk out before there were any more discussions about how she felt. She didn't want to share the odd sensation of belonging to a wreck of a house she hadn't known existed until quite recently. Nor could she explain to him what looking at the plans of the land around it had done to her. The thought of owning the area around O'Rourke's tower and the slopes down to Wild Rose Bay made her nearly dizzy. She needed to talk about it to someone who would understand completely how she felt. And there was only one such person.

Once she had her things, she cycled back to Sandy Cove down the road that ran along the coast. She only glanced at the spectacular views, her mind full of what she had learned today. When she neared the village and glimpsed Wild Rose Bay around a bend in the road, far below her, with its white sand and turquoise water, she nearly fell off her bike, distracted by the idea of owning the slopes covered in a riot of dark pink roses.

It could be all mine, she thought. *And it would once more belong to the O'Rourkes, to Kate and me, and maybe then Daniel can be at peace again with his own family.*

Chapter Fourteen

Tara arrived back at the little cottage at lunchtime. As the weather had improved and the sun shone warmly on the garden, she decided to make herself a sandwich and take it down to the beach, where she could swim before she ate and then relax in the sun for a while. She could look through the photos she had taken, study the plans and upload them to her laptop so she could have a better look before she showed them to Kate, to whom she sent a short text to make plans to have dinner together tonight.

She had just arrived back on the beach after her swim when she heard her phone ping. A text message from Kate probably, Tara thought, drying her hands on her towel before she sat down and squinted at the phone in the bright light. But it wasn't from Kate, it was from Joe. Tara was instantly jolted back to New York and all the troubles with their relationship, wondering why he was texting her despite agreeing not to contact her during her absence. She had wanted some space away from him but maybe he was texting her to say how much he missed her?

Hi, babes. Sorry for contacting you like this, I know it's not very nice, but I think we should call it a day on our relationship.

I don't feel we're compatible, so instead of hanging around all summer long, I want a clean ending. Like ripping off a plaster, you know? Short, sharp and then the pain only lasts for a short while. Thanks for the good times and good luck with the job. Ciao. Joe xx

Shocked, Tara stared at the text, reading it twice before it sank in. Joe was dumping her. By a text message, the lowest form of dumping there was. Tara put her hand to her mouth as it hit her like a punch in the stomach. 'Oh,' she moaned. 'Oh, no, no no…' Paralysed with shock, she sat there and stared at the phone, feeling icy cold despite the hot sun on her back. How was this possible? Joe, the man with whom she thought she was in love, who she was hoping would love her back… Tears pricked her eyes as she read the message again. Then she felt a sudden dislike for this man who had played with her feelings for over six months, with this on-again-off-again relationship. Yes, he was very attractive and fun to be with and she had hoped their dating would evolve into something more serious. But it never had, because of his fear of commitment. She started to feel angry with herself for having been fooled by his flirtatious ways and read more into it than it had been. What she had thought was love on his part was more wishful thinking by her than anything else, she realised, dashing tears out of her eyes, telling herself not to waste them on such a man. But the rejection still stung.

'Tara?'

Tara looked up in a daze, barely aware of someone standing above her, his shadow blocking the sunlight. 'Tara?' he said again. 'Are you all right?'

She shook her head. 'No,' she whispered. Then she looked at him as he crouched by her side. 'Mick?'

'What happened?' he asked, gently prying the phone from her grip.

'He…' She gestured at the phone.

Mick looked at the message. 'He dumped you?'

Tara nodded.

'By text. What a shit.'

'I know.' Tara looked miserably at Mick, her eyes welling up again.

'Come here,' Mick said sinking onto his knees enveloping Tara in his arms, hugging her tight. 'You poor darling.'

Tara pressed her face against Mick's linen shirt, his kind words making her feel even sadder. She started to cry, sobbing into his chest, soaking the shirt with the stream of tears that wouldn't stop. He held her tight, not letting her go, until she stopped. Exhausted, she pulled away, wiping her eyes with her hands. But Mick picked up her towel and dabbed her face, which felt good despite the rough sand scraping her skin. She blinked and took the towel from him, pressing it to her face. 'Thank you,' she said weakly. 'I soaked your shirt.'

'That's a minor problem. It'll teach me to hug women just out of the water.'

'And who are crying their eyes out as well,' Tara added with a weak smile. Feeling foolish at having reacted so strongly to something that wasn't really that sad, she spread the towel back on the sand and sat on it, looking at him bleakly. 'And I was so happy just then, after my swim and looking forward to dinner with Kate and everything.'

'And then he hit you with that. "Thanks for the good times",' Mick quoted. 'How pathetic.'

'Yeah.'

Mick brushed the sand off her face with his finger. 'Don't waste your tears on him, Tara. He doesn't deserve it, doesn't deserve someone as lovely as you, I mean.'

Tara sighed. 'That's very kind of you, Mick, but it's not true. I'm not good enough for a man like Joe. Not pretty enough, not smart enough, or sexy enough, or…'

'Stop it,' Mick ordered. 'Don't let him destroy your belief in yourself.'

Their eyes locked for a moment and Tara felt a surge of sympathy for him. He'd been hit a lot harder than her and now she felt silly to have reacted like that. It had probably reminded him of the break-up with that woman he had been in love with. His brown eyes were full of sadness and she suddenly wanted to comfort him in turn, tell him how much she liked him and that she appreciated his friendship and sympathy. 'You're a very nice man,' she said.

'Thank you. That's good to hear.' He sat back on the sand and looked up at the sky. 'It's such a lovely day. What a pity it was ruined by that guy.'

'I'm not going to let him spoil it,' Tara said, a surge of anger rising in her chest. 'I was feeling happy earlier and I will again. Soon.' She picked up her phone and blew the sand off it. 'I'm just going to do something that might annoy him.'

'What?' Mick asked. 'You're not going to reply to that text?'

'Of course not. Hang on just a second.' Tara quickly located the selfie she had taken with Liam earlier and posted that on both her Instagram and Facebook page. Then she typed in the words:

*Wonderful morning with a handsome captain of the skies, Liam
O'Rourke, a very old friend who doesn't feel so distant any more.*

She held out her phone for Mick to see. 'There. How does that
look?'

'Like you've found someone to console yourself with. Who's the
handsome captain?'

'Liam O'Rourke who owns Riverside Farm. We were talking
about the farm that he's selling.'

'Captain of the skies?' Mick asked.

'He's an airline pilot.' Tara looked at Mick. 'How do you think
it'll make Joe feel when he sees it?'

Mick thought for a moment. 'Possibly a little miffed that you're
not crying into your beer. Officially. And that photo saves you from
looking like a loser. Well done,' Mick said, sounding impressed. 'I
wish I had thought of something like that when the same thing
happened to me.'

'Oh, you will. It's not too late. Revenge is a dish best eaten cold,
they say. I'll help you think of something really good. Something
that'll really flatten the horrible biddy who made you so sad,' Tara
said with feeling.

Mick laughed. 'Thank you. That made me feel a lot better. I
wish she could hear what you said. She wouldn't like being called
a horrible biddy.'

Tara sat up and put her arms around her knees. 'Tell me about her.
I haven't wanted to ask before, but now that we're in the same club...'

'You're entitled?' Mick sat back and leaned on his elbows,
looking out at the sea as he talked. 'We met in London at one of

those glamorous parties where you get a lot to drink and nothing much to eat after the premiere of my play. Everyone's in a tux or tight little dress with sequins.'

'Would have looked good on you,' Tara cut in.

Mick smirked. 'Oh yeah, I wore a little number from Harvey Nicks.'

'I meant the tux.'

'I know.'

Mick smiled and turned to look at Tara. 'She was absolutely gorgeous. Shiny black hair that hung down to her tiny waist. She wore a red dress and stilettos. A dancer with the Royal Ballet, so you can imagine how gorgeous she was. And I was the bright new star on the West End with my new play and having been cast in the main role. We were partying away until the small hours, waiting for the reviews in the main newspapers. Tatiana and I were getting to know each other really well by the time the morning editions arrived. The reviews were good, even if not actually rave ones, but we were all happy. The play was on the way and we all thought it would run and run for a long time. But it only lasted three months. It was weird, because it had started so well, but then we got more reviews and they were awful. Audiences shrank to nearly nothing and we had to close. I could have coped with it all if Tatiana hadn't dumped me nearly at the same time. We had been dating ever since that opening-night party – well,' he corrected himself, 'dating isn't the right word for two people spending every night together and as much as they can during the day, and then texting like mad when we were apart. I thought she was the love of my life, that I had finally found the woman I would settle down with and love until death did us part.' He drew breath and looked at Tara with eyes so sad it made her feel like crying again. Then he sat up and turned his back to her, his arms around his knees.

'I'm so sorry, Mick,' she said and gently touched his shoulder.

'Thanks.' He sighed and looked at her over his shoulder. 'I could give you all the details of how happy she made me, how special I felt when I was with her and how she lit up any room she entered. But you can perhaps imagine all of that.'

'Yes, I can,' Tara said.

'It was only three months, but it felt like a lot longer and a lot more important than just a fling or short romance. For me, anyway. Possibly not for her, of course. I have a feeling she doesn't like losers.'

'You're not a loser, Mick,' Tara protested.

'Neither are you, Tara,' Mick said.

'That's not how I feel right now.'

'I know, but...' He scrambled to his feet. 'I came here to walk and think, trying to find a way out, a way forward. And then, here you were, in bits over that... that...' He stopped. 'Never mind. Let's try to put it behind us, eh? Cheer each other up, do something fun, what do you say?'

'Like what?' Tara asked, feeling numb. 'I don't have the energy to do anything.'

'I know, but I don't think sitting here feeling miserable will help. I have a few errands in the village. Why don't you come with me for a stroll and I'll introduce you to the folks around here? I have heard them talk about you, but they don't know you yet.'

Tara brightened. 'Yes, that would be great,' she said and held out her hand. 'Pull me up. I seem to have sunk into the sand.'

Mick grabbed her hand and pulled her up to stand close beside him. 'There,' he said, looking into her eyes. 'You're standing up. That's a good sign. Now let's go and meet the locals.'

Tara looked at his handsome face, the golden skin, straight nose, strong jaw and nice mouth. His deep brown eyes were a strong contrast to his fair hair that had been bleached by the sun. And that smile and the voice were just as attractive as they had been years ago when she had watched him on stage. He was so kind, doing everything he could to cheer Tara up and help her out of the black hole she had fallen into. What a stupid woman that Tatiana was to have dumped such a gorgeous man.

'Okay. I'll come with you,' she said, feeling a little better. But she suddenly realised that she must look awful after the swim and then crying her eyes out. Her hands went to her hair, tangled with salt and sand. 'I'm a mess. Will you give me five minutes to have a quick shower?'

'Right. Off you go. I'll wait outside your front door.'

'Thanks. See you in a minute.' Tara half-ran up the path to the cottage, Mick following behind at a leisurely pace.

Still smarting after the shock of Joe's text, she began to recover, even if the pain of his rejection would stay with her for a long time. She had to admit to herself that she had been afraid this would happen, but she had felt she needed to put his feelings for her to the test, which he had failed. She had only herself to blame, but she couldn't have continued the relationship the way it was, with him holding her at arm's length, only reeling her in when it suited him and he needed her company and full attention.

All these thoughts ran through her mind as she had a quick shower, untangled her hair and pulled on a white cotton shirt and a pair of navy shorts. She put on her white trainers, stuck her phone in her pocket and glanced at her image in the mirror by the door. She was not yet convinced the natural look was for her, but she found she looked fine despite her hair being a little messy and her face devoid of make-up. She had a light tan, a few more freckles across her nose and her eyes were still red and swollen from crying, which didn't worry her. She was only going to the village with Mick, and he didn't seem to care what she looked like. Why would he anyway? They were friends and now members of 'the club of the dumped'. The thought made her laugh despite the lingering sadness.

She stuck on her sunglasses, opened the door and stepped outside where Mick was waiting for her, smiling broadly. He held out his elbow. 'Take my arm, pretty lady, and I'll introduce you to the hoi polloi of Sandy Cove.'

And off they went, supporting each other. Tara felt lucky to have a friend like him who knew exactly how she felt.

Mick looked down at Tara as they walked down the path towards the village. 'So, what were you up to with the captain of the skies?'

'Up to?' Tara asked. 'Nothing much. He's selling the house I told you about the other evening.'

'Oh. The wreck you have your heart set on?'

'That's it. So we looked at the plans and stuff.'

'Why would you want to buy it?' Mick asked, looking intrigued. 'You didn't really tell me the whole story.'

'It was the home of my great-grandfather Daniel before he left suddenly and went to Dublin. He never came back and we think there was some kind of feud that made him leave.' Tara told Mick the rest of the story, explaining about the wedding photograph that had disappeared from the chest of drawers.

'It disappeared?' he said. 'But are you sure you saw it?'

'Of course I'm sure. I even took a photo of it with my phone before I put it back.'

'Strange. Well, while I was listening to your story, I realised that the first stop on our grand tour will have to be the church.'

'Why?' Tara asked.

'Because we'll ask Father O'Malley to look up the O'Rourkes in the church records. Births, marriages and deaths.'

'Oh,' Tara said, feeling stupid. 'Of course. Why didn't I think of that?'

'Because you were hit by that text message and your whole world collapsed.'

'Yes, that's what it felt like just then.' Tara smiled and squeezed his arm. 'But now I feel a little better. Not great, but better.'

'That's the spirit,' Mick said approvingly. 'And I think doing this, finding out about your great-grandfather, will help turn your mind away from that man and what he did to you.'

'I think it will,' Tara agreed. 'And if you want to join me on my journey, you'll be very welcome.'

'Really?' Mick beamed her a happy smile. 'That'd be terrific. I'll do my best to help in any way.'

Tara nodded. 'You probably know a lot of people in the village who might help put all the pieces together.'

'I might. Your captain fellow didn't know anything?'

'Not much, no. He grew up in Limerick and his great-uncle – who left him the farm –has been dead for over five years. They weren't close at all.'

Tara's thoughts drifted to Liam and the morning they had spent together. She had liked him a lot from the start, and with those blue eyes, his charm and the wide smile, he must appeal to a lot of women. But now on further reflection, she wondered fleetingly if he was really all that he appeared to be. There was something not quite right about the way he had behaved, something a little shifty in his eyes… Was he trying to stop her finding out something that happened in the past? Something connected to her great-grandfather and his sudden departure to Dublin? Tara was suddenly even more determined to delve deeper into this mystery.

Chapter Fifteen

Tara was amused by the effect Mick had on most people. As they walked up the main street on the way to the church, he had to stop several times to chat and answer questions. He introduced Tara to everyone, but they soon turned back to Mick, who handled the attention with ease, joking and laughing, slapping backs and kissing women on the cheek, even picking up small children and swinging them around making them squeal with laughter. It wasn't his obvious charisma that impressed her the most, it was the fact that he clearly cared about the people he met, and that he was interested in their lives and their families. That was something that couldn't be faked.

'You have the knack,' Tara remarked as they left a group of chatting women.

'What knack?'

'Of charming the birds out of the trees. I had no idea you were so popular here. It's like walking down the street with Elvis. You should go into politics. You'd be a shoo-in at any election.'

'Politics?' Mick said, looking surprised. 'I've never thought of that.'

'Why not? As you said to me recently: "go for it!"'

'Well, that was about your dream. I never dreamed about going into politics. But…' He paused. 'You have planted a seed in my mind. Maybe that's my destiny?' He looked at her with a glint of excitement. 'Thanks for giving me the idea. I'm going to consider it.'

'Seriously?' Tara said, taking her little camera from her pocket and aiming it up the street.

'Absolutely.' He looked suddenly thoughtful and Tara realised she had sowed the grain of an idea that might develop into something new and exciting.

'I meant it as a joke,' she said, lowering her camera. 'But now that I think of it, I'm beginning to wonder if it's something you'd be very good at. You seem so interested in other people and their problems.'

'I love finding out about what's going on in their lives. Could be something to work on.' He glanced at the camera in her hand. 'What are you doing?'

Tara aimed the camera up the street. 'What does it look like?'

'You're taking photographs. Is this for your assignment?' He looked at her suspiciously.

'Of course. It's such a cute little street with wonderful shopfronts.'

'I thought you said you wouldn't feature Sandy Cove.'

'I changed my mind.' Tara smirked at him, feeling an irresistible urge to tease him. 'When I'm finished, this village will be packed with tourists and backpackers and day-trippers and all kinds of other folk who want to gape at the natives. This quiet main street will be thronged with people who'll peer into windows and take snapshots of everyone. You'll be up to your ankles in litter and debris that they'll throw around. And I forgot to mention the gridlock of cars and tourist buses.'

'You're having me on,' Mick said, giving her a little shove.

'And you believed me!' she exclaimed, laughing.

'For a second,' he admitted, smiling at her. 'You make me nervous carrying that camera around. I don't know what you're going to do next.'

Tara stopped, still holding the camera. 'Is that what you think of me?' she asked.

'I mean, you know what you want and you're gonna do it, come hell or high water,' he said. Tara knew he was joking, but something had touched a nerve.

'I won't go too far.' She raised her hand. 'I swear I will not mention Sandy Cove by name. I will only include these photos in my articles as examples of villages on the Wild Atlantic Way, nothing more. It will be quite anonymous, I promise,' she said, feeling as though she should explain herself.

He still looked doubtful. 'Okay. I'll try to believe it. But if I'm honest I would still prefer it if you didn't take any photos at all.'

'Try to understand,' Tara pleaded, pulling at his arm. 'I just can't help being completely bowled over by the beauty of these little villages. It's like a time warp here. All these shopfronts and cottages and painted doorways and front gardens full of flowers, they're so idyllic. I want to share it with the world. I'm painting a picture with this,' she said, waving her camera. 'Can't you see that?'

As they stood there, in the middle of the street, jostled by passers-by who wanted to say hello, Mick's expression changed and he looked at her thoughtfully with the beginning of a smile. 'I love your passion,' he said. 'And yes, I do understand. You're an artist and you have to be allowed to create.'

She nodded. 'Exactly. And I will be respectful of your home. I want to protect it too.'

'Great,' he said, dropping the subject. 'So let's get going and see if we can catch the parish priest and ask him to look up the church records for you.'

They resumed their walk, the peace between them restored. Mick stopped when they reached the churchyard. 'Here we are. I hope Father O'Malley is around.'

They walked up the gravel path to the old church and stepped within, where it was blissfully cool after the heat outside. Tara looked at the beautiful stained-glass windows above the altar and felt a peace settle on her like a comfort blanket. 'It's such a beautiful little church,' she said in a hushed tone to Mick. 'Do you mind if I take a few shots? Just for me.'

'Of course.'

Mick stood back while Tara walked around the church, waiting for the right moment when the sun shone in through those beautiful windows, casting a lovely light into the still church. She took a few shots and showed them to Mick when she had finished.

'Gorgeous,' he said and then looked around the empty church. 'But where is Father O'Malley?'

'No sign of him or anyone,' Tara remarked.

The door to the sacristy suddenly opened and a rotund white-haired man appeared, dressed in a dark suit and a dog collar. 'Hello?' he said. 'Isn't it Mick O'Dwyer?' He held out his hand as he approached. He shook Mick's hand, then turned to Tara. 'And Dr Kate.'

'No, I'm her sister,' Tara explained, shaking his hand. 'Tara. We met last year at my father's memorial service.'

'Oh yes, I remember,' Father O'Malley said, his kindly eyes glinting behind his glasses. 'You're Kate's twin.'

'That's right,' Tara said.

'So, can I do anything for you?' the priest asked. 'Or did you just come in to look at the church and say a prayer, perhaps?'

'No,' Mick replied. 'We're here to do a little research into the O'Rourke family. Not Tara's dad, but her great-grandfather Daniel, who we believe was born into this parish. We're trying to find out who his parents were. But of course we'll say a little prayer as well,' he added, looking a little guilty.

Father O'Malley laughed. 'Prayer is always good, but that's up to you. It's what's in your heart that counts, not what I think.' He paused and checked his watch. 'But unfortunately, I have to go to a meeting with the bishop in Killarney. So if you could come back in a few days, I'll have more time to look everything up. Give me a buzz and we'll meet up in the parish office in the parochial house next door and I'll look up the records. Would that suit you?'

'Of course, Father,' Mick said. 'I know how busy you are. Could you get in touch when you have time to look this up for us? We'll be back at the end of the week if that's okay.'

'Certainly,' Father O'Malley said. 'God bless for now.'

'Sorry about that,' Mick said to Tara when the priest had left. 'But he'll look it all up when he comes back.'

'It's okay. No rush,' Tara assured him despite being disappointed not to continue her research.

'Let's get out of here, then,' Mick urged.

'You go on out. I'd like to light a candle for my father,' Tara said, walking to the stand where a row of candles burned.

Mick nodded and touched her shoulder. 'Okay. See you in a minute.'

When he had left, Tara lit a candle and stood there for a while, breathing in the smell of it and the faint scent of incense that seemed have impregnated the walls through the centuries. The smell and the flickering light of the many candles took her back to her childhood and going to Mass with her parents and other religious events: the first communion with Kate, both in white dresses and veils, their confirmation and then… the funerals of both their parents, who had died far too soon. Tara stifled a sob and turned away, not wanting to linger and relive painful memories. Today had been upsetting, but Joe's behaviour was a minor event compared to the tragedies she had lived through and she knew she would get over it fairly quickly, even if it still hurt like a fresh wound.

Tara walked down the aisle of the church and out through the door into the sunshine and birdsong and what felt like a fresh beginning. She suddenly knew that the house would be hers one day, and she would make it come alive again even if it took all her savings and the rest of her life. It had been disappointing that Father O'Malley couldn't look up the parish records today, but she would soon get some clues into what had driven Daniel O'Rourke away from it a hundred years ago.

Chapter Sixteen

Over a dinner of roast chicken and potato gratin on the patio at Kate's house, Tara told her sister what she was planning to do. As Mick was there, too, she felt more confident, knowing she had his full support for her plan. His presence was comforting and reassuring and his glance at her across the table felt like a silent encouragement. 'I haven't been able to find out exactly what happened in the past,' she started. 'But I will do, and in any case the farm is for sale and I think we should make an offer for it.'

Kate put down her knife and fork and stared at Tara. 'What? You mean we should buy it?'

'Of course,' Tara said, taking Kate's hand across the table. 'Can't you see how wonderful it would be? Daniel had to leave for some reason, and now we can put right whatever forced him away.'

'I was only joking when I said that in front of Liam. We don't know what happened to Daniel,' Kate argued. 'He might have done something wrong and ran away because of that.'

'I don't think that was the case, somehow,' Tara said, disappointed that Kate didn't share her passion. 'He came to Dublin and joined the very first Irish police force after Ireland became independent. He must have been very brave.'

'An upstanding young man,' Mick said, taking a swig from his wine glass.

'Possibly,' Kate said without much conviction, and picked up her knife and fork again.

'Possibly?' Tara exclaimed. 'Of course he was. Maybe he was kicked out of his own farm, denied his inheritance? He must have been so sad and lonely, but very brave. But now we can make it up to his memory and buy the farm together, using the money in our joint account. We can afford that, and to do it up and make it shine again.'

'No, we can't,' Kate said. 'I don't want to get into something that would end up costing everything we have.'

'What?' Tara said, staring at Kate, taken aback. 'It would be a great investment for us. It's a big place. You could live there and then I'd come over on my holidays and breaks to help develop it into something wonderful. A nature reserve, or a centre for hiking and bird watching and all sorts of things like that. I am thinking of doing a feature about it for one of the bigger magazines in the US, once I find out more about what happened to Daniel. It would make such a great story and then people would want to come over to see the real thing. Wouldn't it be wonderful to share it with people who love nature and hiking?'

'No, it wouldn't,' Kate replied with a stern expression in her eyes. 'You're letting your imagination run away with you, Tara. That place is a hopeless wreck. I know you think you'd be doing something fantastic buying it and trying to repair it, but it's just romantic nonsense. And I don't want our family history splashed all over some magazine.' Kate shook her head, her mouth pinched. 'I'm not going to be a part of it.'

'But…' Tara argued, the idea of not owning the house already making her sad. 'I thought, after what I told you, that you'd share my conviction that this was meant to happen. Daniel lost his part of that wonderful place because of something that happened to him. But now we can get it back. And the magazine story would pay for some of the costs to do it up.' She tried to enjoy the roast chicken on her plate, but she had suddenly lost her appetite.

'It's all pie in the sky, Tara,' Kate snapped, pushing away her plate.

'I don't agree,' Mick cut in. 'I think Tara is on to something here. I haven't seen the place, but Tara showed me some photos she's taken there. And I saw the plans. You would own the land around O'Rourke's tower and the slopes all the way down to Wild Rose Bay. I can't imagine anything more wonderful for the two of you. And you know what?' he added. 'I know Tara would make a fantastic feature with her amazing talent for taking beautiful, compelling photographs.'

'I don't think this has anything to do with you,' Kate replied.

'You mean it's none of my business?' Mick asked, looking hurt.

'Well, yes, actually.' Kate sighed and looked at Mick as if she regretted what she had just said. 'I'm sorry, I'm tired tonight. It's been a long day and I've been feeling a little off.'

'Off?' Tara said, suddenly noticing how pale Kate was. 'In what way?'

'I think you're overdoing it at the practice,' Cormac said, getting up and gathering their plates. 'I'll get the dessert and then you should go to bed. I made chocolate cake. Your favourite.'

'Yummy,' Tara said. 'With whipped cream?'

Kate let out a groan and suddenly shot up, her hand over her mouth. 'Excuse me,' she mumbled and ran inside.

Tara shot Cormac a worried look. 'What's up with Kate? Is she all right?'

'No, she's been feeling sick on and off for the past week or so,' Cormac replied. 'And she's been very tired. I've told her to let Pat take a look at her. But I'll let her tell you what's going on.' He walked back into the house to put the plates in the kitchen.

'Oh, no,' Tara mumbled, shooting Mick a worried look, getting up from her chair. 'Kate's seriously ill. I'll go and see if I can do anything to help her.'

But Kate came back out with Cormac and met Tara at the door. 'I'm fine again,' she said, looking better despite her pallor. 'I'm just…'

'Just what?' Tara exclaimed. 'There's something wrong with you, and it's serious. I can tell. You look so pale and wan and awful.'

Kate smiled and put her arm around Tara. 'It's nothing to worry about.'

'Nothing?' Tara said, alarmed. 'You look like a ghost and you tell me it's nothing?'

Kate suddenly laughed. 'Calm down. No need to panic. But I think I should tell you that you're going to be an aunt.'

'An… Oh my God!' Tara hugged Kate tight. 'You're pregnant! Cormac, you're going to be a daddy!' Tara ran to Cormac and threw her arms around him. 'Congratulations. This is the best news ever!'

Cormac laughed and hugged Tara back. 'Thank you, dear future aunt.'

'You knew about it all along, didn't you?' Tara said with a laugh. 'That's why you sat there looking smug. But maybe the chocolate cake wasn't such a good idea.'

'Kate seems to be hooked on chocolate when she's not feeling sick,' Cormac remarked. 'I didn't know she'd be off it tonight.'

'Such fabulous news,' Tara said and hugged him again. 'Isn't it, Mick?'

'Terrific,' Mick said, getting up and kissing Kate on the cheek. 'Congratulations, dear Kate.'

'Thank you. Sorry about the sudden nausea. I don't seem to be able to control it.' Kate walked back to the table and sat down. 'So now you know why I was acting a bit strange. My hormones are all over the place.'

'I'm so happy for you,' Tara replied. 'When's the baby due?'

'Early January,' Kate said. She looked at Cormac and shot him a little smile. 'But we're getting married first. So I'd like you to be my maid of honour, Tara. We'll be married in the church here in Sandy Cove.'

'Hooray!' Tara shouted, her arms in the air. 'A wedding! I love weddings. Don't you love weddings, Mick?'

'Sure. A wedding is always good fun,' Mick agreed.

'Funny that Father O'Malley didn't say anything,' Tara remarked.

'He doesn't know,' Cormac replied. 'We only just decided, so there is no date yet. Probably in August, though.'

'Great. Just before I go back to New York,' Tara declared.

'That's right.' Kate nodded. 'You can send Joe a save-the-date message as soon as we know. I'm dying to meet him.'

'Oh, er…' Tara suddenly realised she hadn't told Kate what Joe had done. It had receded to the back of her mind as she had been so intent on the research into her family history. 'He won't be coming.

I mean we… he… We broke up for good,' she ended after a glance in Mick's direction.

'You broke up?' Kate asked, looking concerned. 'I'm sorry, Tara. That's so sad for you. It seemed like he meant a lot to you.'

'Ah, well, maybe it was for the best,' Tara said, putting on a brave face as the pain hit her again. But despite the hurt, she knew it was true. She was better off without the tension and worry about their relationship that never really took off. 'I'm going to try to forget it.'

'Good idea,' Kate said approvingly. 'He probably isn't worth crying over.'

'No, but it's still kind of sad,' Tara confessed.

'We'll cheer you up,' Cormac promised, getting up. 'How about that chocolate cake, Kate? Will it make you sick again if I bring it out?'

Kate laughed. 'No. It's funny, but once I've thrown up, I'm starving. So yes, Cormac, bring it out and we'll attack it.'

'We should have champagne with that,' Mick suggested. 'Except you won't be drinking anything alcoholic for a while.'

'That's true,' Kate replied. 'I have to stay off it for a year or so.'

'But back to the house,' Tara said, looking at Kate's happy face. 'I realise that you might be reluctant to take the house on being pregnant. You have too much to cope with right now, so I'll take charge of the project. We could go to the bank together once I've made an offer and then—'

'No,' Kate interrupted. 'We won't.'

Tara stared at her. 'What?'

'I'm not saying I don't want to do this because I'm pregnant. It's not my hormones talking. All I see is a very foolish idea,' Kate said sternly. 'You want to sink a lot of money into that wreck that might not even be possible to rescue? That seems completely mad to me.'

'But the land… the tower… Wild Rose Bay…' Tara couldn't believe what Kate was saying. Could she not see that owning all that would be important for them and the memory of their O'Rourke ancestors?

'What do we do with it?' Kate asked. 'It's not valuable in any way. It's a terrible waste of money.'

'But we could develop it into something else. Get nature lovers, bird watchers and hikers to come and see it. And we could have a glamping site at the river. That would earn us an income during the summer months. I'd be here then to run it and spend the rest of the year in New York.'

'There you go again with your scheme of luring hordes of tourists here,' Kate said with a dismissive snort. 'Haven't I explained to you that it would be terrible for our village?' Kate sighed and shook her head. 'You always stir up trouble with your mad schemes, Tara. I see that hasn't changed even though you're supposed to be an adult.'

'That's a bit harsh,' Mick protested.

'Well, maybe,' Kate said, looking contrite. 'I didn't mean to sound so critical. It's just that… well, Cormac and I are planning to buy a plot near the surgery, where we'll build a house. So my half of the money from Dad's house will go towards that. And I was hoping you might lend me a bit of yours, should the house cost more than my share.'

'Oh,' Tara said, realising what was going on. 'I see.' She glanced at Cormac and Mick. 'Maybe we should leave this until another time? We can discuss it when we're on our own.'

'I think that's a very good idea,' Cormac said.

The atmosphere improved somewhat as they ate Cormac's delicious chocolate cake and chatted about the wedding and the baby. Tara felt slightly better as she thought of the prospect of becoming an aunt and how she would spoil that baby as much as she could. She'd be the eccentric aunt from New York who brought amazing gifts and played fun games with her niece or nephew.

But as she walked home with Mick, the subject of the house came up again. 'I'll have to give up on my dream,' Tara said sadly when they stopped outside the little cottage.

'Do you really have to?' Mick asked.

'I think I do. If Kate needs the money for that house, I'll have to lend it to her. She'll pay me back, of course, but it'll take a while.'

'Could you get a loan?'

'What bank would approve a loan for a wreck?' Tara remarked hopelessly. 'No, I'll have to let go of it. And Kate is probably right. It's a mad project.'

'It's your dream,' Mick said softly.

'I know.' Tara felt tears threatening to well up. 'But Kate's baby is more important.'

'More important than you?'

'Yes. Oh Mick, you don't understand how we think. I know we're not as close as we were when we were younger, but this brings us together in a strange way. Kate would do the same for me.'

'Yes, but…'

'No. I have to give up any thought of buying that house.' She turned away from him. 'I'm so tired. I need to sleep. And then, tomorrow I have to catch up on some work. It's already the end of

June. I only have a month left to work on it before the deadline in August.'

'And you're still going to feature Sandy Cove?' Mick asked, looking doubtful, despite his earlier support of her dream.

'No, I told you I wouldn't. Just the area. Maybe I'll include a few of the shots I took of the gorgeous cottages with the lovely window boxes full of flowers without saying where it is.'

Mick nodded. 'Okay. Sounds like a good idea.'

'I thought that'd calm your fears.'

'It does.' Mick smiled fondly at Tara. 'Okay, then, I think we'll say good night. It's been quite a day.'

'You could say that again,' Tara said with feeling. 'Good night, Mick. Thank you for all your help. See you soon.'

'I hope so.' Mick hesitated and then leaned over and kissed Tara on the cheek. 'Don't give up on your dream,' he whispered before she had a chance to ask him what he meant.

Chapter Seventeen

Work on the magazine feature provided Tara with a welcome distraction from all of her worries. During the following week, she threw herself into the various parts of the project, and as the weather was still beautiful, she managed to get up early to take gorgeous photos in the wonderful light that was so unique to Kerry. Every evening, she went through the photos she had taken, organising them into files to use for her articles. She also went around to all the activity centres she could find in Kerry, such as surfing schools, hiking centres, pony trekking stables, kayaking clubs and others in order to interview the organisers and instructors, asking them questions about what prospective clients should do to join in. She collected facts and figures and notes about equipment needed for the various sports, costs and schedules and the best time of year to pursue them.

All this took a lot of time and hard work and she didn't have much opportunity for socialising except for the occasional cup of tea with Kate, whose nausea seemed to have abated even though she was going through 'the sleepy stage', as she called it, falling asleep the minute she came home from work. They didn't mention the old house, despite often talking about the story Tara had discovered, and drew up a kind of family tree, looking at the other photos from the old desk and trying to guess who the people in them were. Tara also told Kate about meeting Father O'Malley and how he would look up the parish records when he had the time, promising to report back when she had all the facts.

The subject of the money came up later that week, as Cormac and Kate had to put up a deposit on the purchase of the plot where they were going to build their house. They all walked over to the site: an acre of land near the surgery with beautiful ocean views. Tara pushed aside her disappointment about having to give up her dream and agreed to go to Killarney with Kate to withdraw the money from the branch there. It was for the best, she told herself. Buying an old wreck was a bad idea, despite the connection to their great-grandfather. Kate's baby was more important. It would, after all, be her little niece or nephew. Tara nearly felt pregnant herself, as she closely followed Kate's progress and listened to all her symptoms and even went with her and Cormac to the first ultrasound test, where they could see the image of the foetus and hear the rapid heartbeat.

Tara was touched by the fact that Kate and Cormac shared their happiness with her. It seemed churlish to be yearning for an old house that would turn out to be a huge burden in the end. An impossible dream that she had to let go of. But despite managing to push it away while she worked or spent time with Kate and Cormac, it still popped up in her thoughts during idle moments. She imagined owning that old house and doing it up, turning it into the most beautiful house in Kerry. It could still be done if the house wasn't sold and stayed on the market for a long time, which was a possibility. Who would be mad enough to buy such a wreck?

That's what Tara told herself over and over again, thinking that once she could afford it, she'd get the house for a song.

When Liam called later that week, asking her to meet him at the pub in Ballinskelligs for 'dinner and a chat', Tara accepted at once, delighted to meet him again and to get out of her routine for a night. It was nice to dress up after weeks in jeans and T-shirts, Tara realised as she got ready to meet Liam. In her dressy black trousers and a pink linen shirt, she got on her bike and cycled down the coast road to Ballinskelligs, trying not to even glance down at Wild Rose Bay, or the lane that led to Riverside Farm. If she didn't think about it too much, her dream would come true, even if she had to wait a long time.

Liam, dressed casually in beige chinos, a white shirt and a red sweater across his shoulders, was waiting for her at a table in the back garden of the pub that looked out over a lovely beach, the sun dipping behind the Skellig Islands and pale pink clouds drifting across the darkening sky.

'Hi, Tara,' he said and pulled out a chair. 'I thought we could eat outside as it's so warm.'

'Perfect,' Tara said and sat down.

Liam settled on a chair opposite her. 'You look fabulous,' he said, his eyes full of admiration.

'You don't look too bad yourself,' she replied, returning his smile. She meant it. He did look more than 'not too bad' with his light tan, tousled black hair and brilliant blue eyes that were full of fun. Despite not being sure of what was underneath the glossy surface, she couldn't help enjoying spending the evening with such a good-looking man. 'Thanks for asking me out,' she continued. 'I really needed a break from work and stuff.'

A waiter appeared with two glasses of rosé wine on a tray.

'I ordered for both of us,' Liam said as he handed her a glass. 'I thought it would be the right drink for a warm summer evening. We could pretend we're in the south of France.'

'We don't need to,' Tara said, taking the glass. 'I can't think a better place to be than here right now.' She nearly said 'with you', but stopped herself.

Liam smiled and held up his glass. 'Neither can I. Cheers, Tara.'

'Cheers,' she said and took a careful sip. 'This is delicious wine.'

'It's good,' he agreed as he drank. Then his expression changed and he put down his glass. 'Tara, I'm afraid I have something to tell you that might upset you.'

'What?' she asked, startled.

'I got an offer for the house. And I've accepted it.'

'Oh.' Tara stared at him, trying to understand what he had just said. 'The house? Riverside Farm?' she asked just to make sure she had heard right. 'You… you sold it?' she said in a near whisper.

'Yes. It was a very good offer. Just below the asking price,' Liam said, looking slightly guilty. 'I know I should have told you before I accepted, to give you a chance to bid, but the agent thought I should grab it before they changed their mind. The buyer has already signed the contract. I'm really sorry, Tara, but the market is so tight at the moment, and—'

Tara bit her lip and tried to appear as if it didn't matter. 'It's okay, Liam,' she said, her voice as steady as she could manage. 'Don't worry. I couldn't buy the house anyway at the moment.'

He looked only slightly relieved. 'You did say I should accept if I got an offer, remember?'

'Yes,' Tara said, 'I did.' It was true. She had said something like that. But she hadn't really meant it. She had hoped it wouldn't happen, that nobody would want to buy such a wreck and spend a fortune doing it up. But obviously someone had and now her dream was truly shattered.

'I'm sorry,' he said again, looking uncomfortable.

Tara realised he must have noticed the shock and sorrow in her eyes. 'Don't be sorry, Liam. It's okay, really. Maybe it's for the best. It's probably too much for me to take on anyway. Yes, I'm a little sad, but I'll get over it.'

'Yes, but I knew you liked the house so much. I should have held off until you could buy it.'

He had done nothing wrong, but what he had just told her had hurt more than he could ever know. 'You don't owe me anything,' she said.

Liam looked at her with a touch of regret. 'I suppose not.'

Tara forgot about the wine and leaned forward, hoping that Liam would be more in the mood to talk today, after a glass or two. Trying to distract herself from her misery, she decided to concentrate on the mystery of her family history. 'I've been trying to find out a little more about my ancestors. Is there much else you could tell me about yours?' she asked.

'Not much,' Liam replied, looking mystified. 'Why should I?'

'Only if you've done some research into your family's past.'

'I haven't done any such research,' he said with a disinterested shrug. 'I'm not really into that kind of thing.'

'I see.' Tara thought for a moment, trying yet again to figure out how Liam would have been related to Daniel. 'Your branch of the

O'Rourkes…' she started, but stopped when she realised she had reached an impasse. She was itching to find out more, but Liam wasn't the person to ask. She wouldn't get any further until she found out more from the parish priest. 'It's very complicated,' she said. 'I have to see if I can draw up a family tree when I know more. And I'll be looking up the church records and then let you know.'

'Sounds like a good idea,' Liam agreed.

'Maybe you could ask your father if he knows anything about his family?' Tara suggested. 'His grandfather and so on.'

'I will when I meet him the next time.' Liam put his hand on hers. 'I feel bad about all this. But I had no choice. I couldn't leave the place unsold any longer.'

'Of course. I do understand.' Tara nodded, trying to look cheerful even though part of her was dying inside. 'It was just a silly dream,' she added, the touch of his hand on hers making her feel comforted. 'I get these crazy ideas sometimes.'

'Could be because of your artistic nature?' he suggested without taking his eyes off her face.

She shot him a smile. 'Could be,' she said, and drank some wine to avoid his probing look. It wasn't his fault, but she suddenly wanted to get away and be alone. She felt so emotional. It was another reminder that her beautiful dream that had seemed so fresh and new was gone forever. 'Who is it?' she asked Liam suddenly. 'Who's buying the house?'

'I don't know. I only just heard about it and thought I'd tell you before you found out some other way.'

'That was considerate of you.' Tara didn't know what else to say. It was unfair of her to take out her disappointment on him when he was being so nice. 'Can we forget about it for tonight?' she asked. 'Let's have dinner and get to know each other and try to have fun.'

Liam looked a little brighter. 'That's a very good idea.' He picked up the menu. 'They have good seafood here. Crab claws for starters and then baked sole would be my choice.'

'Make that two,' Tara said, her spirits lifting.

It was a beautiful evening and here she was with this handsome airline pilot who was kind, polite and maybe even fun, when given a chance. She was still suspicious of him but decided to give him that chance and show him she was not going to sit here and be miserable, even if his news had made her sad. Life was about taking it on the chin and moving on, and she was good at that. She smiled at Liam when they had placed their order and fired him a few questions about his job and what it was like to travel all over the world.

During their dinner, Liam launched into some funny anecdotes of all the mishaps and adventures of an airline pilot and even some truly frightening stories of near crashes and dangerous situations he had faced.

'Gosh,' she said when he drew breath. 'I think I'll be more nervous of flying than ever after tonight.'

Liam laughed and pushed his plate away. 'I was exaggerating a bit just to impress you with my heroism.'

Tara laughed, thinking he didn't have to make much of an effort. He was attractive enough without having to boast about bravery. 'Consider me impressed,' she said.

Liam leaned forward and gazed intently at her. 'So what about you? I've looked at all your amazing photos on Instagram and Facebook. You've certainly been around. The Amazon, the Rockies, the Caribbean… And you're some photographer. I was blown away by your work.'

'Thank you,' Tara said, her face turning pink. 'I love my job.'

'And New York?'

'Oh yes,' she said with a sudden pang of longing. 'It's my hometown. I love everything about it, except the summer heat and humidity.'

'Your boyfriend is a New Yorker, then?'

Tara sighed and looked away. 'Yes, but he's not my boyfriend any more.'

Liam touched her hand. 'I'm sorry. Didn't mean to pry…'

'Yes, you did,' Tara said with a cheeky grin, cheered by the admiration she saw in his eyes.

'Yes,' he confessed sheepishly. 'I did. You put our selfie there with a cheeky little comment. Was that for him to see?'

'I suppose.' Tara cringed over the comment on that selfie. 'Stupid thing to do, but I was so hurt by being dumped like that.'

'I'd say he wouldn't have liked seeing that selfie much.'

'That was the idea. He broke up with me by a text message.'

'What a twit.' Liam topped up Tara's glass from the bottle of white wine they had ordered. 'Him, I mean. Not you.'

'Oh, please, I don't want to talk about. I'm trying to move on.' Tara smiled warmly at Liam. 'You're a great help, you know.'

'I'm glad you think so. Pity I had to deliver news that made you sad. But maybe, as you said, it was for the best. My father didn't want me to keep the house. He thought it was too much trouble and he had bad memories of it from when he was a child. My great-uncle used to tell him stories that gave him nightmares.'

'How sad. Can't have been nice for a little boy.'

'No.' Liam paused and looked out over the ocean. 'This is a gorgeous place.'

'Sandy Cove is even nicer. Why don't you come to visit me there next time you're free?'

'I might,' Liam said, his gaze drifting back to Tara. 'But I prefer Ballinskelligs.'

'I've never been here before.'

'I'll show you around. Do you want to go for a walk on the beach?'

Tara nodded. 'Why not? It's still quite early and it doesn't get dark until after ten, so I'll have time for a walk and then I can still cycle back while it's still daylight.'

Liam got up. 'Great. We can pay at the bar. I'm staying the night here and then I have to get up early for the flight to Newark.'

They paid the bill and walked out of the restaurant and started to walk up the street. It was a lovely little village, but Tara felt less at home here than in Sandy Cove as it was a lot more touristy with many pubs, souvenir shops and takeaways. Throngs of people were gathered outside the pubs and the air smelled of chips and garlic. She began to understand why Kate was so against an influx of tourists to Sandy Cove.

Liam casually draped his arm over Tara's shoulders which felt protective and sweet. She looked up at him and returned his smile and didn't protest when he pulled her closer as they reached the path along the cliffs from where there was a beautiful view of the Skellig Islands. Then he took her hand and pulled her along the path, joining other couples wandering out to the promontory to watch the sun slowly sinking behind the horizon.

'Beautiful,' she said with a long sigh, thinking that it was, if not a perfect moment, the nicest part of a week that had been full of upsets and disappointments. But who could complain about being at this beautiful spot with an attractive man who seemed to be equally drawn to her? She glanced at him and tried to analyse her feelings. Was he the kind of man she could fall in love with? It was too soon after her painful break-up, but there was nothing wrong with considering one's options. And he was good for her self-esteem that had taken such a plunge, thanks to Joe.

'A penny for your thoughts,' Liam said as he met her gaze.

'Oh, I was just thinking how nice it is to be here with you,' Tara said.

Liam's smile widened. 'That's a thought worth every penny. Happy to be here with you, too.' He pulled her closer. 'I would like to see you again,' he said.

She smiled at him, a little confused about how she felt. He seemed to have avoided the subject of his family history, but maybe she was overreacting and he simply didn't know much after all? 'I'd love that,' she heard herself say, hoping he didn't detect her hesitation. She did like him, but at the same time she wasn't sure if she felt attracted to him in that special way.

As if he could sense her uncertainty, Liam sidled away from her. 'I think I'll go to the hotel and turn in. Early start tomorrow.'

'Me too.' Tara turned around and slowly started walking back the way they had come.

Liam fell in step with her. 'So how about meeting up again? We could go down to that lovely bay. The beach is very private. We could have a picnic and swim if the weather holds.'

She met his eyes and couldn't help smiling. 'Yes, why not?' she said without thinking. She hadn't been down to that beautiful beach yet; she was saving it for last. But going there with Liam seemed a nice idea. 'Next week, when you're free?'

His face brightened. 'Okay. It's a deal. I'll bring the food. You just bring your swimsuit.'

'Brilliant.' Tara glanced at him and suddenly looked forward to seeing him again. 'Give me a call when you're free.'

'I will.'

They had reached the front of the pub where Tara had parked her bike. 'Well, good night, then,' he said with a light kiss on her cheek. 'See you soon. I'll check with the agent to find out who bought the house.'

'No, don't,' Tara said. 'I don't want to know. I'm going to try to forget about it.'

'Probably a good idea,' Liam agreed.

Tara put on her bicycle helmet and got on her bike. 'Have a good trip to Newark. Fly carefully.'

'I will. Good night. See you soon, Tara.'

'Thanks for dinner. Good night, Liam,' Tara said and slowly pedalled down the street, feeling happy despite the news that she had lost the chance to buy the old farm. It had been a shock and a huge disappointment, but probably a good thing in the end, she mused, to console herself. It might only result in a lot of problems financially and emotionally. The new owner was probably more capable of restoring it to its former glory.

As she cycled back to Sandy Cove in the light of the setting sun, Tara's thoughts turned to Liam's great-uncle. It puzzled her that

Liam knew so little about his own family history and she wondered if he was telling the truth, or trying to hide something he didn't want her to know. She had enjoyed his company and was looking forward to seeing him again, despite her misgivings. And maybe, in time, if she played her cards right, he would trust her enough to share whatever he knew about his family history.

Chapter Eighteen

Tara arrived home just after ten o'clock. She could see that the lights were on in Kate's living-room window, and on a whim decided to call in to say hello. She left the bike at the side of the little cottage and walked the short distance to Kate's house and knocked.

Kate opened the door, greeting Tara with a wide smile. 'There you are. Come in. I was just going to call you. I know it's late, but we're looking at the drawings of the new house that the architect made up for us. It's just a preliminary sketch, but we want you to tell us what you think. The project includes you, too, you see.'

'Me?' Tara said, stepping inside.

'Yes. Go into the kitchen. Cormac has put the drawings on the table in there.'

Tara went into the kitchen and found Cormac studying a big sheet of paper. 'Hi,' he said without taking his eyes off the drawings. 'We were just discussing your part of the house.'

Tara moved closer and looked. 'My part?'

'Yes,' Kate said behind her. 'We're planning to include a large room for you with your own entrance. You did say that you wanted to come over more often, so this would be ideal for you. And me, of course. I'd love to see you whenever you come over and this way, you'll have your own little pad in Ireland. You'll have a kitchenette and a bathroom and it will be a little separate from our quarters, as you can see,' she said, tapping her finger on the drawing.

'Oh.' Tara was overwhelmed by this news. 'Like a granny flat, you mean?'

'Or the auntie flat,' Cormac suggested. 'Much better than sinking all your cash into that old farm.'

Tara leaned over the plans and saw what they meant. The house would have a big living room, a kitchen-diner and a family room downstairs and then three double bedrooms upstairs with a study off the master bedroom. But there was an addition to the downstairs layout which seemed to be a separate studio and bathroom. 'So that's where I'd be?' she asked, pointing at the plan.

'Exactly.' Kate put her hand on Tara's back. 'It'll be there for you when you come over in the summer. Your very own base in Sandy Cove. What do you think?'

'It's a fabulous idea,' Tara said, touched by their generosity. It was a sensible plan that would work perfectly for her. This way she would be very much part of their family when she came back to Ireland for visits. It would be her own little flat and she could come and go as she wanted but still be close to Kate and the new baby.

'It'll cost more than what we thought originally,' Kate said. 'So we'll have to ask you to lend us a little more than we said. That's not a problem, is it?'

'I suppose not,' Tara said glumly. 'In any case I don't need it right now. Riverside Farm has been sold.'

'Really?' Kate looked startled. 'Who's mad enough to take that on?'

'I don't know,' Tara replied. 'But that's not important. It's gone.'

Kate put her hand on Tara's arm. 'I'm sorry.'

'Ah sure, it was a bit of madness,' Tara said with a resigned sigh. 'The new owner will probably turn it into a nice place.' Swallowing the lump of sadness in her throat, she switched her attention to the plans of the house. 'This looks great. I'll be very happy with my own space so close to you.'

'Beats doing up an old wreck, doesn't it?' Kate said happily. 'I mean, that old farm is a lovely place but sinking your money into it would have been foolish.'

'That's true.' Tara looked at the drawings again and the little private wing she was going to have. An auntie flat, they had said as a joke. It was a good idea, but deep down she felt somehow that they were pushing her into the role of the old aunt who didn't have a family of her own – and never would. Was that how they saw her? Perhaps Kate was trying to distract her, but it didn't in any way compete with her dream of owning Riverside Farm.

A sensible compromise, Tara thought. *But oh, how I wish I could have done the foolish thing…*

Tara buried herself in work during the following week, filing her photos and writing the articles, despite being ahead in her schedule and very close to completing the whole project. She saw no one apart from Mick, who she bumped into on a misty, drizzly morning as she walked on the beach. As the drizzle turned to rain, she invited him back to the cottage for a cup of tea. He accepted enthusiastically, declaring he had also been working hard on something he couldn't talk about just yet. 'A new departure in my working life,' he said. 'A new beginning, a whole new career.' Tara assumed he was turning to a different area of the theatre, like directing instead of acting, and didn't ask any questions, thinking he wasn't allowed to say anything before some kind of contract had been signed.

They had tea in the little kitchen as the sun broke through the clouds and sent a warm beam through the window, just when they had agreed it was a dreary day compared to the glorious weather the day before.

Mick looked out the window, squinting in the sunlight. 'Ah, that's a bit of Kerry magic for you. You never know what the day will bring.'

'That's true,' Tara said, cradling the teacup in both her hands. 'You can never predict the weather here.'

'That's the charm of it,' Mick declared, turning from the window to look at her. 'So what have you been up to these past weeks?'

'Work mostly,' Tara said and put the cup on the table. 'And spending time with Kate and Cormac. They're building a house next door to the surgery.'

'I know. That plot of land has been for sale for a while. I'm glad they've decided to build there.'

'It's a gorgeous spot. They showed me the architect's drawings. It's going to be a big house.'

'And you're going to help out with the finances?'

'Yes. They didn't have quite enough to pay for the whole project.'

Mick frowned. 'Why couldn't they borrow the money like most people do?'

Tara slid her cup away. 'Oh, well… I suppose they could, but Kate's salary isn't huge and Cormac is launching into a new business, so I thought I'd help out.'

'Very generous of you,' Mick remarked with slightly sour note in his voice. 'And they accepted it just like that?'

Tara nodded, puzzled by his tone. 'I felt they needed the money more than I do. And they're going to make a little flat for me so I'll have somewhere to stay when I come over for the summer. A granny flat,' she said with a wan smile.

'A what?' Mick asked, looking shocked.

'A granny flat.'

'That's what I thought you said. Who's the granny, then?' he asked, lifting an eyebrow.

'Me. But it's meant to be a place for me to stay when I come over for the summer holidays.' Tara saw his expression mirroring what she felt deep down. 'I know what you're going to say.'

Mick pushed away his mug with more force than was necessary. 'That they're a little bit selfish? First asking you to give them your money for their Shangri-La and then throwing you a consolation prize of a "granny flat"?' he said, making quotation marks.

'It's not as bad as that.'

'Isn't it? But what about your own future and your life in New York? Where did owning this house fit into that?'

'The farmhouse has just been sold,' Tara said miserably. 'But maybe that was a good thing. My life's in New York, after all. Buying this house and doing it up when I can only come over for a few weeks in the summer might have been a bit tricky. It was a silly idea that was doomed to fail from the start.'

'I never thought so,' Mick said with a strange expression in his eyes.

'You were the only one. Kate and Cormac thought I was completely mad. So now I'll be staying with them and be the unmarried aunt who comes from New York with great presents for the kids. Not a bad way to end up.'

'Stop it,' Mick said, his eyes blazing. 'You're a beautiful, talented young woman, Tara, with your whole life ahead of you. Buying that house was a great idea that didn't work out, but you might find something else you'd want to spend money on. Your own place somewhere, maybe even in the States. But you gave it all up for them. Don't they realise that?'

'It's not for them, as such,' Tara protested. 'It's for Kate and her baby. And in any case, they're right in a way. I don't think I'll ever have children.'

'What makes you say that?' Mick asked.

Tara shrugged. 'I don't seem to be able to find a man who'll want to commit to a relationship. I always fall for these bounders with some kind of Peter Pan complex. And I'm not getting any younger, you know.'

'Is anyone?'

'You don't understand what I'm talking about. It's just the way it is. I probably wasn't meant to be a wife and mother. So Kate and Cormac will be the only family I'll ever have. And that's not all bad, you know.'

'Oh, Holy Mother, what a load of rubbish,' Mick said and suddenly grabbed her hand across the table. 'Please stop this nonsense. You're not an old spinster aunt, Tara.'

'Not yet anyway.'

'You never will be. And about your dream of owning the house…
It might not be lost after all.'

'What do you mean?' Tara asked, wondering why he was looking
so flustered.

Mick let go of her hand and brushed his hair out of his eyes. 'I
have something to tell you. Something that'll change everything
you've just said. Promise you won't be angry.'

'Why would I be angry?' Tara asked, puzzled by his behaviour.
She had been happy to meet him at the beach by accident, as she
had missed him and wondered why he hadn't been in touch for
over a week. She had become used to spending time with him, as
they had fallen into a comfortable, close friendship. Mick was her
solid rock – she could talk to him about anything. And here he was,
staring at her with a wild look in his eyes as if he was about to tell
her he had done something terrible.

'Because…' He stopped, looking as if he was fighting with
himself. 'I bought the house.'

'What house?' she asked, bewildered.

'Your house. Your dream house. Riverside Farm.' He let go of
her hand and sat back, looking at her as if he already regretted what
he had just said.

Tara was speechless. 'The house?' she finally whispered. 'You're
the new owner? But why?'

'I did it for you and Kate,' Mick said softly. He leaned forward.
'I thought if I bought it, I could keep it safe for you until you could
afford to buy it – from me. We don't know what happened in the

past, but I have the same feeling you do that your great-grandfather was cheated out of his inheritance.'

'We don't know that for sure,' Tara argued, still dizzy with shock.

'But we're already so much closer to finding out,' Mick countered. 'I sold my house in Dublin a few months ago and got a lot of money for it. I decided only a week ago that I'd use some of it to buy Riverside Farm. I went to have look and knew at once why you fell in love with it. So I put down an offer just under the asking price and it was accepted. I bought that house so that nobody else would. It's going to be yours one day, I swear. I'll keep it until Kate pays you back.'

'But that could take years,' Tara argued. Her mind reeled as she tried to take it all in and she suddenly understood what Mick meant. 'It's a lovely thing to do, but I don't know if I can accept it. Or if…' She shook her head, trying to clear her thoughts. 'This is a bit of a shock, to be honest.'

'I know. I wasn't going to tell you like this, but when you told me about Kate and Cormac and what they're planning for you, I thought it might cheer you up.'

Tara looked at Mick, her feelings for him shifting from friendship to something else that shook her. Was it possible that she was beginning to feel something quite different for him? She looked at him, wondering if he could see what she was thinking. Their eyes met for an instant during which something passed between them, gone before she could be sure what it was. 'Cheer me up doesn't quite describe it,' she said after a while. 'It did a lot more than that. It's a wonderful gift, Mick, but I don't think I've done anything to deserve it.'

'You have no idea how much you deserve it,' Mick said with feeling. He put both his hands on Tara's arm. 'You have pulled me out of a long and miserable time in my life and made me feel so good and so different. By talking to you, I was in a way talking to myself and managed to see where I was going – or should be going, I mean. You opened my eyes and made me see that I don't have to keep plodding on in the old tracks. I can do something completely different if I want. I'm not too old to change my direction to another area altogether.'

'You mean, buying the house?' Tara asked, intrigued by the new fire in his eyes.

'No, something else. I can't tell you what it is yet. But you'll be the first to know when it's all in place.' His eyes were full of emotion as he ran his finger down her cheek. 'You're so like Kate on the outside, which has blinded me to the real you inside.'

'She's the sensible one and I'm the flighty, wild one,' Tara said.

'But look at what you've achieved,' Mick said with a touch of wonder in his voice. 'You've made a name for yourself in America, in an industry that's so tough. And you've done it all in record time. That takes a rare talent and a lot of guts.'

'Oh, it's not as amazing as you think,' Tara protested.

'Yes, it is,' Mick said in a tone that didn't allow argument. 'Stop being so modest and own it, for God's sake.'

Tara got up from the table. She was grateful to Mick, but she needed to think about what she wanted to do. He might believe he knew what was right for her, but she wasn't so sure. 'Can we stop this now? Do you want more tea?'

'No, thanks.' Mick got to his feet. 'I have to go. I have a meeting in Killarney, so I'd better be off.' He took his cup and put it on the draining board. 'Think about what I just told you. And maybe, if you prefer, we could buy the house together?'

'Oh.' Tara stared at him, thinking hard. 'That's not a bad idea,' she said after a while. 'I could give half of my money to Kate and use the other half for the farm. In any case, if they don't build that granny flat, their house will cost less to build, don't you think?'

'I'm sure that'll reduce the cost by quite a lot,' Mick agreed.

Tara nodded. 'I love the idea. I won't own all of it but sharing it with you seems like a great solution,' she said, her heart beating faster at the thought of working on the project with Mick. 'I wouldn't be able to manage all of the work by myself, anyway.'

'It would be too much for one person, I think,' Mick agreed. 'This way I'll look after it all when you're in New York. And once we've bought the place, we could start making plans for the house and start doing a bit of work on it together. And then I'll keep going when you've left.'

'You will?' Tara asked, as the enormity of what he had told her hit home. 'You mean you're going to look after the whole project?'

'Yes, I am,' he declared.

She looked at him, trying to figure out his motives. Had he bought the farm, just because he wanted to help her achieve her dream – or for another reason altogether? Was he trying to get her to feel a sense of ownership so she'd want to protect this area from a tourist invasion? He had been so against her assignment from the start, but had seemed to be more relaxed about it lately. Maybe he was still a little worried? 'You're doing this for me?' she asked, trying to figure out what was on his mind.

'And for me.'

'Why?'

'Because I love that kind of work. Making a house live again in a way. There is a lot I can do myself, with your help and artistic flair. And then… at the end of the month, it might be possible for me to move in.'

'You're moving into Riverside Farm?' Tara asked incredulously. 'But it's a wreck.'

He nodded, smiling broadly. 'I know. But it's quite possible to stay there if one's into camping. In any case I have to move out of my dad's house. My mother is retiring from running the family pharmaceutical firm in Killarney and moving back into the house here. God knows how my parents will get on, but I won't be there to listen to them bicker. It's time to cut the umbilical, you know? So camping in an old wreck seems like heaven in comparison. There's water and a loo and I can wash in the river. Just for the summer, really. Quite romantic, don't you think?'

'Amazing,' Tara said, trying to imagine what it would be like to do what he suggested. Exciting and new and totally crazy. She suddenly understood why he had bought the farm and why he was so enthusiastic about it. It wasn't some kind of underhand trick to make her change her mind about her job. He had fallen just as much in love with it as she had and that touched her more than anything. He needed this project after all his disappointments. It would be as much his creation as hers and she couldn't wait to get started, whatever Kate or anyone else thought. And the restoration project would add huge interest to the article she was planning in her head. But she'd raise that with him at a later date. 'I'd love to join you,' she said as it dawned on her what fun it would be. 'I'm quite good at camping.'

'You are?' he asked, eyeing her Versace T-shirt and Armani jeans. 'It'll seriously mess up that glamorous look you have. Not to mention your lovely hairdo.'

Tara touched her smooth bob. 'I know. But I've been roughing it before on assignments. This'll be easy compared with some of those,' she said, casting her mind back to that trip up the Amazon when she had put up with conditions that made Riverside Farm look like a five-star hotel in comparison. 'I'm not worried about a little less comfort. In any case, I'll have to move out of here in a few weeks, when Jasmine and Aiden arrive for their holiday. It'd be fun to do this with you.'

'Are you sure?' Mick asked, looking doubtful. 'I mean, yeah, it'd be fun to have you on board, but…' He paused looking slightly awkward.

Tara laughed. 'Don't worry, I have no ulterior motives. It'll be like summer camp.'

Mick made a strange sound. 'Yeah, right. Exactly like that. But why don't you wait until it's a little more inhabitable? We could do up two of the bedrooms and then get a few other bits of furniture from that fun second-hand furniture warehouse near Killarney. Have you ever been there?'

'No, but it sounds just like my kind of place.'

Mick nodded, looking nearly as excited as Tara. 'Let's go there next week, then. We'll be closing the sale this coming Friday. So if you're on board with what I suggested, we'll get together and sign the contract with the solicitor.'

Tara smiled, her heart doing a little flip at the thought of buying the place with Mick. 'I've kind of made my mind up already.'

He laughed. 'I know you have. But there's no rush. You have time to think about it a bit more before Friday.'

'I will,' Tara promised.

'Great. But whatever happens, I'd love you to come with me to the furniture warehouse. So we'll do that on Sunday, whether you'll be signing on the dotted line or not.'

'Fantastic,' Tara replied, with a dart of pure joy. He was offering her an adventure of the kind she couldn't resist. The dream she'd thought was lost was suddenly real again and it was even better when she could share it with this sweet, caring man. Looking at him, the spark in his eyes and hearing the excitement in his voice, she realised that she might be beginning to have deeper feelings for him.

Mick smiled at her as he opened the door to leave. 'Let me know what you decide and then we'll take it from there.'

'Yes, that's fine. I'll have another think about what you suggested and do a few sums. Could you text me the amount you bought it for and the stamp duty? It's a big step, so I'll have to weigh up everything. But the outing seems like fun whatever I decide. See you soon, Mick.'

Mick made a little salute and disappeared through the front door, leaving Tara feeling slightly dizzy with everything that had just happened. She couldn't believe it. As she stood there by the window watching Mick walk down the path away from the cottage, Tara felt a stab of fear about having said she'd move into the old house. What was she getting herself into? Camping in a wreck of a house when she was in the throes of finishing her project. With Mick of all people? Especially with what she was beginning to feel for him? It all seemed quite risky all of a sudden. But staying safe wasn't in Tara's nature and the dangers ahead seemed a lot more enticing.

Chapter Nineteen

The following day, Tara sat on a beach blanket in a heavenly spot, drinking champagne from a plastic cup and looking out across the turquoise water that lapped gently against the soft white sand. It was her first time in Wild Rose Bay and it was everything she had heard about, and more. She looked up the steep slopes covered in wild roses, the jagged cliffs above and the ruined tower outlined against the cerulean sky and took a deep breath.

'How magical this place is,' she said to Liam, who was taking food out of his rucksack and laying it out on front of her. She felt relaxed despite not having had a chance to think about her chat with Mick. She decided to go through it all later and just enjoy this lovely day. 'And what a fantastic picnic,' she said. 'Smoked salmon pâté, chicken drumsticks, Camembert and fresh rolls… Where did you get all this?'

'The little café in your village,' Liam replied, smearing smoked salmon pâté on a cracker and handing it to Tara. 'The Two Marys', it's called. Fun place with amazing food.'

'They know their stuff,' Tara mumbled through her bite of salmon and crisp cracker. 'You're really spoiling me, Liam.'

'I was hungry,' he replied with a grin, grabbing a chicken drumstick.

Tara tucked her legs under her and enjoyed the food, the sunshine and the stunning views. They had met on the cliff path above and made their way down the steep slope together, slipping and sliding as the path turned nearly perpendicular, finally arriving on the beach, laughing and panting, happy to have escaped a bad fall. Then Liam had unpacked his rucksack and laid out this fabulous spread before her.

Tara swallowed her bite and looked at Liam. 'Amazing to be here, the two of us, isn't it?' she started. 'Two O'Rourkes on O'Rourke land. I'm sure our ancestors would be happy.'

'I'd say they'd be delighted,' Liam said, wiping his mouth.

'I've been thinking about how we are related,' Tara continued. 'Your great-grandfather and mine must have been brothers.'

Liam looked into his plastic cup. 'I suppose,' he muttered.

'What was his name?'

'Not sure, I think it was Tom or something.'

'You don't know? Did your father never talk about the family around here? I mean, the farm was quite big and they must have been quite prosperous.'

Liam shot her a look, his eyes dark. 'I said I don't know much about them. I've sold the place and now I want to move on and enjoy the money I made,' he said.

'What are you going to do with the money from the sale?' Tara asked, disappointed he didn't want to talk about his family and at the same time puzzled by his annoyed expression. She had thought perhaps he was beginning to trust her. She probably needed to humour him a bit instead of asking direct questions.

'I'm going to buy a new car for a start,' Liam said, looking brighter. 'I'm looking at a few sports cars at the moment. Always wanted to own one. And when I get one I'll take you for a trip around Kerry.'

'Sounds like fun.' She watched Liam as he tucked into the rest of the picnic, smiling as he offered her strawberries in a little basket. 'This is like a dream,' she said. 'I'm sure I'll wake up with a smile on my face. Do you treat all the girls you go out with like this?'

'Only the ones called Tara,' he replied, moving closer and putting his hand on her bare knee. 'And you're not a girl, but a beautiful woman that I feel very lucky to have met.'

'Thank you,' Tara mumbled, overwhelmed. It was suddenly too much: the food, the champagne, the compliments – it was like being force-fed a too-sweet dessert. He was a handsome, fun guy, but this kind of wooing suddenly felt patronising and a little too slick for her taste. She hadn't meant for this to be a date, more like an outing with a friend during which she had hoped to find out as much as she could about his family – and her own. But he seemed to have different ideas and now she felt a strong urge to get away from his flirty blue eyes and wide toothpaste smile. She put the little basket on the blanket and stood up. 'I think I'll go for a swim.'

'After all that food?' Liam asked, looking startled.

'It's a myth that you can't swim after eating.' Tara walked away and quickly pulled off her T-shirt and shorts revealing her swimsuit she had put on underneath. Then, without another word, she ran into the water and threw herself into the waves, swimming fast out into the bay until she had to stop and float to catch her breath. She looked at him standing on the beach, shading his eyes against the sunlight, peering at her, his whole stance telling her he was both startled and confused by her behaviour.

She had the impression that he was a fun, sweet man with whom she would have a good time and maybe even form a lasting friendship. But now it was slowly dawning on her that he wasn't at all what she had hoped. She mentally kicked herself for not seeing the signs earlier; it was written all over his Facebook timeline. The flirty comments to other women, the innuendos they flung back at him and the fact that very few of his friends were men. She didn't know much about him, she told herself, only his occupation that had seemed so glamorous and the fact that he was distantly related to her, but now she realised that he was very similar to Joe. *How stupid I am*, she thought. *But I needed someone to have fun with after what Joe did to me, someone to help me forget the hurt and disappointment.* She wished she hadn't come with him at all but now here she was at this beautiful spot with the wrong man. How was she going to get out of here without telling him why?

As she floated on her back, trying to think her way out of this awkward situation, she heard noises that made her lift her head and listen. It was a clicking, squeaking, creaking sound. She glanced at the shore but Liam hadn't moved. Then the noise became louder and a little rowing boat came slowly into view as it rounded the headland. The man at the oars rested them in the air as he spotted her and then started to row again. 'Ahoy?' he shouted. 'Are you all right over there?'

Tara waved. 'Yes. I'm fine,' she shouted back and started to laugh as she recognised him. 'Hi, Pat,' she called. 'What are you doing here?'

Pat squinted at her. 'Who—? Tara, is it? Aren't you a long way from home, girl?' He drew closer and Tara grabbed on to the side of the little rowing boat, nearly tipping it over.

'Oops,' she said, laughing, and let go. 'I don't want to land you in the water.'

'You'd better not,' Pat warned. 'I have fishing gear here that I won't want to lose.'

'You're going to fish here?' Tara asked.

'I was going to do some sea angling from that beach, but if you and your friend want some privacy, I'll go somewhere else,' Pat said, taking in Liam standing on the beach and the remnants of their picnic.

'No, no!' Tara exclaimed as she remained bobbing in the water. 'We don't need any privacy at all. In fact, I couldn't be happier to see you. I'm really interested in sea angling actually. Could be a great addition to my article.'

'Oh,' Pat said, looking puzzled for a moment. Then he looked over at Liam and seemed to understand why Tara would welcome his company. 'I see what you mean,' he continued and grabbed the oars. 'I'll row this thing ashore and you can hang on to the aft if you like.'

'Okay,' Tara panted, grabbing the rope that hung from the aft of the rowing boat. 'Row away. I'll hang on to this.'

Pat slowly rowed to the beach, where he jumped out and pulled the little boat onto the sand. He held out his hand to Liam. 'Hello, there. I'm Pat O'Dwyer. Who are you, young man?'

'Liam O'Rourke,' Liam replied, shaking Pat's hand absentmindedly while he stared at Tara.

'O'Rourke, eh?' Pat asked. 'You must be the lad who sold that farmhouse to my son.'

'That's right,' Liam said.

'We've never met, but I think I might have seen your great-uncle,' Pat continued.

'That's possible,' Liam replied. 'I inherited the farm from him, but I grew up in Limerick.'

'Nice property,' Pat remarked as he unloaded his fishing gear. 'I'm going to set up the pole here, if you don't mind, as Tara invited me. She wants to watch me fishing and take a few photographs for her magazine, she says.'

'Did she now?' Liam said, shooting Tara a confused look.

'That's right,' Tara replied. 'I kind of forgot this activity in my article, so I'm going to add it and send it once I've taken a few shots and asked some questions.'

'With your phone?' Liam asked, his voice laced with irony.

'No. With my camera.' Tara went to her bag she had left on the beach blanket and pulled out the small Canon camera she always brought with her just in case. 'Here it is.' She held it up for Liam to see.

'Fabulous,' he muttered.

Pat busied himself with setting up a tripod on which he put a long rod after having cast out the line with the bait. 'This is what I do,' he said to Tara. 'Then there's a little bit of waiting around until I get a bite. This beach is one of the best on this coast for bass and flounder. I even get a sole or two sometimes. Helen bakes it with butter and lemon and we eat it straight away. So I'm hoping I'll get lucky today. In one way or the other,' he added with a smirk in Tara's direction.

Tara giggled. 'I hope you will.'

'Yeah, well,' Liam muttered, gathering up the remnants of their picnic. 'I think I'll get going.'

'Don't you want to stay and watch the fishing?' Tara asked with an innocent air, knowing he was livid that their romantic outing had been interrupted and that she had been so obviously happy about that.

'No thanks.' Liam stuffed the containers and the empty champagne bottle into his rucksack.

'Look,' Tara said, feeling an urge to clear the air between them. 'I really enjoyed our outing. You went to a lot of trouble with the picnic and everything. But...' She hesitated. 'We might have got our wires crossed a little.'

Liam looked back at her without smiling. 'Yeah, I think so. I might have read your vibes wrong or something. I get it, don't worry.'

Relieved, Tara nodded. 'No need to leave in a huff, then, is there?'

Liam finally smiled. 'No, but I have to go anyway. It'll take a while to climb up that slope and get to my car. I take it you'll be okay, Tara?'

'I'll be fine,' Tara replied.

Pat turned to look at them. 'You can come back with me in the boat, Tara,' he offered.

'Brilliant,' Tara said. 'I'd love to. I walked here so that'd be much better.'

'We could fit you in, if you squeeze together,' Pat said to Liam. 'But then you'll have to sit very still not to tip us all in the water.'

'Nah, I'm fine.' Liam hitched the rucksack onto his back. 'I'll see you around, Tara.'

'See you,' Tara replied. 'Thanks for the picnic. It was lovely.'

'You're welcome. Bye for now.' And with that Liam started to scramble up the steep slope, without looking back.

'Bye, Liam.' Tara looked at his departing figure, relieved that the date had ended on a reasonably friendly note, even if Liam was disappointed.

Pat glanced over his shoulder. 'That's one of those O'Rourkes,' he remarked. 'The ones from the other side, I mean.'

'The other side?' Tara asked walking to his side, camera ready.

'Yes. That's what they were called in Sandy Cove way back then. I never knew why but there was some kind of rumour that they weren't acceptable in some way.' Pat shrugged. 'Just one of those old stories that gets added to until the original is lost.'

'I suppose,' Tara said, wondering what the original story had been. She looked up the slopes covered in wild rose bushes, amazed at the beauty but at the same time wondering what kind of tragedies and family feuds had happened here in the past. It had to have been something terrible to have driven a young man away, never to return to his land and his people. She was sure Liam knew the story and she was in a way sorry the date had ended so abruptly preventing her demanding answers to her questions. Would she ever find out the truth?

Chapter Twenty

Morrissey's Household and Furniture Emporium was possibly the quirkiest shop Tara had ever been to. Housed in an old barn off a back road on the way to Killarney, it had everything anyone could possibly need to furnish a house. Furniture from every era of the past two hundred years lined the walls, competing for space with shelves full of china, glassware, cutlery and pots and pans.

Tara had finally agreed to move into the farmhouse after her disastrous date with Liam. She had to leave the cottage at the end of the month anyway, so when Mick called in after completing the sale and asked if she really wanted to camp in the farmhouse with him until she went back to New York, she had happily agreed. She fleetingly asked herself if her excitement was more to do with Mick or the house, but chose not to worry about her motives. They had decided between them that he should buy it in his name and then sell half of it to Tara once she had organised with the bank to deposit half of the purchase price into his account. She knew moving in with Mick might cause raised eyebrows in the village, but as their friendship was growing and there were never any undertones of a different nature from him, she felt that it would be nice to share this adventure with him and put her own stamp on the house – it was big enough for them to have separate quarters and this way they would be company for each other when they felt they needed it.

Mick had listened to her plan and finally agreed that the house and grounds should eventually be developed into a centre for hikers and people who wanted a place off the beaten track to enjoy the stunning surroundings. It could also be a haven for bird watchers and botanists, Tara explained, with small numbers and not the crowds he had feared. What had been the original farmhouse would be restored, the roof thatched and four bedrooms with en-suite showers would be created eventually. But that was a long way away. Right now they were just getting the basics so Mick could live there while the main house was being done up. Tara felt excited every time she thought of their plans, which had more to do with how she was beginning to feel about him than the actual project. But he showed no signs of being anything other than a friend, so she hid her feelings and just enjoyed his company. And now, here in this incredible furniture store, she was simply having fun and enjoying picking out things that would suit the old house.

'Gosh,' Tara exclaimed, looking around the warehouse. 'What a lot of stuff.'

'We could spend a whole week here and not see all of it,' Mick said as he charged ahead, wading through an assortment of easy chairs and padded footstools. 'Try to concentrate and don't get distracted by the curiosa. We're here for just the bare essentials, so we have to stick to the list we made and not buy things just because they're fun.'

'Okay,' Tara said, looking longingly at a porcelain basin decorated with pink roses and a matching water jug. 'But that set would be so cute in the master bedroom. And look at that mirror with the seashells around the frame!'

'You can have those,' Mick agreed after checking the price. 'Only because you'll need them and you can put them on the chest of drawers and hang the mirror over it.'

'What about the rocking chair?' Tara asked, pointing at it. 'So adorable.'

'No,' Mick snapped. 'Come on. We have to get kitchen chairs and a sofa and some easy chairs for the living room now that I've thrown out the awful old sofa bed the old man used. But I think we'll be spending the colder evenings in front of the range in the kitchen.'

'When we're not in the back garden,' Tara filled in. 'So we need some garden furniture.'

'Exactly,' Mick agreed. 'But just a few chairs and a table. What we're doing now is getting things for a temporary arrangement and then I'll be working on the repairs during the winter when you'll be in New York. So I think when you come over for Christmas, the house should be fairly liveable in, if the builder I've hired sticks to his schedule.'

'I'm sure you'll manage that as well,' Tara said. 'I was gobsmacked by all you'd done already when we went there this morning.'

Mick had done an amazing job clearing the house, washing the floors, fixing the front door and getting rid of most of the musty old stuff that Liam's old uncle had left behind. He had hired three lads from the village to help out and got a skip from the recycling centre nearby. What was left was the now polished old table in the dining room, the four-poster bed in what would be Tara's bedroom, the chest of drawers and a mahogany wardrobe in another, smaller bedroom. Mick would sleep in the shed that had been the original farmhouse, he said, so he could guard against intruders, but Tara knew he wanted to give her some privacy, a gesture she hugely appreciated.

Mick ran his hand across a mahogany sideboard that looked as if it would match the dining-room table, but walked on as Tara gave him a warning glance, silently reminding him that however nice it was they didn't need it now. But Mick had found a sturdy bed with a wicker headboard that only needed a mattress, two small bedside tables and a small kerosene oil lamp for Tara's room as the house needed rewiring and they didn't dare turn on any of the switches. 'We don't want to burn it down just now,' Mick had remarked. He had bought a camping fridge and they would order a load of logs for the range and that would have to do until they had sorted out the electricity problem. They had already bought two mattresses, sheets, towels and duvets online to be delivered next week.

'Look,' Tara exclaimed as they entered the antiques section. 'More kerosene lamps. We can take that big one with the glass shade for the kitchen and one more for your bedside table. And have you seen the gorgeous old velvet curtains over there?'

'We don't need curtains right now,' Mick argued. 'We can close the shutters. You can do all the cute stuff later on.'

'I suppose,' Tara said, disappointed she couldn't decorate the house just yet. But Mick was right, and in any case she wouldn't move in until the end of the month, which was nearly two weeks away, during which time she had a lot to do. The magazine project had to be finished, she had to pack all her things and thoroughly clean Jasmine and Aiden's cottage before they came back for their holidays. And last but not least, the biggest hurdle: she had to tell Kate what was going on.

Mick's phone pinged as they got back into his car. It was Father O'Malley saying he was in his office and would be happy to look at the parish records for Tara if they wanted to call in straight away. They drove back to Sandy Cove, excited to find out at last what the situation with Tara's great-grandfather's family had been.

They found Father O'Malley sitting at the computer in the parish office next door to the church. He beamed at them as they entered.

'There you are,' he said, putting his glasses on his head. 'As I said to young Mick, I've been putting all the parish records on the computer, year by year.'

Mick gestured at the chair beside the old man. 'Here, Tara, sit down and tell Father O'Malley what you want to know and he'll look it up.'

'Thanks.' Tara walked around the desk and sat down beside Father O'Malley.

'So,' Father O'Malley said, putting on his glasses again. 'What year should we look up?'

'I'm not sure where to start,' Tara said, thinking hard. 'Let's try 1900. I think that was when my great-grandfather Daniel O'Rourke was born.'

'Okay...' Father O'Malley muttered and scrolled down the pages from the nineteen twenties. '1900... O'Rourke... Oh yes, here we are. *Daniel O'Rourke, born October 2, to John and Sarah O'Rourke.*'

Tara stared at the screen and the old script that had been copied from the parish records. 'There he is,' she said, feeling a dart of excitement. '*Daniel Cornelius O'Rourke*, it says. To John and Sarah?'

Father O'Malley nodded. 'Yes. But then…' He scrolled down and looked suddenly glum. 'Sarah seems to have died only a month later.'

'Oh,' Tara said with a sad little sigh. 'That's terrible. How sad that Daniel had to live with this loss from the very beginning of his life. Not knowing his mother would have been so hard for the little boy.'

'Yes,' Father O'Malley said. 'Awful. It often happened in those days, I'm afraid.'

Mick leaned over Tara's shoulder to see the screen. 'But then if the groom in your wedding photo is John, he must have remarried? What year did you say that photo was taken, Tara?'

'It said 1904,' Tara replied, her heart beating as all the pieces fell into place.

'Nineteen-oh-four?' Father O'Malley scrolled down. 'Here we are… Marriages… Yes, *May 20, 1904, John O'Rourke married Mary Corrigan, widow*, it says here. Born Mary Quirke from Kenmare, it seems.'

'And did she have children?' Tara asked. 'There are two young boys in that photo.'

'No idea,' Father O'Malley said. 'You'd have to go to Kenmare to find that out. She was from there, so she might have married her first husband there and possibly had children.'

'Oh,' Tara said, disappointed.

'Those lads could be her nephews or something,' Mick suggested.

'Yes but then why are they in the wedding photo?' Tara asked. 'I'm assuming this one is Daniel,' she said, pointing at the little boy in the photo on her phone. 'He does look about four, the poor little thing.' She pocketed the phone.

'Why do you say that?' Mick asked. 'He'd been motherless since he was born, and now he has a stepmother to look after him.'

Tara took her phone out of her pocket again and pulled up the photo. 'He doesn't look very happy.'

'Nobody does in photos at the time,' Mick remarked, looking at Tara's phone. 'They had to sit like that without moving when they had their photos taken. I'd say that'd be hard for a little boy.'

'Yes, but that woman looks grim,' Tara replied, staring at the stern face of John O'Rourke's new wife. 'Not exactly motherly. And her new husband doesn't look very happy for a newlywed.'

'He might not be feeling very well,' Father O'Malley suggested as he kept scrolling. 'Look, here we are in 1906. John O'Rourke died in January that year.'

'Oh, no,' Tara exclaimed, looking at the page. 'What did he die of?'

'It doesn't say. Could have been TB, or the flu, or any number of illnesses that weren't curable in those days.'

Tara looked at the face of the little boy in the photo on her phone. 'So Daniel was brought up by his stepmother?' she said with a pang of sadness. 'She might not have been nice to him. Maybe that's why he left the family farm when he was only twenty.'

'But he would have been the heir to the property,' Mick mused. 'It was a big farm in those days, with that house and all the land that came with it.'

'Mary O'Rourke died in 1920, it says here,' Father O'Malley announced, looking at the computer screen. 'And someone called

Tom O'Rourke… Just a moment, I'll go through the years… died in 1960, age sixty-eight,' he continued a few minutes later. 'Tom O'Rourke of Riverside Farm.'

'What? But…' Tara nearly pushed Father O'Malley from his seat as she leaned in to see. 'Then he was older than Daniel, who would have been only sixty by then. But who was he? Why was he the owner of the farm, if Daniel was an only child? If he had stepbrothers, they must have been called…'

'Corrigan,' Father O'Malley filled in. 'From Kenmare.' He tapped his head. 'I have a very good memory, you see.'

'Amazing,' Mick said. 'But that doesn't solve the riddle. Was Tom O'Rourke a cousin or nephew of Tara's great-great grandfather, John? Why would he have inherited the farm?'

Father O'Malley looked confused. 'No idea.'

'Was it the stepmother who disinherited Daniel?' Tara suggested, her breath caught in her throat. 'Oh God, that must have been awful for him. No wonder he never came back.'

'I think that's what must have happened,' Mick agreed. 'Often did in rural Ireland. Family feuds were mostly about land and inheritance. The O'Rourkes were not unusual.'

'But we're still in the dark about what happened,' Tara said, disappointed. 'Could you print all this out for me? I want to show it to my sister.'

'Of course,' Father O'Malley chirped. 'I have a brand-new printer. Wireless,' he said, looking proud of himself. 'I love all this new technology.'

'You're very good with it, too,' Mick said.

Father O'Malley's face turned pink. 'Not at all. I'm still learning. But it's most enjoyable.'

'You're a gifted man,' Mick said.

Speechless, Tara sat there, looking at the computer screen, thinking of everything she had just learned. She couldn't wait to share it with Kate. She knew now that something terrible had happened; it wasn't just a feeling she'd had. She had been right to try to return the farmhouse to the family. She had been keeping her and Mick's plans from Kate, but she knew now that she could tell her.

Chapter Twenty-One

'Are you out of your mind?' Kate asked, staring at Tara as they stood in the living room of the little cottage the following morning. 'You and Mick are moving into that old wreck? And he has bought it? For you?'

'He's not giving it to me,' Tara protested. 'We're investing in it together.' She stopped wondering how she could explain how much that house meant to her and why she wanted it so badly. 'It's our house, you know. I've found out that Daniel was definitely disinherited.' Tara drew breath. 'And now we have a chance to get it back,' she ended. 'Don't you understand how wonderful that is?'

'No.' Kate shook her head. 'I can't believe I'm hearing this. I had no idea that you were still thinking of buying it. And that old story you were talking about. How do you know what happened or who should have inherited the farm? Wasn't Daniel the youngest brother in the family? How could he possibly have expected to inherit it?'

'It's more complicated than that. He was the only son of John O'Rourke, who owned the farm at the time and then…' Tara launched into the family history she had heard from Father O'Malley while Kate listened, her eyes widening as Tara came to the end.

Kate sat down on the white sofa looking shaken. 'If it's true what you seem to think, Daniel was somehow cheated out of his inheritance by his stepmother. But how? And why?'

'I don't know that yet. I don't even know if this woman had children. Daniel might have left for some other reason.'

'The feud?'

'Possibly,' Tara agreed. 'The Civil War was raging at that time and they could have been on opposite sides, one with Fianna Fáil and the other with Fine Gael, which was the case with a lot of families.'

'Still is, I would imagine,' Kate remarked. 'Those two parties are still the most important ones in Irish politics. But back to the house and your plans. Not the best investment, is it? How can you trust Mick, when you barely know him?'

'I can, because that's what he promised. We're buying the house together and he'll sign over half of it when I put in my share.'

'Have you signed some kind of contract?' Kate enquired, looking sceptical.

Tara turned away from Kate. 'No, but we have an agreement.'

'Oh, okay,' Kate said with a resigned sigh. 'Let's leave that for the moment. But if you're planning to use the house when you're here for the summer, we won't have to build that little flat for you, will we?'

'No,' Tara said, flashing a thin smile at Kate. 'I'll wait to be the auld aunt until later in my life.'

'But that wasn't at all what we thought,' Kate protested. 'We want to include you in our new home and our family.' Kate looked up at Tara. 'Sit down, will you, instead of standing there looking at me like that.'

'Like what?' Tara asked and plopped down beside Kate. 'I'm trying to explain why buying the farm is so important to me.'

'Yes, tell me. Why?' Kate asked.

Tara took her phone from the small table beside the sofa and produced the old wedding photo. She held it out to Kate. 'Look at the eyes of that little boy. So utterly sad. And he has the same expression in the photo taken years later, just before he left for Dublin.'

Kate studied the photo. 'Well, yes, but they all look serious, just like all old photos of people who had to stay stock-still when they were having their photographs taken.'

'It's more than that,' Tara argued, looking at the screen. 'There is an expression of deep sorrow in his face. Can't you see that? And it never left him. That's what's urging me to buy the farm and to make it ours again. It's as if Daniel is reaching out to me across the span of a hundred years.'

'I think you're seeing it with a photographer's eye,' Kate remarked. 'You notice things others don't.'

Tara put down the phone and looked at Kate thoughtfully. 'I suppose you're right. And it could be because of my way of taking photos. I have to feel it in my gut before I can press the shutter. Right here.' Tara put her hand on her stomach. 'Not in my heart or my head. It's very strange, but I know exactly when to take the shot.'

Kate nodded. 'That's why you're such a great photographer. But I think you should try to put it all in the right perspective.' She pointed at the phone. 'Those pictures were taken a hundred years ago. The people in it lived very differently to how we live and think and feel today. What seems tragic now was simply part of life to them. I don't think you can look at what happened to them from a modern perspective. And they are long gone and no longer feel pain or sorrow.' Kate put her hand on Tara's arm. 'Let it go, Tara. Don't throw away your money on a wreck of a house because you think you can right some wrong that happened in the past.'

'It's a lot more than that.' Tara shook off Kate's hand and stood up. 'I want that house more than I've ever wanted anything in my whole life. I know it's unpractical and foolish and all those things you've just said, but…' She stopped, unable to go on. It hurt her deeply that Kate didn't understand how she felt, didn't share her conviction that Riverside Farm should be returned to them, the descendants of that young man with the sad eyes in the photo. Kate didn't appear to have seen the beauty of the garden, the view of the river and the weeping willows trailing their branches in its gushing water. 'You were there,' Tara said in a near whisper. 'Didn't you feel it?'

Kate sighed and got up. 'It's a lovely place all right. But it didn't pull me in like it did you. Maybe that's because other things are a lot more important to me right now. I can't afford all these romantic notions. I was so happy sharing the plans for our new house with you, but now I see that it doesn't matter much to you. That pile of rubble is more important than me and my baby. That makes me so sad.'

'It's not like that,' Tara protested, close to tears. 'Of course I care about you and the baby. And Cormac, too. But I also have my own life to live and the freedom to make mistakes – or not, as the case may be. I know deep down it's a huge risk, but I think there is a lot I could do with that property. Something amazing for other people to enjoy.'

Kate frowned. 'More tourists. Just what we need,' she muttered and got up. 'I have to go. I have to take afternoon surgery. And the house is being redecorated. Pat's wife is planning to come and live there for good, now that she has turned over her business in Killarney to her niece.'

'I know. Mick told me. That's partly why he wants to move.'

'I suppose it's the best thing for him. Helen can be very domineering. She says she can't wait to move back in. Pity, because I initially had the idea to take over the house once Pat retired. He wanted to buy a little bungalow nearby, but Helen thought it was too small.' She looked levelly at Tara. 'I love that house, you know. It's so like the house we grew up in. So not buying it was a huge disappointment. I have to admit that deep down, I do understand how you feel about the farm. But that doesn't mean I think it's a good idea.' She gave Tara a peck on the cheek. 'Let me know if you need help to move your stuff. I'll drive you over to Riverside Farm when you're ready. And then, when Jasmine and Aiden arrive, we'll have a little party at our house so you can meet them, and Sally and her husband, too.'

'That'll be great,' Tara said, her spirits lifting. 'I'm looking forward to meeting them.'

'You'll love them. Oh, and with all this, I nearly forgot that we've set a date for the wedding. It's going to be on the twentieth of August. The wedding ceremony will be in the church with Father O'Malley officiating, but we haven't found a venue for the reception yet. And you'll be maid of honour and Cormac's brother Darragh will be best man. So we'll have to go to Killarney to find dresses very soon.'

'That'll be so much fun,' Tara exclaimed.

'Like old times,' Kate said, smiling fondly at Tara. She got to her feet. 'So after all that, I'll be on my way. Let me know if you need help with your move.'

'I will,' Tara promised and jumped up from the sofa. 'And let me know when you're free for that shopping trip.'

'Of course. Bye for now. I'm so glad we've sorted everything out,' Kate said.

Cheered by Kate's words, Tara hugged her sister and felt slightly better when Kate had left. There had been a chill between them during their conversation, but then Kate had admitted she understood how Tara felt, even if she wasn't prepared to endorse the purchase of the old farm. Kate had shown a chink in her armour, however. Buying the surgery would have been perfect for her, and the new house was some kind of compromise. And as they'd talked, a grain of an idea had popped into Tara's head. Something that would solve Kate's predicament and make her very happy. Tara had to get all the parties involved and that included a woman who wouldn't be ready to agree to a scheme she hadn't thought of herself. It would require some hard negotiating with a dash of deviousness.

But that was for later. Right now, she had to pack and get ready for her own adventure. What would it feel like to sleep in that bedroom in the old house? Would the ghosts of the past frighten her away?

Chapter Twenty-Two

When Tara and Kate arrived at Riverside Farm a week later, the front of the house looked very different from the sad and lonely place Tara had seen that first time a month earlier. The gate had been fixed and painted, the gravel raked and weeded and the front door had been painted a dark green. Two huge planters with red geraniums flanked the front steps and the broken windows had been repaired and their trims painted white.

Kate pulled the car up in front of the house and stared, her eyes huge with surprise. 'Oh my God,' she mumbled.

'I know,' Tara said beside her. 'Mick has done an amazing job.'

'All on his own?' Kate asked incredulously.

'No, he's been hiring lads from the village. Loads of them on summer holidays and very keen to earn a few bob.' Tara leaned over and pressed the horn.

The door opened and Mick, in a paint-stained shirt and old baggy trousers, peered out. The happy look in his eyes, his messy hair and the perspiration on his brow made him look so endearing, Tara felt a strong urge to hug him. 'What's the bloody racket?' he shouted and ran down the steps. 'Oh, it's my partner in crime.' He opened the passenger door. 'Please step out, my lady. All is ready for your stay in the manor. The staff will serve tea on the lawn shortly.'

Kate leaned over and smiled at him. 'Hi, Mick. You've done an amazing job. The house looks great.'

'On the outside,' Mick replied. 'The inside is a lot less elegant. But don't worry, the master bedroom has been fixed up fit for a princess, the outside loo cleaned up and, well, the river bathroom is what it is. But the trees provide a lot of privacy and the water is cold but crystal clear.'

Tara giggled. 'Stop messing and help me get my stuff inside,' she ordered.

'At once, my lady,' Mick said and grabbed Tara's suitcase.

'Come on,' Tara said to Kate over her shoulder. 'Let's have a look at what he's done inside.'

The interior of the house wasn't much different to what it had been before, except for the newly sanded floors, the repaired windows and the empty living room. In the dining room, the table was still there with twelve chairs that Mick had discovered stacked up in the shed.

'Lovely room,' Kate said, walking to the tall window. 'And a gorgeous view of the river.'

'Oh my God,' Tara suddenly exclaimed behind Kate.

'What, what?' Kate looked around the room, panic-stricken. 'What's wrong? Did you see a rat?'

'No,' Tara said. 'It's not something like that. But I just realised… Wouldn't this be a lovely place to have your wedding reception? We could rent round tables and those lovely gilt chairs and put roses from the garden on all the tables and have a band in the living room and dance on that gorgeous floor. And…'

'Stop,' Kate protested. 'You're getting too excited. I'm not sure this could be done at all. I mean, the kitchen is probably not suitable for that kind of catering and the lane here is full of potholes…' She stopped. 'But…' She laughed suddenly and rushed to Tara, hugging her tightly. 'What a beautiful, perfect idea.'

'I know,' Tara said, beaming. 'An O'Rourke wedding at the O'Rourke farm. It feels so right somehow.'

'Let's see the kitchen before we get carried away,' Kate suggested. 'It could be too rundown for any kind of food preparation, let alone catering for over fifty people.'

But they found the kitchen in amazing order: the range polished with two fireside chairs in front of it, a brand-new fridge purring in the corner, the pine table scrubbed clean, the flagstone floor gleaming and the half-door to the back garden open to reveal the rose bushes and cobblestones.

Tara stopped and stared. 'Wow,' she whispered.

'I've been playing house,' Mick said behind her. 'You like?'

'I love,' Tara said in a near whisper. 'Oh, Mick, you're a genius.'

'But of course I am,' Mick replied. 'Didn't you know that already?'

'But the fridge,' Tara asked, confused. 'There's no electricity, so how?'

'It's running on a generator I set up in the utility room. I thought you might have heard the noise.'

'Oh. Of course,' Tara said, even more impressed.

'Where are you going to sleep?' Kate asked Mick.

Mick gestured out the window. 'Out there in that building which was the original farmhouse. I've cleared out one of the rooms and put a bed and a table in there with one of those paraffin oil lamps on top of it.'

Kate looked out the window at the little house. 'The original farmhouse?'

'Yes, Liam told me about it,' Tara said. 'That was where they lived before one of the O'Rourkes married a rich girl from Tipperary in 1860. Then the big house was built. Before that, they were a lot less grand.'

'Dirt poor, like everyone around here,' Mick said cheerfully.

Kate looked at Tara, her cheerful expression gone. 'You seem to know a lot more than you told me. Is there anything else?'

'No,' Tara replied. 'I've told you all I know about the family history. The last little bit about how the big house was built I learned from Liam. But there are so many other things I don't know. Like *why* Daniel didn't inherit this place and why he left for Dublin. But I have no idea how we could find that out.' She drew breath and looked pleadingly at Kate. 'I'm not trying to hide anything from you, if that's what you're wondering.'

Kate didn't look convinced. 'Maybe not about the family stuff, but I think you have plans you're not sharing with me.'

'Like what?' Tara asked, standing back and folding her arms. Kate's sudden animosity and suspicions tore at her heart, but it also made her feel slightly guilty about not having said anything about the feature she was hoping to get published in a magazine.

'Like you want to turn this into some kind of B&B? Or you'll start a restaurant or something?' Kate suggested.

'What?' Tara exclaimed. 'A restaurant? B&B? No, that's not at all what I had in mind.'

'So tell me, then,' Kate said, her voice cold. 'What *are* your plans? I have a feeling you're going to milk this place for all you can take out of it, possibly starting with a series of articles about some kind of magical old house with a fascinating history, accompanied by your incredibly enticing photographs that are sure to make everyone want to come here in droves.'

'Oh, well…' Tara squirmed as Kate's words hit home. She had somehow read Tara's mind with that odd twin-telepathy they had often marvelled at. Now it suddenly didn't seem so wonderful.

'Well, what?' Kate asked.

Tara looked down at the floor. Then she looked back at Kate. 'Okay, yeah. I had been playing with the idea to write the story of the house, and also include the restoration in a kind of series for one of the high-profile magazines. But not for the reasons you said.'

'Hey, you didn't say anything about this to me,' Mick cut in.

'I was going to,' Tara tried to explain. 'I thought, you see, that it would help pay some of the bills. Like the rewiring and the new bathroom.'

'Oh.' Mick nodded. 'I see. Well, we could talk about that later.'

'You mean you'll talk her out of it,' Kate said. 'Because I don't approve of this. In fact, I don't approve of the whole mad scheme of Tara buying into the place at all.'

'Well, it's her decision,' Mick stated. 'I'm not twisting her arm.'

'No, but you're encouraging her,' Kate said, her voice a little softer. 'I don't blame you, really. The idea of doing up the house is nice, but you have to be realistic.'

'Realism isn't my idea of fun,' Tara quipped. 'And I'll decide for myself, thank you very much.' She stared at Kate, daring her to object. Then the puff went out of her and she was suddenly terrified that Kate would never support her. 'Please don't kill my dream,' she said in a near whisper. 'This means so much to me. More than anything ever in my life.'

They looked at each other for minute or two, an uncomfortable silence hanging between them. Then Kate let out a resigned sigh. 'All right. On your head be it. I officially wash my hands of the whole affair. I'll transfer your part of the money to you and then you can do what you want with it. But don't come crying to me when it all goes belly-up.'

'Nobody's crying,' Mick said. 'But I'm glad you came to your senses, Miss Pontius Pilate.'

'Yeah, well, I don't want to be a killjoy,' Kate said with a contrite look at Tara. 'We'll never really agree about this, but let's not fall out over it.'

'No, I'd hate that,' Tara said, relief washing over her like a warm shower. 'And there will be no hordes of tourists here, I promise.'

'Hmm, I should hope not,' Kate muttered. 'But let's not worry about that until it happens.'

'It won't.'

'We'll stop them at the gate,' Mick joked. 'With pitchforks and torches.' He looked from one to the other. 'I hope you two won't be rowing about this.'

'No, we won't,' Kate said. 'Case closed, even if it's not what I'd want for Tara.'

'No more arguing, then. And we'll have the wedding here?' Tara asked, her voice still shaking slightly. 'I mean it would be so lovely.'

'I'll think about it,' Kate replied.

'Great idea, though,' Mick said.

The sound of wheels on the gravel made them all stop and listen. 'Are you expecting anyone?' Kate asked.

'No,' Mick replied, going to the door. 'All my little helpers have gone home for the day. I'll go and have a look who's here.'

'Maybe the postman?' Tara suggested, following him down the corridor.

'Can't be,' Mick said over his shoulder. 'I haven't changed my address yet. Nobody knows I'm here, not even my mother.'

'She wouldn't approve,' Kate whispered in Tara's ear.

'Really?' Tara whispered back. 'Why not?'

'She wants to be in control,' Kate mouthed behind Mick's back.

They arrived at the front door and Mick opened it, swearing under his breath as he looked at the tall blonde woman dressed in a beige skirt, white shirt and red espadrilles alighting from a silver Audi.

'Talk about the devil,' Kate said with a suppressed giggle. She ran down the steps and greeted the woman with a kiss on the cheek. 'Helen,' she gushed. 'How lovely to see you. Have you come to inspect Mick's new home?'

Helen backed away from Kate and looked at Mick and Tara with confusion. 'Kate,' she said. 'And… You must be Tara, as you're the spit of your sister.'

'I am,' Tara said and went to shake the woman's hand. 'And you must be Mick's mum, right?'

Helen nodded. 'Yes. Nice to meet you, Tara. Hello, Mick.'

'Hi, Mum,' Mick replied glumly. 'How the hell did you know where I was?'

'Kate hinted at what was happening,' Helen O'Dwyer replied as she looked up at the house. 'I had no idea what she meant exactly, but then I met Cormac and he accidentally revealed what was going on. So I had to come here to find out what you were up to. And now I'm standing here wondering how on earth you could be so foolish. You spent the money from the sale of your house in Dublin on this? It's a wreck. It'll take all you have to make it habitable.'

'So what?' Mick said with a grin. 'Won't it be worth it?'

Helen's blue eyes focused on Tara and Kate. 'Maybe we should talk in private?'

'Why?' Mick asked, his voice cool. 'Kate and Tara are friends of mine. Close friends. No need to hide anything from them. And I need witnesses,' he added in a frivolous tone.

'Very funny.' Helen walked up the steps and peered inside. 'Is it safe to go inside? I could do with a cup of tea.'

'I'll put the kettle on,' Tara said. 'But I'll have to light the range first so it'll take a while.'

'Why?' Helen asked in a thin voice.

'Because there is no electricity, Mum,' Mick said. 'We didn't dare turn anything on as the switches seem to be from the nineteen fifties and the place hasn't been rewired since then. I didn't want to burn it down when I've just bought it.'

'No electricity?' Helen looked appalled. 'And what about plumbing?'

Mick shrugged. 'Water seems to come when you turn the tap in the kitchen. I think the outside loo has some kind of pump affair, but I've applied for planning permission for a new septic tank that'll be very eco-friendly. It'll be installed next week.'

Helen folded her arms across her chest. 'You got planning permission already?'

Mick looked back at her with a touch of rebelliousness. 'No, but I will. Better not to wait, don't you think? We don't want things to be unpleasant in that area, do we?'

'We?' Helen asked, looking even more appalled. 'There's someone else involved in this madness?'

'Yes.' Mick pulled Tara to his side. 'Tara is my partner in crime. We're going to own this house together and we're going to turn it into…' He stopped and looked at Tara. 'Not sure what exactly, but it'll be great.'

Helen's eyes homed in on Tara. 'Is this true?' she enquired, her voice sharper than a razorblade, her eyes colder than a Norwegian mountain lake.

Tara felt a chill go up her spine as she met those icy blue eyes. She stuck out her chin. 'Yes, it is. I will be putting money into this project. We have great plans, but we prefer not to share them with anyone yet.'

'I,' Helen said very slowly. 'Am. His. Mother.'

'And Kate's my twin sister,' Tara retorted. 'And I won't tell her either. Not until we reveal everything officially.' She was making things up as she went along as Helen's stance was so irritating. She couldn't believe this woman treated a grown man like Mick as if he was five years old and didn't know better. But maybe it was because she loved him so much and couldn't let him go? There had been a touch of fear and sadness in those blue eyes before they turned hostile, and Tara felt sorry for her. Didn't she know that love couldn't be forced or bought or controlled? Letting go of Mick would make him love her more than if she tried to hold on. She suddenly wanted to hug Helen's stiff body and whisper in her ear not to be afraid and explain that Mick would love her more if she let him be.

'Mick has done an amazing job already,' she said in a softer voice. 'He's incredibly hardworking and clever at this sort of thing.' She made a sweeping gesture at the two rooms. 'Look at what he's done already. Aren't you impressed?'

'He gave up a great acting career,' Helen remarked. 'That's not what I call impressive.'

'But now he's doing something that he loves,' Kate cut in.

'Life's about changes, not being stuck in a rut,' Mick interjected.

'That's all very well for other people,' Helen argued. 'But you've given everything up – for this?'

'Not just for this,' Mick said. 'For another project that I can't talk about yet. But I'm certain you'll be over the moon when I announce it.'

'If it's anything as mad as this, I doubt it,' Helen said dryly. 'I hope it's not what I think it is. That would be horrific.'

Mick put his hand on Helen's shoulder and swung her around to face him. 'Mum, trust me. I will soon make an announcement that will make you very happy. I'm changing careers to something completely different and you will be the first to know before it goes public.'

'Are you turning this into some kind of hotel?' Helen asked, looking confused. 'With Tara?'

'No,' Mick said. 'That's not what I'm talking about. My new career will only involve me. And the rest of the county,' he added, looking mysterious. He hugged his mother and her stiff form softened. 'Don't worry, Mum. It'll be all right. And you and Dad can live together at the surgery and Kate will be next door and I will be here and Tara will be in New York.'

Helen looked at Tara. 'New York? You're going back?'

Tara nodded. 'Yes. At the end of August. After Kate's wedding.'

Helen pulled out of Mick's arms and tidied her hair. 'But what about the house and your project with Mick?'

'That's a seasonal thing,' Tara said. 'I'll be here in the summers to run the project. And then, eventually, I will buy the house from Mick. And it will be an O'Rourke property again.'

'Well, that's as it should be,' Helen said. 'My grandmother always said it was a crying shame that this place was lost to those dreadful people.'

'What?' Kate asked.

'You must know that old story,' Helen said.

Tara stared at Helen, suddenly breathless, wondering if they would finally find the final, most important piece of the jigsaw. And from Helen of all people. 'What do you mean?' she asked, waiting with bated breath for the reply.

Chapter Twenty-Three

'You heard what I said,' Helen replied. 'Those dreadful people cheated that young man out of his inheritance.'

Kate and Tara looked at each other, then back at Helen. 'Excuse me?' Tara said. 'What dreadful people?'

'The ones who stole the farm from the rightful heir, of course,' Helen said. 'Didn't you know?'

'No,' Tara replied, her stomach in a knot of excitement. 'But you obviously do.'

'Well, my grandmother did, of course,' Helen stated.

Tara blinked. 'Your grandmother knew about this house and the O'Rourkes?'

Helen nodded. 'Yes. She often talked about this poor young man who had to run off to Dublin after the fighting and how the widow gave the farm away.'

'The widow?' Tara asked, her heart beating.

'Yes,' Helen replied. 'The widow who married the farmer here. She somehow managed to give the farm and all the land to her own son from her first marriage. It was a huge scandal in those days, apparently.'

'What?' Kate exclaimed. 'Hey, we have to hear the story. We've been trying to find out all summer what happened to our great-grandfather and why he lost the right to this farm. And you knew this story all along?'

'Well,' Helen said with a little sniff. 'Nobody asked me.'

'We're asking you now,' Tara exclaimed and pulled at Helen's arm. 'Please, can we go and sit down somewhere and you can tell us everything you know?'

Helen seemed to soften now that the spotlight was on her. 'I don't suppose there are seats in the back garden?'

'Yes, there are,' Mick replied. 'I got a garden set from IKEA when we ordered everything else. Four chairs and a round table. You go on and sit down and I'll make tea, which will take a while, so please be patient.'

'All right. Thank you,' Helen said graciously. 'Come along, girls, we'll let Mick get the refreshments and I'll tell you all I know.'

They walked back to the kitchen and out through the back door into the little garden where Mick had placed four wooden chairs around a table with an umbrella over it. The roses emitted a sweet scent in the hot sun and a blackbird treated them to a serenade as they sat down.

'A nice spot,' Helen said as she smoothed her skirt. 'Lovely roses. Must have been planted many years ago.'

'I'm sure they were. So tell us,' Tara urged as she and Kate settled on their chairs. 'What do you know about this old feud or whatever it was that chased our great-grandfather away from here?'

'And how come your grandmother knew so much about it?' Kate asked.

Helen folded her hands in her lap. 'Well, you see, my grandmother was the village vicar's wife. As Kate might have told you, Tara, our house was once the vicarage. So anyway,' she breezed on, 'my grandmother loved gossiping about the old days and what happened in the village when she was a child. It was during the time just after the Civil War and of course, the First World War in Europe, so things were tough and people were poor. Land was important and anyone who owned a few acres was better off than those who had to struggle. And Riverside Farm was the biggest property around here then. Whatever happened here was big news. It was common knowledge that John O'Rourke had married again after his first wife died shortly after giving birth to her son.'

'That little boy was Daniel, our great-grandfather,' Kate cut in.

Helen looked taken aback. 'Really? I never realised that... There are so many O'Rourkes around this area, it's hard to keep track of you all.'

'Did John's new wife have any children?' Tara asked, eager to hear the rest.

'Yes, she did,' Helen replied. 'Mary Corrigan had two sons by her first marriage. And her new husband adopted them and gave them his name. Poor John died of pneumonia a few years after their marriage, and when Mary died years later, she left the farm to her eldest son, Tom. That meant that Daniel lost his right to his father's farm.'

'So unfair,' Tara muttered.

'Yes,' Helen agreed. 'That's what they thought in the village, too, my grandmother said. They all felt sorry for the poor boy. And he left very soon after that.'

'He went to Dublin,' Kate filled in. 'Probably heartbroken.'

Helen nodded. 'Oh yes, that's what they all said. Poor boy, only twenty years old.'

'He joined the newly formed police force,' Tara said. 'And married very young and had a family of his own. But he never came back to Sandy Cove.'

'It was said that he cut all ties with his stepbrother,' Helen said. 'Tom O'Rourke wasn't a nice man and everyone knew it. My grandmother said the villagers turned against him when Daniel left. He turned into a very solitary, grumpy man. He married late in life and had two sons, but that's all I know about them.' Helen drew breath.

'One of them must have been Liam's great-uncle,' Tara mused.

'That seems to fit,' Kate agreed.

'So Liam is not a real O'Rourke,' Tara said as if to herself. 'And his old uncle must have been Tom O'Rourke's son. Maybe he knew that all along? And maybe he also took that photo because he didn't want me to find it and start asking questions.'

'Why would he care?' Helen asked. 'It was a long time ago. People around here have mostly forgotten that old story. There's just a touch of negativity attached to people from this farm, but most people don't know why.'

Kate winked at Tara. 'Maybe Liam O'Rourke was trying to impress you? He might have been afraid that touch of negativity would put you off him.'

Tara rolled her eyes. 'Oh please. I told you I'm not interested in him. Or any man at the moment.'

Helen looked pleased. 'Not even Mick?'

'We're friends and business partners,' Tara said coolly, trying to keep herself from blushing. 'That's all.'

'In that case, maybe you could persuade him to sell on this pile of rubbish and spend his money on something sensible,' Helen suggested, leaning back in her chair and looking up at the façade. 'He's put a lot of effort into improvements, so someone might want to take it off his hands. I really don't understand why he won't live with us when he's in Sandy Cove. The house is going to be so comfortable when we've finished the repairs and new additions. Much better than camping in this place. You must see that yourself, Tara. It's not a good investment for you either.'

'You're right, Helen,' Kate cut in. 'That's what I was trying to tell them a while ago.'

'We're keeping it,' Tara said, sticking her chin out defiantly as she stared at Helen.

Kate sighed. 'I wish you would let go of that idea. It's a lovely place right now, but in the depth of winter it'll be a nightmare.'

'I don't care,' Tara replied. 'And you promised to stop arguing, Kate.'

They were interrupted by Mick carrying a tray with mugs of tea and a plate of gingernut biscuits. 'Tea and bikkies for the ladies.'

'Wonderful.' Helen took one of the mugs and sipped it. 'Very nice.'

'The water here makes great tea,' Mick remarked. 'So what have you been talking about while I slaved in the kitchen?'

'This house,' Helen said. 'And its early history. Amazing that Kate and Tara's great-grandfather grew up here.'

'And even more amazing that your mum knew the whole story all along,' Tara filled in. She told Mick the gist of what Helen had revealed, which made his eyes widen.

'Really?' he said. 'So that's what happened. And you knew it all along, Mum?'

Helen put the mug on the table and reached for a biscuit. 'Yes. It was one of my grandmother's old stories. I had nearly forgotten about it until I came here and talked to Kate and Tara. I had no idea they were part of that O'Rourke family.'

'I'm so glad we know,' Kate said, smiling at Helen. She grabbed a mug and drank most of her tea before she put it back on the tray. 'I have to get back to the surgery soon.'

Helen got up. 'And I'd like to see the rest of the house, Mick.'

'Of course. I'll show you around.' Mick walked ahead of his mother, opening the door. 'This way.'

Tara looked at Kate when Mick and his mother had gone into the house. 'You asked her to come here, didn't you?'

'Not really,' Kate protested. 'She asked me in such a persuasive way I couldn't help telling her. But it was only a hint, really.'

'And then Cormac told her the rest?'

'I suppose.'

'You were hoping she'd persuade Mick to drop the whole project, weren't you? And that maybe she would also manage to talk me out of it as well.' Tara looked at Kate, knowing this was a watershed moment in their relationship. They would either make their peace and move on, getting back what they had lost during this strange summer, or... Tara couldn't bear thinking about the alternative. 'Weren't you?' she asked again, her voice hoarse.

Kate looked back at her and nodded. 'Yes. I suppose I was. But that was before...'

'Before what?'

'Before I saw the house again. Before I found out that the little house in the yard is the original farmhouse, and long before I found out Daniel's story. Then, I thought it was just a madcap scheme and a subject for one of your articles.'

'That was just an idea,' Tara interjected. 'I mightn't even do it.'

Kate nodded. 'I know. But I was sitting here, listening to Helen and then I felt suddenly that perhaps it was meant to happen.'

'What was?'

'That one of us would get the house back and do it up and maybe even live in it.'

'Oh,' Tara whispered, taking Kate's hand. 'You have no idea how much that means to me.'

Kate put her other hand on top of Tara's and looked into her eyes. 'I'm sorry. I should have understood how you felt. But now I do. And you know what? I think you should write that article and do a feature on how this house is rising from the ashes of a lot of pain and suffering. I think it'll be wonderful.'

Tara's eyes filled with tears of joy. 'I'm so glad to hear that. And I will do it.'

'I'm looking forward to seeing it in one of the glossies,' Kate said and got up at the same time as Helen and Mick emerged from the back door.

'How did you like the house?' Tara asked.

'It must have been a fine house once,' Helen replied, picking up her handbag from the chair where she had left it. Mick looked at

Helen with an expression that said he wasn't going to listen to any more negative comments from her.

'I wish you'd listen,' Helen said, looking miffed. 'But I feel there's no persuading you, so I'll stop trying. I'm leaving now. Pat wants to play golf in Waterville this evening and I think I'll join him.'

'I'm off too,' Kate said, starting to walk into the house.

'Hang on a second,' Tara said. 'Kate, Helen, don't go yet. I want to discuss something that has occurred to me. About your houses, I mean.'

'A curse on both of them?' Mick joked.

Tara waved him away. 'No, this is serious.' She looked at Helen and cleared her throat, trying to gather up enough courage to say what was on her mind. 'Helen, I was wondering… If maybe you would consider swapping with Kate?'

Helen frowned. 'How do you mean? Swap houses?'

'Yes,' Tara said. 'It just popped into my head, but I thought that if you and Pat bought that plot next door to the surgery from Kate and Cormac, you could build a house that has all the things you're trying to put into the old house. This way, it would be modern, warm, comfortable and a lot more suitable for an old… I mean for you.'

'Oh,' Kate said and blinked. Tara could see that the idea was music to her ears. 'My God, that would be…'

'Perfect for you both,' Mick cut in, grinning from ear to ear. 'You could buy the surgery, like you always wanted, Kate.'

'If Helen agrees.' Kate looked doubtful that this was going to happen.

Helen said nothing while they all looked at her, waiting for her reaction. 'I…' she said. 'Oh, but… I don't know…'

'Ocean views, a big garden, a house with all the luxuries you always wanted,' Mick mumbled in his mother's ear. 'Walk-in closets, power-shower, jacuzzi... Oh my God, I can see it all now. A big picture window looking out at the ocean. I mean, in our old house, you'd have to hang out of the bathroom window to catch a glimpse of the sea. But in that house... It would be the most glamorous place in Kerry.'

'A real wow factor,' Tara said, beaming at Helen.

Helen's eyes slowly lit up. 'I see what you mean,' she said. 'Yes... well... I'll have to discuss this with your father.'

'Of course,' Mick said in a serious tone, his mouth twitching.

'So we'll see.' Helen got up and kissed Mick on the cheek. 'See you soon, sweetheart. Bye, Tara. Good luck with everything.'

'Bye,' Tara replied.

'I'll give you a call later, Kate,' Helen said and sailed out of the garden.

They all looked at each other in silence when Helen had left. 'It's a done deal,' Mick said. 'Dad will love the idea. I just know it.'

Kate looked at Tara with stars in her eyes. 'Do you know how happy you've made me? I never thought of that idea at all. And I would have had great trouble persuading Helen. But here you are, having thrown her this plan and then Mick with his marketing genius sold it to her in two minutes flat.'

'Ah, sure it was easy,' Mick said with mock modesty.

Kate jumped up and hugged them both. 'Bye, lovelies. See you soon. Have fun with the house.'

Chapter Twenty-Four

Tara was the first to speak when Kate had left. 'I never realised how alike Kate and your mother are. They're both so sure that neither of us knows what we're doing or that we're even adults.'

'They mean well,' Mick argued.

'That's the most irritating kind,' Tara replied. 'Well-meaning people who're convinced they know what's best for others. And they haven't a clue what's best for them.'

'And they can't let go. Kate can't let go of her sister, and my mother can't let go of her only child. Maybe they're the ones who need support?'

'I'm beginning to think that's true. But Kate and I were talking while you were showing Helen around. And she has changed her mind completely.'

'Really?' Mick said, looking surprised. 'And I thought it was set in stone as far as she was concerned. What made her change her mind?'

'She was already wavering when she saw how great the house looked,' Tara explained. 'But finding out what had happened to Daniel was the tipping point. It dawned on her how great it is that the house goes back to the right family. She won't argue with us any more, and neither, I think, will Helen.'

'Now they have other things to worry about, so they'll leave us alone,' Mick said, grinning.

'Of course they will.'

'We hope. But that idea you threw them was brilliant. The work of a true genius.'

'But of course.' Tara finished the biscuit she had been nibbling on and drained her mug. She looked at Mick. 'So what's this project we said we would be doing with the house? I was just stringing them along, but I have a feeling you have some ideas.'

'One or two,' Mick said, looking annoyingly mysterious. 'I'll tell you over dinner.'

'Oh God,' Tara said. 'Dinner! I forgot all about food. I should have brought some but I can easily order some online, or ask Kate to bring us some later.'

'Relax,' Mick said, grinning. 'It's all organised. I ordered some takeaway and the fridge is full of milk and butter and all kinds of stuff for lunch and breakfast.'

'Oh.' Tara looked at Mick with respect. 'You're incredible.'

'I know,' he said with mock modesty. 'There is no end to my ingenuity.'

'Apparently not.'

'The electrician is coming on Monday to start the rewiring. It's a big job, but he thinks he'll have part of the house connected by the evening, so we can at least have hot water and charge our laptops and phones.'

'Fantastic.' Tara stretched her arms over her head and smiled. 'I feel so free here, suddenly. As if I could run naked through the fields without anyone seeing me.' She stopped and felt her face flush as she realised what she had just said. 'That was just a metaphor. I wouldn't actually do that. I mean,' she babbled on, flustered by Mick's expression of amusement mixed with something else that she didn't even want to analyse. 'It's just the feeling of being so in tune with nature here.'

Mick laughed. 'I know exactly what you mean. And don't worry. I wouldn't ever take advantage of your feelings of freedom.'

'That's a relief,' Tara said, feeling quite the opposite. She pushed away the thoughts that flickered through her mind. It was just the heat combined with the scent of roses and the sweet song of the blackbird still sitting on the roof of the shed that made her feel mellow and slightly romantic. She fanned her face. 'It's getting really hot.'

'Why don't you go and have a dip in the river?' Mick suggested. 'It's not deep, just about waist high. The water feels lovely. I cooled off there after finishing the work for the day.' He got up. 'I have to make a few calls and the signal is better in the dining room. You go on down to the river. There are towels in the linen cupboard on the upstairs landing.'

'Wonderful idea.' Tara jumped up and put the mugs on the tray. 'I'll take these in on my way.'

'Great.' Mick paused. 'Could I ask you to do something for me?'

'Of course.' Tara looked at him wondering why he seemed suddenly awkward.

'Could you take my portrait?' Mick asked. 'I mean, take my photo and make me look good. Serious. Professional, caring, that kind of thing.'

'What for?' Tara said teasingly. 'Are you going on Tinder?'

Mick let out a laugh. 'No. Not that kind of photo. It's for my new project.'

'Oh.' Tara suddenly remembered what Helen had said. 'The project your mother thought would be horrific?'

'Yes. But she was only guessing.'

'But she was right?'

'She was. Quite eerie, I thought. And she'll be as horrified as she was about the house when I tell her.'

'So what is it?' Tara asked. 'Go on. Spit it out, willya?'

Mick cleared his throat. 'Promise not to laugh.'

'Yes,' Tara said with an impatient sigh, preparing herself for the news he was going to tell her, thinking he was auditioning for a movie, or a play on Broadway, or something equally challenging. But it was nothing like that. Tara nearly dropped the tray she was holding when she heard what he was getting into.

'Politics?' Tara said after a long silence. 'You're going for a seat in the Irish parliament?'

'Not yet,' Mick replied. 'I'll start a little smaller and try for the county council at the local elections next month. I've been having meetings with my party and they think I'll do well.'

'Well?' Tara exclaimed. 'You'll win hands down. With your charm and charisma and kindness and everything else you exude, you'll win by a landslide,' she continued, remembering how everyone had responded to his warmth, and what a fantastic job he had done on the farm house already. He was such a solid, honest sweet man with no secret agenda and that came through in everything he did and said.

'I'm not so sure of that,' he argued, looking slightly embarrassed at her comments.

'But I am. Councillor Mick O'Dwyer,' she said, testing the sound of it. 'Yes, that'll work.'

'I'm not there yet,' Mick protested, laughing.

'But you will be.' Tara gripped the tray she was holding. 'How can you lose?'

'Don't count any chickens yet. In any case, it's all your fault. You gave me the idea.'

'I did?' Tara asked, mystified, trying to remember ever suggesting Mick should go into politics.

'Yes. Remember when we were walking through the village and you said something about Elvis and that I should be a politician?'

'Oh. Yes, I remember now. But I was only half-serious.'

'But I'm a hundred per cent serious. What you said got me thinking. I've always been interested in politics, and I realised that I can do something useful instead of acting. Something that will benefit the country I love so much, especially this part of it. This village has done so much for me. And now I can give something back.' He paused for breath, looking earnestly at Tara. 'So… what do you honestly think?'

'It's amazing,' she replied, moved by the passion in his voice. 'I think it's also the perfect time in your life to do it. You're at the right age for a politician and people will trust you.'

'Thank you for saying that.'

'I meant it.' Tara smiled, studying him for a moment. 'I know exactly the kind of photo I'll take of you. It'll go on all the election posters, won't it?'

'I think so. If I'm elected as candidate for the party.'

'You will be.' Tara looked down at the tray as if she had just noticed she was holding it. 'I'd better bring this in before I drop it. I'll have to think about that portrait and how I'll do it. I'll go for that dip in the river and then we'll talk.'

'That's a date, then. Enjoy your dip.' He smiled, turned on his heel and walked into the house.

Tara quickly put the tea things on the kitchen counter and ran upstairs to get her swimsuit. The master bedroom was all cleaned, the window open to let in the summer breeze, the floor shining, a new mattress on the bed and a pile of sheets waiting to be put on it, along with a stack of pillows and down-filled duvet. She'd make up the bed later and hang her clothes in the huge mahogany wardrobe. That dip in the cool water of the river was her top priority right now.

Tara put on the swimsuit she found in her suitcase, grabbed a towel from the linen cupboard on the landing and ran down the stairs again, smiling as she heard Mick's voice on the phone in the dining room. He'd probably set up an office there later. Then she went outside and walked down the slope to the river, the sun hot on her back and the air filled with the smell of wildflowers and heather. Bees buzzed among the blooms and a seagull emitted a plaintive cry above Tara's head before it glided away across the fields. She reached the river and ducked under the branches of the weeping willow before she tossed the towel on a branch and sank gratefully into the chilly water that gushed over the rocks, forming a little pool below. It was only waist deep but when she crouched down and sat on the smooth stones of the bottom, the water washed over her shoulders, instantly cooling her.

Tara found she could lean her back against the bank and relax, enjoying the soft water washing over her. The sound of the river was soothing, calming her after the hectic few hours she had just been through. But the greatest concern of all were her feelings for Mick that were beginning to trouble and confuse her. Was the affection she felt just a close friendship, or something deeper, more serious and a lot more complicated to deal with? And how did he feel? She knew he liked her a lot and considered her such a close friend that he shared his deepest thoughts and feelings with her.

There was a strong trust between them. It was like they were also kindred spirits. But was there also a physical attraction? Yes, she decided, at least for her. But she knew it was the wrong time for romance, especially for him. He had to concentrate on his campaign and prepare for the eventuality of his winning a seat on the county council. It might not be as important as a seat in the Irish parliament, but it carried a lot of responsibility and would be the cornerstone of a future political career. This was where he would establish his reputation and his credibility while making a huge difference to his fellow Kerrymen. He might even be elected Cathaoirleach – or chairman – of the council if he did well. And he would, she was very sure of that. So it would be best to put her own feelings for him aside and do her very best to help him succeed. She felt in her bones how important it was. Because if he failed it would be another blow for him after such a difficult year.

The photo shoot took place in the dining room later that day, as the light from the windows and the backdrop of the wood panelling were perfect for a head-and-shoulders portrait that would look good on the posters and flyers. Mick, dressed in a navy blazer, white shirt and red-and-blue patterned tie sat on one of the dining-room chairs composing his features.

'Trustworthy and dependable?' he said, looking at Tara, who was taking a few preliminary shots to test the light and contrast.

Tara lowered her camera. 'Just be yourself. This is not a part in a play, remember.'

'Myself,' Mick mused. 'How do I do that? I keep thinking I should act the politician.'

'Just relax for a moment,' Tara suggested. 'Close your eyes, lower your shoulders, breathe in and out slowly. We have all the time in the world.'

Mick closed his eyes and seemed to relax. Then he let out a deep sigh and opened his eyes. 'Okay. I'm ready.'

Tara looked at him and as their eyes met, she felt that pull in her gut that told her to take the shot. She pressed the shutter several times as Mick's expression changed ever so slightly, his eyes full of hope and yearning, looking at Tara as if he trusted her with his life.

'Are any of them good?' he asked as she checked the photos she had just taken.

'Hang on,' she muttered. 'I might have to take some more.' But when she looked at the first few shots, she knew she had captured exactly the right image. He was looking straight into the camera with a confident air that inspired trust. 'Not bad,' she said as if to herself. 'I think the second one is the best.'

Mick got up from his chair. 'Can I see?' he asked, leaning over Tara to look at the photos.

'This one,' she said, showing him the shot. 'It's very good. What were you thinking about when I took it?'

'I just thought of all the people I love around here... I could do so much for them if I got involved. I could improve the roads, build a bicycle lane to Waterville, add more walking trails and sort all the little things that need fixing in the village.'

Tara smiled at him. 'Well, it worked.'

'All thanks to you,' he said, looking at her with an odd expression. 'Everything I've done lately is thanks to you.'

'Ah, you would have drifted into it anyway,' Tara protested. 'I just gave you a push to get started.'

'Don't be too modest. You've been wonderful.' Mick looked into her eyes as if to say more, but took a step back instead. 'Could you send me that photo?'

'Okay.'

'Brilliant. And send your invoice to me as well.'

'But that's not...' Tara started, but then realised he would hate for her to do this as some kind of favour instead of a job by a professional photographer. 'I will,' she corrected herself.

'Good.' He checked his watch. 'I'll have to go back to my parents' house to use the Internet connection there. Do you need to do anything like that?'

'No,' Tara replied. 'I can use the hotspot on my phone to send you the photos. And I'll send the whole project to the magazine in New York tonight. I'm officially on holiday from now on.'

Mick smiled. 'That's great. I know how hard you've worked. And the weather is set to continue warm and sunny.'

'That's good. I hope it stays like that until Kate's wedding. Lots to do around that, so I'm happy to be able to help.'

'I'm sure you'll be a great help.' Mick took off his blazer. 'I'll just change and then I'll be off. I'm picking up a takeaway meal for us on the way back. Something nice from the Harbour pub. What would you like? Fish and chips? Or something else?'

'I don't know. Surprise me,' Tara suggested.

Mick laughed. 'I'll do my best.' He hesitated. 'I know I shouldn't say this, but I want to make sure. Please don't tell anyone about all of this for now. Especially not my mother.'

'I swear,' Tara said with feeling.

'Good. I'll be making an announcement in a couple of days.'

Tara nodded. 'Better to wait and tell everyone at the same time.'

'Exactly. See you later, so.'

'Bye,' Tara said absentmindedly, busying herself with the camera, ready to send the best photos to Mick's email address.

Mick's footsteps died away as Tara looked through the series of photos she had just taken. His car door slammed and the engine started, the wheels crunched on the gravel, but Tara hardly heard those sounds as she stared at the very last photo she had taken of Mick. In this shot, his expression had changed from the earnest politician to something completely different. She shivered as she felt he was looking straight into her eyes. Was she imagining it? But no, it was too obvious. Mick wasn't looking at the camera, he was looking at *her*, and the expression in his eyes took her breath away. She could nearly feel him touching her as she stared at the image and suddenly knew that something important was happening between them.

Chapter Twenty-Five

The house rang with the hammering and drilling from the electricity team during the following weeks and, as promised, the whole house was connected by the weekend. But Tara continued to use her little kerosene lamp in her bedroom for reading in bed. The soft light was restful, and she liked the smell of the kerosene which gave her the feeling of being back in time. She didn't see Mick apart from dinnertimes when they shared a meal either in the little garden or in the kitchen, cooked on the new induction hob that had been installed in the old wooden worktop. The wood-burning stove would be used in the colder months but only for heating and slow-cooking when Mick felt like a stew. But that wouldn't happen until later in the year, when Tara was back in America and Mick was living here on his own.

New York already beckoned, with the magazine having been in touch raving about the photos and articles Tara had sent. They were already sending feelers about future trips to far-flung places all over the world. And they asked her to a meeting in early September to plan a schedule. Other magazines had also been in touch, offering her all kinds of jobs from fashion to celebrity portraits, all of which looked very enticing to Tara.

Jasmine and Aiden had arrived back in Sandy Cove and were staying in their beloved cottage, which made Tara happy as she had been able to move into her new accommodation at the perfect time for both parties.

Kate's wedding was looming nearer and Tara was busy helping out with the arrangements as Kate didn't have much free time. They had slowly begun to mend the bonds that had been broken and they were nearly as close as ever. But Kate still wasn't so sure about Tara's arrangement with Mick. 'Have you ever thought that Mick might want to stay when he finally finds the right woman and wants to start a family?' she asked one evening.

The mere thought of Mick marrying and having children was like a knife in Tara's chest, but she knew it was bound to happen one day and she'd better face it and move on. The attraction and friendship between them were sweet but it couldn't last.

Mick was working hard on his campaign and the election was only a week away which prevented any thought of romance or even the slightest flirtation between them. He was a bundle of nerves and all she could do was to try to soothe and calm and keep boosting his morale. She even shouted at him when in a fit of nerves he said he couldn't go on and he'd call the party and tell them to choose another candidate. That was a week ago, when he was about to start calling from door to door to talk to prospective voters and convince them he was the best man for the job.

The posters with the photo Tara had taken already adorned every lamp post in the village and she had to smile as she looked at his earnest, caring face, promising to make Kerry an even better place for everyone. She accompanied him on the very first evening of door stepping and he was met with enthusiasm and promises to elect him by nearly everyone who came to the door. After that she announced he was on his own.

'Go for it, Mick,' she said one evening as he was getting ready to go out campaigning yet again, straightening his tie and smoothing his hair in front of the hall mirror. 'What have you got to lose?'

He turned from the mirror and looked at her, standing there in a pair of old shorts and a paint-stained T-shirt, a dripping roller in her hand, having started on the wall of the living room. 'You look a sight. You're a far cry from the fashion plate you were when you arrived, I have to say.'

'I know. I'm getting to like the messy new me. It's very liberating. And I don't have to go around shaking hands and kissing babies,' Tara declared.

'Lucky for you.'

'Are you getting cold feet again?'

'No.' He stared at her for a moment. 'I'm actually beginning to enjoy it. All thanks to you.'

'I just gave you the first little push,' Tara said modestly. 'I never thought anything would come of it.'

'But it did. And then…' He paused, his eyes tender as he kept looking at her. 'You helped me through that first bout of stage fright. Then I went out there feeling I had nothing to lose. And I even had the courage to break the news to my mother.'

'What did she say?'

Mick laughed. 'She was speechless for over a minute, would you believe. Then she started to cry and said she wasn't sure she could take the disappointment if I lost and what would everyone say? But I told her I had no intention of losing, so she should just shut up and let me do it.'

'You told your mother to shut up?' Tara asked, amazed.

Mick grinned. 'Yes, I did. Rude, I know, but it was the only way to make her do just that. And my father thinks my entry into politics is terrific despite my mother's misgivings. In any case she and Dad are so busy shouting at each other about the new house and what should go where, they don't have the time to worry about me. So that's all sorted and I can go out there and face the public without them leaning over me and making sure I have clean underwear before I go out. Metaphorically speaking, of course.'

'And now you're walking the walk and talking the talk and everyone adores you.'

His eyes glittered and he took a step closer. 'Even you?'

'Me? Well, I…' Suddenly frightened by the way he looked at her, she stepped back and shooed at him with the roller. 'Go on, get out of here. I want to get back to painting. Never knew how much fun it was.'

'I think you know what I'm talking about,' Mick said, the expression in his eyes making her cheeks glow.

She moved back again. 'We should be concentrating on your campaign and the house and the wedding and…' She tried desperately to find something to say to defuse the situation but her heart had other ideas, hammering in her chest, making her breathless.

'I'd rather concentrate on us right now.' He took the roller from her suddenly weak hand and dropped it on the floor. Then he put his arms around her and looked deep into her eyes. 'Tara,' he murmured. 'Let's stop this. I think we both know what's going on here.'

Unable to speak, Tara nodded. 'Yes…' she stammered as he continued looking at her, and she felt again the spark she had been trying so hard to ignore. The fact that he seemed to share her feelings made her heart soar.

'I'm mad about you,' he said.

'Oh, Mick,' she whispered.

His lips met hers as she tried to say something, to tell him it wasn't the right time, that it was a very bad idea, that she was going back to New York after Kate's wedding, that… Whatever else she meant to say flew out of her head as he kissed her and she felt her body melt into his, his soft lips chasing away all thoughts of paint stains on the newly sanded and polished floor, replaced by a feeling of pure bliss as the kiss went on and on. Tara closed her eyes, the smell of lemon soap and the feel of his body making her dizzy with desire and love.

They finally drew apart, staring at each other, laughing, then kissing again until Mick had to step away, smoothing his hair and clothes.

'Do you trust me?' he suddenly asked, looking into her eyes.

'Of course,' she replied. 'What about you? Do you trust *me*?'

'Absolutely,' he said. 'But now I really must go. We'll talk later.' Then he smiled and stepped out of the room and Tara could hear him get down the steps and drive off in a shower of gravel before she had a chance to pull herself together.

She stood there looking at the paint stains on the floor wondering if she was dreaming. But she could still feel his kisses on her mouth, his arms around her and his voice…

She was leaving. What did this mean? Did this change things? She had no idea. All she knew was what Mick had said and his words kept ringing through her mind, making her smile. Tara shook herself, picked up the roller and went out to the utility room to find some white spirits to clean the floor. What would Kate say about all of this? she wondered. But then she pushed that particular worry out of her head. She didn't have to ask for anyone's permission to fall in love.

Chapter Twenty-Six

Tara and Kate left for Killarney the following day to find Kate's wedding dress. Tara was still in a daze after what had happened between her and Mick the day before. She had waited for him to come back until very late, but then he had sent her a text saying he'd been called to a last-minute meeting with the local party members and not to wait up. She had reluctantly gone to bed, and gone to sleep, tired after a day of painting the living room and doing other little DIY jobs around the house. Kate had arrived in her car as she was having breakfast, Mick still asleep in the old farmhouse across the little garden, which removed any chance of a romantic interlude before she set off to Killarney. But they had plenty of time, she told herself, leaving him a sweet note and a rose bud in a jam jar on the kitchen table.

As they made their way to Killarney, Kate explained that she didn't want anything fancy from a bridal boutique, preferring to try her luck in a vintage shop just off the main street. It was a little like the furniture emporium, Tara thought, as they walked inside the former drapery shop in a charming old building, with a huge array of clothes from bygone days hanging in row after row.

'Wow,' Tara said, fingering a soft velvet coat from the nineteen thirties with an appliqué of flowers on the collar. 'This is gorgeous.'

'But not suitable for a wedding,' Kate said, trying on a cloche hat, striking a pose. 'How do I look?'

'Like Greta Garbo,' Tara said with a giggle. 'Come on, stop messing. We have to find you a wedding dress.'

They walked further into the shop, finding a section with Victorian dresses. It didn't take long before Kate squealed with delight, holding up a floor-length broderie anglaise dress with a high neck, puffed sleeves and a light blue velvet sash. 'Isn't this beautiful?'

'Adorable,' Tara said. 'Try it on.'

'I hope it's the right size,' Kate said. 'My waist has expanded a little.'

'Not that much,' Tara said, eyeing Kate's still slim midriff. 'The wedding is quite soon so your waist won't have changed that much. And then you can put it away and wear it after you've had the baby. Try it on, anyway. I'm sure it'll fit.'

'Well, we'll see.' Kate disappeared into the fitting room and, after a little while, called out to Tara for help with all the tiny buttons at the back.

Tara stepped inside the fitting room where Kate stood in front of a tall, ornate mirror in the beautiful dress that made her look like a woman in an impressionist painting, ethereal and incredibly beautiful. 'Is it okay?' Kate asked, her eyes huge with wonder at her own image.

Tara looked at Kate's reflection and felt tears well up. 'Oh, Kate, you look gorgeous,' she said in a near whisper. 'More than beautiful. It's the perfect dress for you.'

'Do up the buttons to see if it fits. My waist seems to have thickened the last week or so.'

'But you won't have a real bump until months after the wedding,' Tara said. But when she started to push the tiny pearl button into the buttonholes she discovered the dress was indeed a little tight. 'I'm sure it can be taken out,' she said, examining the seams. 'There's plenty of material at the seams.'

'Are you sure?' Kate asked, her voice wobbling. 'I want this dress even if I have to walk up the aisle with it open at the back.'

'That won't be necessary,' Tara assured her. 'I think I could have a go. It'll only need a little snip just here,' she said, pinching at the middle of the waist area. 'And I can put in an elastic band to allow for any expansion.'

Kate turned around and looked at Tara with gratitude. 'Could you? You're so good at that sort of thing.'

'No problem,' Tara assured her. 'Do you want to wear a veil or some kind of headband?'

'No. Cormac is making flower wreaths for us both.'

'Oh. How lovely.' Tara started to undo the buttons.

'I didn't want all that bridal stuff,' Kate declared, slowly taking the dress off. 'Not really my thing.'

'No. Absolutely not.'

'And Pat is giving me away,' Kate continued. 'I asked him yesterday. He was so touched he teared up. He pretended to blow his nose, but I saw him dabbing at his eyes and then he polished his glasses and looked at me with his lovely kind eyes and said it would be an honour to take my father's place.'

'Oh,' Tara said, hugging Kate. 'That's perfect. He's been a real father figure to you, hasn't he?'

'Oh yes, he has.' Kate carefully put the dress back on its hanger and turned to Tara. 'I haven't thanked you properly for what you did for me and Cormac. He's over the moon about the house. And Helen and Pat are both so pleased. They're having a great time bickering over the plans of the new house they're going to build. I have a feeling they'll end up in separate wings.'

Tara laughed. 'Wouldn't surprise me.'

'And we're not changing the surgery house much,' Kate continued as she put her jeans and shirt back on. 'We like it the way it is.'

'That's good.'

'And I'll pay you back the money I borrowed from our shared account. We don't need it now that the house was so cheap. So you can buy the farm from Mick as soon as you want.'

'That's fantastic,' Tara said, hugging Kate again. 'It's all working out, isn't it?'

'Sort of,' Kate said. 'I mean, you're going back to New York and I will miss you more than ever.'

'I know.' Tara felt a pang of sadness at the thought of being apart from Kate again. 'But I will be back every summer to run the farm and the hiking and nature centre, or whatever we'll call it.'

'I like that idea, actually,' Kate said. 'It doesn't seem so scary any more.'

'It never was,' Tara replied. 'You were exaggerating the whole situation.'

'I know,' Kate admitted. 'But I think it will be fine. And Mick looks so happy now. I think politics will suit him. It's a tough world, but he'll cope, I think. He's strong and determined and after all he's been through in show business, he'll be able to deal with the dirty world of politics.'

'I'm sure he will,' Tara said airily, not wanting to discuss Mick in case her own feelings and their budding romance were revealed. She didn't want to tell anyone what was going on between them yet, not even Kate. It was too new and fragile to be talked about. In any case, Mick's political career was only beginning and he didn't need rumours about his personal life to start flying around.

'But now we have to find a dress for you,' Kate declared as if she had sensed Tara's reticence.

'I'd like something simple, if we can find it,' Tara said, walking out of the fitting room with Kate's dress over her arm.

It took them over an hour of searching through the entire shop before they found a dress – or 'The *perfect* dress for you,' Kate squealed, holding up a long flowing kaftan-type garment with a pattern of tiny blue, light green and pink flowers and butterflies on a white background. 'Look, Tara, it's gorgeous!'

'Edwardian tea gown,' Tara read from the label. 'It's made of printed muslin, it says.' She stepped away and looked at the dress. Not strictly speaking a suitable dress for a maid of honour, but she wanted it more than any dress she had ever seen. 'I'll be tripping over it down the aisle.'

'You'll just have to be careful,' Kate stated. 'I want to see you in this dress.'

'Me too.' Tara walked swiftly back to the fitting rooms and found a cubicle that was free. She undressed and slipped the dress on over her head, feeling the soft fabric skim her body like a whisper. She closed her eyes for a moment and then opened them, blinking as she saw her reflection. The tea gown sat on her body as if it was made for her, the soft colours complementing her shiny hair that had grown to nearly shoulder length, her light tan, accentuating the shifting colours of her hazel eyes. 'Isn't this lovely?' she said to Kate, who had stuck her head in to check.

'It's divine,' Kate said with a happy little sigh. 'Buy it. You'll be the belle of the wedding.'

'But I don't want to outshine you,' Tara said, her enthusiasm waning. 'It's your special day.'

'It'll be even more special with you looking like that. Buy it,' Kate ordered in a voice that didn't allow argument. 'I'll pay for it. It's the least I can do after all the negativity about your project and the way I tried to stop you buying the farm.'

'Oh, but…' Tara started. 'I want to forget all that and move on. I know you meant well and that's all that matters, isn't it?' she said, not wanting to go back to a place that had been so hurtful. They had started to drift apart at the beginning of Tara's visit, but now they had come full circle and there was a new understanding between them that felt stronger than ever. Today was a happy day and Tara felt it was a new beginning for them both. Why rake up old hurts when they were getting on so well? Better not to carry grudges and let sleeping dogs lie, she thought. Kate was so happy and that was the most important thing.

Kate sighed happily and hugged Tara. 'Yes. And we'll look stunning, won't we?'

Tara looked at their reflection in the mirror and nodded. 'Amazing,' she said.

They paid for the dresses and watched as the shop assistant wrapped them up in tissue paper and put them in individual paper carrier bags. 'Lovely dresses,' she said as she handed them their bags. 'I know you'll both look gorgeous in them.'

'Mine is my wedding dress,' Kate told her.

The woman beamed. 'Really? That's wonderful. I love these vintage clothes. Much nicer than the modern stuff. And I know for a fact that the broderie anglaise dress was worn by a local woman for her wedding. She was married somewhere nearby over a hundred years ago and then the dress was packed away and they only found it when the house was sold. The new owners brought it in.'

'That's amazing,' Tara said. 'Did they know anything about this woman?'

'No. Only that her name was Sarah. It's embroidered on a label inside the dress.'

Tara and Kate exchanged a glance. 'Our great-great-grandmother was called Sarah,' Tara explained. 'And she would have been married in 1900.'

'Who knows? That could be her,' the woman said, looking excited.

'So that's what we'll imagine,' Kate said with a laugh.

They emerged from the shop in the sunny street with their bags, looking around for a place to have lunch. 'We should go back to the main street,' Kate suggested. 'There's a little French café near the car park that does fabulous salads and stuff.'

'I know the one you mean.' Tara nodded and looked in her bag for her sunglasses but they weren't in her bag as expected. 'I must have left my sunglasses on the counter in there. You go ahead and grab a table and I'll join you in a minute.'

'Okay.'

Tara went back into the shop and found her sunglasses where she had left them on the counter. She smiled at the shop assistant, who was sorting through a pile of scarves. Then she went back outside, put on her sunglasses and was about to follow Kate when someone bumped into her. Startled, she looked at the man.

'Oops, sorry.' She backed away as she recognised him. 'Liam,' she stammered. 'Eh, hi.'

He looked at her over the rim of his sunglasses. 'Hi, Tara. What are you doing in Killarney?'

'Shopping,' she replied, feeling horribly awkward.

'Of course.' He hesitated for a moment. 'I was going to get in touch with you and say… well, sorry about what happened. I think we got our wires crossed or something. I misread the situation completely. I thought we'd… well, you know.'

'I know what you might have hoped would happen,' Tara said, putting her sunglasses back on. 'It was probably my fault, too. I should have made it clear that I just wanted to be friends.'

He smiled and shook his head. 'Nah, that wouldn't be possible. Friendship between men and women is very rare. It just doesn't work that way.'

Tara shrugged. 'Okay. No big deal. But there was another thing…'

'Yes?'

'It's about the family stuff.'

Liam looked suddenly annoyed. 'Oh, that again.'

Tara glared at him. 'Yes. That again. I know the full story now, and so do you, I'm sure.' She folded her arms. 'We should really go and have a coffee and discuss this instead of standing here on the street, but I don't think there's any point.'

'I suppose not,' Liam said and took a step back. 'What is this whole story you think you know?'

'You're not a real O'Rourke, for a start. And your great-grandfather cheated mine out of his inheritance. Not that you're not responsible for that, of course,' she added. 'But I have a feeling you knew and didn't tell me.'

'I don't think that's quite correct,' Liam countered. 'Nobody cheated. He inherited the farm from his mother. In any case,' he added, 'that's not my fault, is it?'

'No, but why weren't you honest with me?'

Liam smiled sheepishly. 'I fancied you…' He paused. 'I suppose I didn't want anything to ruin what might happen between us. I'm sorry. Do you want the wedding photograph? I still have it.'

'No. It's yours. You keep it. It made me sad to look at it.'

'I understand.' Liam took her proffered hand. 'Well, goodbye, then, Tara O'Rourke. It was nice to know you. And, as I heard the property will eventually be yours, I have to tell you that I am happy that Riverside Farm is returned to your family. It never gave them much luck to own it, but I think it will bring you lots of happiness.'

'Thank you, Liam.' Tara shook his hand and smiled, her opinion of him changing for the better. He may have lied about the family history, but she felt he might have had a sense of shame about his great-great-grandmother. 'No hard feelings at all, I assure you. The sins of the fathers and all that, eh?'

'Something like that,' he agreed, still holding her hand. Then he let it go.

Tara waved at him. 'Bye, Liam. Take care.' She walked away, her step light, feeling suddenly as if a cloud had lifted, the cloud of a past tragedy that would now turn into a wonderful future. She looked up at the blue sky. 'A happy ending for us all, don't you think, great-grandpa?' she said to the clouds.

A soft breeze played with her hair, as if replying from somewhere above, a silly thought that made her feel a burst of joy despite knowing she was imagining something that wasn't there. But everything had fallen into place; even meeting Liam like that out of the blue seemed to have happened for a reason. The only thing worrying Tara was the question of where she would go next. Back to New York? It had seemed inevitable, but now she wasn't too sure. So many little bonds and ties had been created all through this summer. Would she be able to cut them all and leave this wonderful place?

Chapter Twenty-Seven

The whole village turned out for Kate's wedding. The church was packed and a lot of people had to stand outside. When Kate arrived at the church with Pat, who was giving her away, there was a hush through the crowd as they looked at the beautiful bride in her white dress, a wreath of daisies and Kerry roses in her hair. As they walked up the aisle, Tara behind them, there wasn't a dry eye in the whole church. Tara felt her eyes prick as she watched Cormac look at Kate with an expression of wonder. He had stayed with his family in Dingle town for a few days before the wedding while Tara and Kate got everything ready, including a day at the spa in the Great Southern Hotel in Sneem, where they were pampered and spoiled and thoroughly enjoyed the luxury of facials, pedicures, manicures, steam room and a swim in the beautiful pool overlooking the ocean. There, Tara had told Kate about Mick and their budding romance.

'We're taking it nice and slow,' she said to Kate. 'No rushing into a relationship that won't last this time. We've both been burned and need time to heal. So we're healing each other and being very careful.' *So careful we haven't slept together yet*, she thought, knowing Kate would understand what she meant. They had indeed been very careful not to rush things, even if their kisses and embraces had been quite lengthy and full of yearning. But as if by a silent agreement, they had always ended each evening with a good-night kiss, going to their separate sleeping quarters and meeting the following morning for a breakfast full of smiles and soft chatter. Mick was gentle and sweet and very considerate which made her love him even more. It felt good and safe and very romantic to Tara, even though she knew they would have to come to some resolution before she left. 'And we haven't told anyone,' she said to Kate. 'We don't want people to start talking. Not that they'd mind, but he has only just been elected, so it's important he finds his feet first, before we start going out in public.'

'Good idea,' Kate said approvingly. 'Must say, I never thought he'd lose. His campaign was incredible, not to mention the photos on the posters.'

'And what a party we had afterwards,' Tara said. 'I'm still trying to recover.'

As Tara walked behind Kate and Pat, she saw Mick out of the corner of her eye and glanced at him, smiling when he shot her a secret wink. As they arrived at the altar, Father O'Malley started the service, the choir from the school sang 'You Raise Me Up' and Kate handed Tara her bouquet with a tender smile. And then Cormac and Kate promised to love each other till death did them part, the groom kissed the bride and they walked out of the church into the sunshine as everyone cheered and threw so much confetti at them it looked like a multicoloured snowstorm. Tara took the wedding photos in the churchyard against the backdrop of the mountains and the glittering ocean in the distance.

*

The wedding reception was a huge success, even if the venue was less elegant than a hotel. But Kate declared it was all perfect, from the food and wine to the dining room with round tables and roses from the back garden in little pots on each one. The local band that usually performed in the pub on Saturday nights played Irish dance music in the large living room to which they all danced until the small hours and the sun rose over the mountains.

Tara danced all night with everyone, drank champagne, laughed and chatted with so many people she had trouble remembering all their names. The other O'Rourkes in the village – Sally, her French husband, her daughter Jasmine and son-in-law Aiden – stood out among the guests and Tara enjoyed long chats and jokes about the wild O'Rourkes and what they had been up to all through the centuries. Sally said she thought her mother had talked about Daniel and the upheaval in the family and how the people in Sandy Cove had turned against his stepbrother after the farm was lost. The bad name had stuck for a long time, she said, and that O'Rourke family had stopped coming to the village and gone to Ballinskelligs instead for supplies. Tara listened to the stories even though she knew them already from what Helen had told them. But now here they were in the house, celebrating Kate's wedding and taking back what was lost, even if they could never heal the wounds that had been inflicted on their great-grandfather.

Later that night, Cormac and Kate left for their honeymoon on the Beara Peninsula, where they would be staying at a little hotel for a week. Tara hugged Kate tight before she got into her car. 'I'm leaving next week,' she whispered in Kate's ear. 'But I'll only be gone a week or so and then I'll be back.'

'For good?' Kate asked, glancing at Mick standing beside them.

'Forever,' Tara whispered back, the words said out loud making it feel real for the first time. She had had a long, serious discussion with Mick the night before and as she looked at him, she suddenly knew she would never be able to live apart from him more than a few days. They hadn't worked out the details, but it was enough that he knew and that it had made him happy to hear her say it. 'But it's still a secret, so don't tell.'

'I'm so happy I could burst,' Kate said, hugging Tara back.

'Me too.' Tara turned to Cormac and hugged him, too. 'Take care of my sister.'

'You know I will,' Cormac replied. 'And you take care of yourself, Tara. I think you'll be very happy here in this old wreck.'

'Thank you, Cormac.' Tara kissed her new brother-in-law and let him go, lining up with the other women as Kate ran up the stairs to throw her bouquet. Everyone laughed as Tara caught it, except Helen, who looked worried, sizing Tara up, as if she didn't quite measure up to standards. Tara winked at Helen and waved the bouquet, laughing. Nothing could ruin the happy feeling tonight, not even Mick's mother.

When the last stragglers had departed, Mick and Tara tidied up the worst of the mess, until Tara had to sit down on the back step outside the kitchen and take off her shoes, leaning her back against the wall.

Mick sat down beside her, handing her a cup of tea. 'Here, beautiful. Camomile tea and then bed.'

'Thank you.' Tara took the cup and sipped the tea, smiling sleepily at him.

He sat down beside her. 'You look gorgeous in that dress. Did I tell you that?'

She leaned her head against his shoulder. 'Yes. Several times. But it's not a dress, it's a tea gown.'

'So you said. I love it. It suits you.'

'You look nice in that blue shirt,' Tara said, admiring his wide shoulders and strong arms outlined against the fabric of the fine cotton. His hair curled at the back of his neck and she reached up to run her fingers through the golden curls.

'We both look great,' Mick agreed.

Tara looked across the rose garden at the roof of the old building outlined against the starry sky. 'What a beautiful night. The stars look so close I feel I could touch them.' She breathed in the scent of roses mixed with Mick's aftershave and felt she could stay there all night like this, her head against his shoulder and his arms around her. 'It was a lovely wedding,' she said. 'But now I'm glad it's just us here in this little garden.'

'Me too. But…' He hesitated, loosening his tie. 'I think we might try to see what we look out of these things.' Tara drew back from him and he looked suddenly shy. 'I mean, only if you feel you could… you know.'

Tara shot him a serious look. 'I think that would be a very good idea. There's plenty of room in my bed, you know.'

'Yes, but I don't want to presume…'

'I feel it's the right time. Don't you?'

'Well, everyone already thinks we're doing it, so why should we disappoint them?' He kissed her cheek. 'I think we've been very, very good until now.'

'We weren't ready,' Tara mumbled against his chest.

'But now we are, don't you think?' he said, sounding hopeful.

'Yes. I do.' Tara struggled to get up. 'Come on, then. It's nearly four o'clock. I'm exhausted.'

Mick stood up and took Tara's mug. 'That the most romantic invitation I ever had.'

Tara laughed. 'That's the only one you'll get tonight – I mean, today. Come on, help me up the stairs.'

Mick had to nearly carry Tara up the stairs to the master bedroom, where he laid her carefully on the bed. He eased off her dress and hung it up in the wardrobe, before he took off his suit, padded to the window and closed the shutters against the early morning sunshine. Walking back across the floor, he got into bed beside Tara and pulled the duvet over them both. 'Let's sleep before we do anything else. I'm so tired I couldn't raise so much as an eyebrow and even that would be too much.'

'Me too,' Tara mumbled. 'I mean, me neither. I mean…'

'Go to sleep, lovely,' Mick whispered in her ear. 'Tomorrow is another day.'

'And tomorrow and tomorrow,' Tara whispered into the darkness. 'And,' she added with a huge yawn, 'I've decided not to go back to New York. Well, I mean, I'll go back for a bit, but then I'll come home and stay here. With you. Forever. Is that okay?'

'I think that would be acceptable. But don't tell my mother. She'll have a fit.'

'You're such a romantic,' Tara mumbled.

Unable to keep her eyes open any longer, she drifted off to sleep, knowing that Mick was there beside her, and always would be, even when they were apart.

Epilogue

Sarah Jane O'Shea was christened on a blustery day in early April. She cried loudly as Father O'Malley poured holy water on her head. Tara, holding her little niece and goddaughter, laughed as the baby squirmed in her arms. She smoothed the lace of the christening gown that had been in the family for generations. Maybe even Daniel had worn it at his christening as it had been from his family and had been found among his things hidden in an old chest in their home in Dublin.

Kate reached out to take her daughter when the ceremony was over. 'Sorry about the crying.'

'She seems to have good lungs,' Tara joked, stroking the baby's soft hair.

'Especially at four in the morning,' Cormac remarked.

'A baby crying at the christening is a good sign,' Father O'Malley said. 'It means she's healthy and strong.'

'Thank you, Father,' Kate said. 'That's good to know.'

'How are things in the new house?' Father O'Malley asked.

'Wonderful,' Kate replied, cuddling little Sarah. 'We moved in before Christmas and now we feel as if we've lived there forever.'

'We'll be serving tea and buns there in a moment,' Cormac said. 'And maybe even a glass or two of wine. I hope you'll join us.'

'I'd be delighted,' Father O'Malley replied. 'I just have one more christening and then I'll be with you. April seems to be the month for christenings.'

'It's a lovely time of year,' Tara agreed.

When Kate had put little Sarah into her pram, they all walked through the village to Kate's house, chatting about the past year and all the things that had happened since Tara had arrived that hot June day nearly a year ago. Tara smiled at Mick, who had to stop several times to chat to people who rushed up to him shake his hand and talk to him about minor problems that always cropped up in the village. He always had a good suggestion and took everything people told him on board, even complaints about the county council that weren't his responsibility. His answers were always polite and honest, and as always, her heart swelled with pride as she watched him deal with people in that special caring way.

How life had changed since that first day they met on the beach and they were both so lost and lonely, somehow adrift without a proper goal or direction. But now, here they were, together, running a little business. Tara had continued as a photographer whilst in Ireland, specialising in nature photos, and had just been hired by the Kerry Tourist Board for their many campaigns.

Riverside Farm was restored to its former glory, the house now updated with bathrooms, central heating, a brand-new kitchen and beautifully furnished. The original farmhouse was thatched, restored and ready to receive guests in the summer season. They already had bookings from Americans who had read Tara's articles in *The Wild Vagabond* that had been such a success. And the series of articles about Riverside Farm, its history and restoration had been a hit in *Vanity Fair*, which had earned Tara a lot of praise, not to mention a cheque for a large amount of money that went towards a new bathroom. The boom of tourists that would destroy Sandy Cove, which Kate had once feared, had never happened, just as Tara had said.

Two weeks in New York was all Tara had managed before she jumped on a plane with all her belongings, rushing into Mick's arms when he met her at the airport. It had been a blast to be back there but it had soon worn off as the beauty and tranquillity of Sandy Cove beckoned, along with one special man she didn't want to be away from for very long.

Their winter had involved many ups and downs as the old house was restored – they even had to camp in the shed while extensive work was being done, which put Tara's resilience to the test as they argued hotly about it – but finally Riverside Farm had been restored. By then Tara and Mick owned it together; that was one thing they had never argued about. They knew they would always be together, even if the little detail of marriage hadn't been decided yet. And they also knew they would have a family, which was already on the way.

Mick took Tara's hand as they caught up with Kate and Cormac. Tara smiled at the baby in the pram and wondered if it was the right time to announce her own wonderful news.

'We'll do a toast and announce our news,' Mick said quietly in Tara's ear as he pulled her close before they went into the house. 'Little Sarah has to be told she'll have a cousin soon.'

'Yes, she does,' Tara said as she tickled Sarah's tummy.

The baby looked at Tara and shot her a toothless grin, as if she knew exactly what was in Tara's heart.

A Letter from Susanne

I want to say a huge thank you for choosing to read *Miracles in Wild Rose Bay*. If you did enjoy it, and want to keep up to date with all my latest releases, just sign up at the following link. Your email address will never be shared and you can unsubscribe at any time.

www.bookouture.com/susanne-oleary

I have hugely enjoyed writing this story and felt such a strong connection to Tara and Kate in their quest to find out about their family history. Old houses have always fascinated me and there are so many all over Ireland with hidden secrets and fascinating stories. If the walls could speak, wouldn't it be amazing to hear the stories they could tell?

I continue to be touched by the huge support from readers which is inspiring me to keep writing. Many thanks to those who have sent me kind emails or chatted with me on my Facebook page. It's so nice to hear your thoughts about the plot and characters!

There will be three more books in the Sandy Cove series and the next one will be just as enjoyable and intriguing, set in an old coastguard station this time.

I hope you loved *Miracles in Wild Rose Bay* and if you did, I would be very grateful if you could write a review. I'd love to hear what you think, and it makes such a difference helping new readers to discover one of my books for the first time.

I love hearing from my readers – you can get in touch on my Facebook page, through Twitter, Goodreads or my website.

Thanks,
Susanne

authoroleary

@susl

837027.Susanne_O-Leary

www.susanne-oleary.co.uk

@susanne.olearyauthor

Acknowledgements

There are so many people to thank for their continued support and encouragement. First of all, I am so happy to have an editor like Jennifer, who is so on my wavelength and nearly as invested in my stories and characters as I am. Many thanks also to all at Bookouture, who continue to be a delight to work with. I must also thank my lovely neighbours in Kerry for the friendship and laughs, and also that cake, Mary! Very much appreciated. My friends in Sweden are close to my heart, and especially Agneta and Maud have been amazing all through my writing journey. My husband deserves, as always, a huge thanks for cheering me on and always being there, willing to discuss plot ideas and characters.

Made in United States
Orlando, FL
23 September 2022

22701579R00152